New Orleans Noir

New Orleans Noir

EDITED BY JULIE SMITH

Akashic Books
New York

This collection is comprised of works of fiction. All names, characters, places, and incidents are the product of the authors' imaginations. Any resemblance to real events or persons, living or dead, is entirely coincidental.

Published by Akashic Books

Series concept by Tim McLoughlin and Johnny Temple
New Orleans map by Sohrab Habibion
Cover photograph ©2006 David G. Spielman, from his book *Katrinaville Chronicles: Images and Observations from a New Orleans Photographer.*

ISBN-13: 978-1-933354-24-8
ISBN-10: 1-933354-24-0
Library of Congress Control Number: 2006938151

First printing

Akashic Books
PO Box 1456
New York, NY 10009
info@akashicbooks.com
www.akashicbooks.com

Also in the Akashic Noir Series:

Baltimore Noir, edited by Laura Lippman

Brooklyn Noir, edited by Tim McLoughlin

Brooklyn Noir 2: The Classics, edited by Tim McLoughlin

Chicago Noir, edited by Neal Pollack

D.C. Noir, edited by George Pelecanos

Dublin Noir, edited by Ken Bruen

London Noir, edited by Cathi Unsworth

Manhattan Noir, edited by Lawrence Block

Miami Noir, edited by Les Standiford

San Francisco Noir, edited by Peter Maravelis

Twin Cities Noir, edited by Julie Schaper & Steven Horwitz

Forthcoming:

Bronx Noir, edited by S.J. Rozan

Detroit Noir, edited by Eric Olsen & Chris Hocking

Havana Noir (Cuba), edited by Achy Obejas

Lagos Noir (Nigeria), edited by Chris Abani

Los Angeles Noir, edited by Denise Hamilton

Paris Noir (France), edited by Aurélien Masson

Queens Noir, edited by Robert Knightly

Rome Noir (Italy), edited by Chiara Stangalino & Maxim Jakubowski

Wall Street Noir, edited by Peter Spiegelman

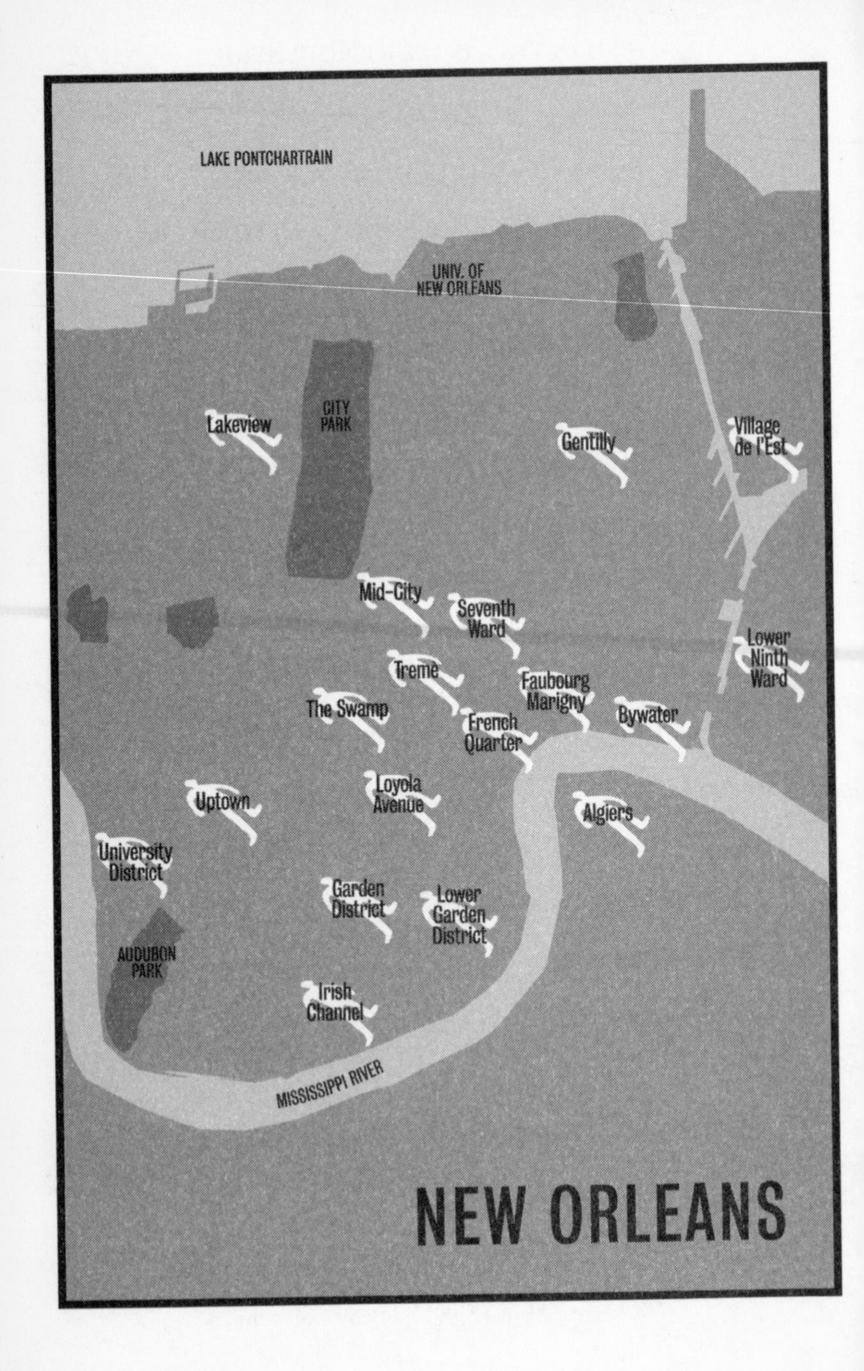
LAKE PONTCHARTRAIN
UNIV. OF NEW ORLEANS
CITY PARK
Lakeview
Gentilly
Village de l'Est
Mid-City
Seventh Ward
Treme
Lower Ninth Ward
Faubourg Marigny
The Swamp
French Quarter
Bywater
Uptown
Loyola Avenue
Algiers
University District
Garden District
Lower Garden District
AUDUBON PARK
Irish Channel
MISSISSIPPI RIVER
NEW ORLEANS

To those who took care of us:
Janet and Steve Haedicke, the first week;
Kiley, Molly, and Tory McGuire, the next month;
and Debra Allen, who saved the cats

Acknowledgments

Thanks have to begin with Tim McLoughlin, who started the Akashic Noir Series with *Brooklyn Noir*, and Johnny Temple, who's turned it into a cultural phenomenon; and then move quickly to the seventeen brilliant authors who agreed to participate in this one. Working with all of you has been a joy.

And so many others helped in so many ways: Laura Lippman, Vicky Bijur, David Simon, Denelle Cowart, Chris Wiltz, Greg Herren, David Spielman, Linda Buczek, Jack Willoughby, Captain Jeff Winn, Paul Willis of the Tennessee Williams Festival, Ron Biava of the New Orleans Public Library, Lee Pryor, and especially Mary Alice Kier and Anna Cottle, who put some serious time in, just as a favor. My most heartfelt thanks to all. Plus a second thank you to Johnny Temple for so generously sharing in our recovery.

TABLE OF CONTENTS

PART II: LIFE IN ATLANTIS

INTRODUCTION

Writing Underwater

Before Hurricane Katrina, New Orleanians used to joke about not really being a part of America, being, in fact, a tiny Third World country unto ourselves. *And proud of it*, we used to say.

The layers of irony in that idea become clearer—and more numerous—with each day that passes since our city was inundated and, well . . . pretty much leveled, except for the skinny strip along the river where we're all hunkered now. (At least those of us who aren't still trying to get home from Houston or haven't packed up and moved to North Carolina.)

The Bubble, we call it, or the Isle of Denial, but some days the denial just doesn't work and neither does the Prozac, and we get all liquid in the eyeballs and have to pull ourselves together.

Little more than a year after the storm, we're still floundering, still in shock, still wondering how to write about such a momentous, life-changing, historic, downright biblical tragedy. We've lost so much that meant so much, and we're struggling so desperately to hold onto what is left. How to convey something like that?

Last Christmas, when we were all just barely home, just starting to get our bearings, a librarian at Tulane University told me she'd already bought twenty-five post-Katrina books for her library. "Nonfiction?" I asked.

"Of course," she said.

She must be up to a hundred by now, but so far as I know, only one post-K novel has been published at this writing. Though I have no doubt hundreds are in the works. Everyone is struggling to find a way to tell his or her story, to tell it in such a way that those who didn't go through this particular bewildering and disorienting loss can understand how it relates to the larger picture, how universal a thing it really is, this destruction and this *potential* for destruction, this aching misery, this indifference on the part of the rest of the country. Never have so many writers in such a small area become so passionate, yet so desperate, all at the same time. We are at once immobilized by the task and inflamed by it.

So a short story is really the perfect way to stick a toe back in the water. Whether set pre- or post-K (these are the terms we use down here), the stories herein, to my mind, are particularly passionate. Some of the post-K ones will sear your eyeballs. And yet . . . so will some of the historic ones.

Patty Friedmann's tale of mean girls at an Uptown private school may well be the most chilling story ever set at a kids' pajama party. The nineteenth-century yarn by Barbara Hambly and David Fulmer's "Algiers," set a century ago, provide ample evidence that, so far as crime is concerned in this French city, *plus ça change, plus c'est la même chose*. We've always had our con artists, our gamblers, our two-bit hustlers, and, God knows, our hookers and femmes fatales. We'd hardly be ourselves without them.

Alas, we also have our racists. Jervey Tervalon offers a peek into the discrimination of the past in his story of two wrangling priests, one a bigot *and proud of it*. Ted O'Brien also tackles the issue of race—with all its tangles and contradictions—in a twenty-first-century mixed neighborhood.

James Nolan's wry and wicked "Open Mike" leads us on

a careening tour of the underside—both past and present—of that gaudy world known as the French Quarter; the part the tourists haven't a clue about. Laura Lippman treats us to an insider's look at the Tremé Mardi Gras, one of the city's most colorful, while providing so hair-raising a take on masking that it ventures into horror territory.

Before reading Tim McLoughlin's worldly-wise Irish Channel story, be sure to pour yourself a couple of fingers of Irish whiskey. You'll need it—especially if you next move on to Olympia Vernon's unnerving tale of love gone wrong in the University District.

The Lower Ninth Ward, perhaps our most famous neighborhood of late, was always a tough place, but it had its tender side too, its neighborly, gentle, almost maternal side, the side that makes people so desperate to go back no matter what—no matter that it mostly doesn't even exist anymore. Kalamu ya Salaam skillfully evokes the complexity of its residents' lives.

Not surprisingly, almost half the writers chose to make their stories contemporary. And it's a good choice, I think. For this is what we live with now—this is the new New Orleans. This messy, ugly, often violent, confusing, difficult, inconvenient, frustrating post-Katrina world.

In "Muddy Pond," Maureen Tan wades into a part of the city most of its black and white citizens are only vaguely aware of, and almost never visit—Village de l'Est in New Orleans East, where the church called Mary Queen of Vietnam is the dominant social organization. Unless you count the gangs.

The Masson boys in Thomas Adcock's "Lawyers' Tongues" are pure New Orleans—one a prosecutor, the other a petty thief. They're Gentilly folks who moved up from the nearby St. Bernard project under the watchful eyes of certain Aunt-tees only too eager to see them stumble.

Jeri Cain Rossi's haunting tale of frustration, despair, and desperation—and heat!— in the very bohemian Bywater will make you long for a refreshing dip. Preferably not in the river.

A little known fact: Lakeview, just the other side of the now-famous 17th Street Canal and once the home of well-off white folks, took on just as much water as the Ninth Ward. But since the houses were newer and stronger and mostly brick, it fared better. So unlike the Lower Ninth, it now looks more like a Western ghost town than a field where the gods played pick-up sticks. "Night Taxi," Christine Wiltz's angry, gritty portrayal of latter-day carpetbagging mines those spooky ruins for nasty truths.

Several years ago, the *Utne Reader* named the Lower Garden District "the hippest neighborhood in America." So naturally plenty of gay people live there and some, just as naturally, have lovers' quarrels. Let's hope most are resolved more peacefully than the one in Greg Herren's "Annunciation Shotgun," a classic noir nightmare in which stepping *just* over the line opens the narrator's personal Pandora's box.

My own story of looting in the Garden District proper (several feet and a planet away from the Lower Garden District) seeks to remind us that we New Orleanians have no monopoly on taking advantage of our fellow humans.

No fewer than six of our intrepid contributors (including our cover photographer) rode out the storm here—Christine Wiltz, who finally left when the looting got nasty; Jeri Cain Rossi, who got out by commandeering a van (along with five other people, five dogs, and a cat); James Nolan, who escaped with musician Allen Toussaint in a stolen schoolbus; Patty Friedmann, who got trapped in her Uptown home, hitched a rowboat ride to her sister's also flooded house, and had to wait four more days for a second rescue; Olympia Vernon, who was marooned for days in Hammond, Louisiana with no gas, food, or electricity; and photographer David Spielman, who took shelter in a convent with a group of cloistered nuns.

But one of us actually came here voluntarily that week. Ace Atkins blew in from Mississippi on a magazine assignment, and saw things that . . . well, that he injected into his powerful story, "Angola South," along with the raw emotion of one who's seen things nobody should have to see.

Last, Eric Overmyer looks through the jaundiced eyes of an Eighth District homicide cop to sing a sort of love song to the noir side of the city. Or maybe it's more like a love-hate song. The first paragraph alone will take the top of your head off—and the funny thing is, it really happened, as did most of the narrator's memories. He reminds us just how violent our history has been, how much of our culture was already lost even before the bitch blew through.

Since the recovery process is more or less a holy cause with most of us, a percentage of the profits from this book will go toward rebuilding the New Orleans Public Library, which is mounting a brave and massive campaign to get the funds it needs to reinvent its broken self.

In addition, the authors were given an opportunity to help their colleagues by waiving their fees and donating the money directly to Katrina K.A.R.E.S. (Katrina Arts Relief and Emergency Support), an arm of the New Orleans Literary Institute that makes small grants to individual authors affected by the storm. We're proud to say we raised money for eleven such grants.

Julie Smith
New Orleans, Louisiana
February 2007

PART I

Before the Levees Broke

WHAT'S THE SCORE?

BY TED O'BRIEN

Mid-City

The door swings open, in walks Reggie. Paul, on the stool next to me, gives him the once-over, shakes his head. "Man," Paul whispers, "they say being black in the South is like being black twice. Being a dwarf, too? Man, what's that like?"

Reggie's eyes are bloodshot, yesterday's clothes soiled. He stands, legs bowed, lets the door swing shut behind him. Give him a cowboy hat, it's like he's sizing up a Western saloon.

He's got the swagger. He should. None of us have ever beat him at pool. Reggie plays up the angle for the newcomers, *What, I'm just a dwarf AND a nigger, think you can't beat me?* Half-hour later your wallet's lighter, and Reggie's drunker.

First time I lost to him, I just shook my head. Maybe it's his height. He sees things we don't.

At the end of the bar, Reggie sidles up to Wayne, the meanest son of a bitch in the bar. Old rugby player from Wales. Reggie says, "My nigga."

"My nigga," says Wayne.

Billy, behind the bar, pulls out a Coke and an Abita, puts them side by side on the counter in front of me. "What'll it be?" he asks in his thick Irish brogue.

"What time is it?"

"Uh," checks the wall clock behind me, which I could've done. "Eight in the morning. What'll it be?"

"You know me," I say, "caffeine before alcohol." Billy hands me a glass of ice. I pour the Coke over the cubes, down it like water. Already hot as a motherfucker outside. You'd think Billy could turn up the a/c. Cheap bastard. Billy waits. "Right," I say, "guess I'll have that beer now."

Billy laughs and pops the top off. I take a swig, survey the crowd. Everybody's baked. I'm always bringing up the rear.

Five televisions hang from the ceiling, various points, all with the pre-match commentary from across the pond. Ireland versus Switzerland. Onscreen, three fellows dressed for a night on Miami Beach break down the X's and O's. Billy's got it turned down low, for now.

"What do you think they're saying?" I ask Paul.

"I'm Scottish, who gives a fuck. What are they saying? Ireland are going to play like shite."

I look around the bar. All familiar faces. The soccer fans in their jerseys, the neighborhood fellows, black, keeping to themselves by the pool table, watching us warily, wearily.

"Once again," I say, "Louisiana's Swiss community has let us down. Maybe they forgot to set their watches."

At the end of the bar, other side of Reggie and Wayne, someone yells, "Fuck Switzerland!"

Hear hear, fuck Switzerland.

"Who plays after this?" I ask Billy.

"England versus Turkey."

Again, from the end of the bar: "Fuck Turkey!"

Billy raises his glass with a hearty, "Fuck England!"

"Think you'll have a good turnout?"

Billy shrugs. "Be plenty of English bastards," he says, so the bastards hear it. "Don't know of many Turks in the city. Wish I had a Turkish flag."

The brothers hang back by the pool table, occasionally

sending an emissary to the bar, whispering PBR orders like sweet nothings.

The Ireland game comes on. Reggie's the only brother watching. He's excited. "Fuck, I didn't know they was any Irish niggas! Look at that one! Who that?"

Billy laughs. "Clinton Morrison."

"Yeah! Clinton Morrison! Man, that ain't no nigga name. The fuck?"

"He plays for shite."

"Nigga plays for *you*, Billy!"

Wayne says, "Irish first, nigga second. Doubly fucked."

"Nigga, *you* Irish."

"Welsh, you dumb fuck."

"Ain't that worse than Irish? Welsh still answer to the Man, don't they? Hell, it ain't even the Man, it's the fucking Queen."

Wayne glares at him, doesn't say anything.

"Yeah, Wayne, you think a dumb nigga don't know nothin' about history, huh? I fuckin' went to school. Probably know just as much as you ignorant Welsh muthafuckas."

Paul's already up out of his chair, gets between Reggie and Wayne. Wayne's got a short fuse. Rugby player, you know.

Reggie backs off. "Come on, Wayne, just fuckin' with ya."

Wayne forces a smile. "You're lucky I like you, man."

White guys in English jerseys begin pouring into the bar, waving Union Jacks, awaiting their game. Don't ever bet the farm on Irish football. They play like shite. Switzerland wins it, two-nil.

Paul nods approvingly at the crowd, better part of a hundred, mostly English now. Waving flags, drinking Budweiser. "That's a lot of English wankers," says Paul.

It's an hour until England-Turkey. The front door bursts open. A collective roar, singing as if in tongues, a wall of people wrapped in red flags, pours into the bar. We're struck numb. The brothers in the corner, by the pool table, scurry out the back door.

Paul speaks first. "Fuck. Al-Qaeda."

There has to be at least two hundred Turks, singing, yelling, waving flags. None of us can move. Literally. Try to fall down, you'll stay upright. Fuck the fire code.

The Turks take over the pool table. They take over the dartboard. They pin Turkish flags up on the wall, over Celtic crosses, over printed lyrics to "Danny Boy," over family photographs.

"Fuck," Billy says, behind the bar. "Muslims. They don't drink."

Happily, not true. Like their English nemeses, it's Budweiser all around.

I step outside for the fresh air. Two buses from Florida, Escambia County plates, parked in the left lane of Banks, next to the neutral ground. Florida?

More Turks are pouring out of the buses, singing.

It's enough for me. Across the street there's a birthday party. Some guy's kids. They've got one of those giant inflatable jungle gyms—moonwalks is what they call them—out front, the kids, six of them, all of four or five years old, catapulting themselves to the top, back down, over and over, happy as hell. Man out front, drinking a High Life, I recognize from nights at the pub.

"Hey, man," I holler, crossing the neutral ground, crossing Banks.

He calls back: "The hell's going on over there?"

I reach his fence. "Turks. Fucking Turks."

"Turks? Ragheads?"

"Well, you'd think. They all drink, though."

"Oh," he says, then "oh" again, as if, well, in that case, they must be all right. "Hey, it's Sharonda's birthday! She's five. She's right there, see her? Jumping up, there!"

Sharonda, on the descent, waves to her daddy.

I approach the giant plastic gym. "Sharonda! Your daddy says it's your birthday! How old are you?"

"I . . . am . . ." She holds up her hand, giggles, counts fingers. "I'm FIVE!!"

The girls resume their jumping, higher now, to entertain the new guest. "Hey, man," the daddy says, never can remember his name, "have a drink, huh?"

We go up the stairs to the front porch. Cooler in front, High Lifes. His lady's sitting on a wooden rocker, glass of iced tea in hand. "How you doin', baby?" she says to me.

"Pretty good. Congratulations on your daughter's birthday."

"Ohhh . . . I can't believe she's five. You got kids?"

"No. No wife either."

She laughs. "'S wrong with you? You got cooties?"

"Lots of angry ex-girlfriends."

We sit and watch the kids, quietly. The music coming out of the house, it's kid music, something like Raffi. My man digs out two more High Lifes, pops the tops off, hands me one. He makes eye contact with his wife, says "Baby?" real quiet, but she shakes her head.

Across the street, the jerseys are gathered outside the front door in shock. Most of them have palms attached to ears, phones cradled between, shaking their heads, you won't fucking *believe* what's going on here.

A kid rides through the crowd, and I watch him lazily

drift toward downtown; he fades out of sight. Kids are everywhere—street, neutral ground, sidewalk. Some are oblivious to the excitement at the pub, a few point and laugh. Makeshift hoops hang off second-floor porches, a few games of horse. The soccer jerseys stand out. Everyone's got torn clothes, matches the paint peeling off crumbling houses.

I slap my friend on the back and rise. "You're a lucky man," I say.

He laughs. "Sometimes, man." I catch the funny look he gives me before he turns his head.

I wish his wife a good day, and run downstairs to the kids in their jungle gym. "Hey, Sharonda, y'all want to make some noise?"

"YEAHHHHHH!!" The kids have been hitting the caffeine.

"Okay, look across the street. There, see the guy in the green shirt? That's Billy. Everybody, on the count of three, yell *Hi, Billy!* Okay? One, two, THREE."

It's a hell of an uproar. Billy peers across the street, shakes his head and waves. As I cross the street, the kids take turns yelling at Billy again.

"Hey, Billy, so what's the story?"

"Ah, mate, there's too many fucking people in there."

"And?"

He shakes his head, smiles. "What are ya gonna do? Drink faster!"

England-Turkey kicks off. The Turks shred their vocal cords, singing. I stand in the corner by the front door. Any trouble breaks out, quick exit.

Fifteen minutes into the game, the door swings open next to me. A bunch of the brothers who had run out after the

Turkish invasion peer in. The one in front chews a plastic straw. "Shee-it," he mutters, slams the door shut.

Drink faster. Billy tosses me another Abita, another, crowd just as packed but becoming less relevant. Halftime approaches. Penalty awarded to England. The Turks roar indignantly, deafeningly.

Paul moves next to me. "Christ," he says, "all fucking hell."

We tense up, awaiting the kick, the goal, the angry Turks to turn as one toward us. David Beckham takes the kick, sends it high into the stands above the posts. The Turks roar again, a gift from the heavens, and they sing aloud to them.

Paul sighs. "Thank God."

Halftime. We move out onto the sidewalk. There's rain. It's light but getting heavier. Clouds darkening. My friend across the street is slowly gathering the kids, ushering them up the steps, into the house. He looks our way, waves. I raise my bottle.

I've lost interest in the game. I wander off to Telemachus Street, to my car. The brothers are out on their porch, safe from the rain, falling harder. They wave me up.

It's not uncommon. Most evenings I come to the pub, I park at their house, hang out for a bit, bring up some forties. Good security. Nobody's going to fuck with my car.

"I was just wondering who that ugly white motherfucker was."

"Yeah? I was wondering who the blind black motherfucker was."

They've got Juvenile pumping out of the house. He's rapping about sets going up, the Third Ward, the UTP. The hell's the UTP?

Rainfall hits the roof, a clatter of buckshot. The brothers

offer me a Colt 45. Shit's strong, goes down smooth. I'm lit. One of them's up out of his chair, rapping over the sound of the rain, smacking an invisible ass in front of him, *baby, let me see you do the rodeo.*

The brothers whisper shit about their girlfriends, look over their shoulders, make sure they can't hear. I offer up an ex-girlfriend, several months vintage. I say mine had a bigger ass.

Nah, man, white bitches don't have no big asses!

Shit, this white bitch had an ass so big an astronaut could see it.

The rain lets up, enough. I'm on the sidewalk in the drizzle, back at the pub. Paul's outside, cigarette in hand.

"What's the score?" I ask.

"Nil-nil, mate. Almost over. Hope it stays a draw. Don't want to have to fight the Turkish bastards."

"Or English bastards."

"Right. Not sure which ones smell worse."

It's the anticlimax we all craved. Fulltime, the Turks drift out of the bar onto their Florida buses. Some sing half-heartedly, most trudge by quickly, making rapid eye contact, then breaking it.

Naturally, the English stick around. They're happier. They only need a draw to go on to the next round.

Soon, it's just twenty of us. Shitfaced. Billy pours himself a draft Harp, leans on the bar. "Without a hitch. What a relief."

Quiet hangs over the establishment. The building sighs, and settles. Zombielike, we sit at the counter watching our drinks, unable to make the effort to lift them. I've developed a dark ring around my line of sight; tunnel vision. Too shit-faced to care.

The front door opens slowly, then four figures pour into the room, slamming it shut behind them.

The first thing that registers is the straw in his mouth. I notice it before I hear him. Everything appears at the end of the tunnel. He says, next to me, wet with rain, "Motherfucker, open the register!"

Hands grab me from behind, throw me to the floor. My palm hits the ground first, my head next. Distantly aware of impact. My wallet's ripped out of the sucker pocket.

There's yelling. I don't move. I make careful observations of the grime on the bottom of Billy's barstools. Mental note.

Paul's down here too. He's looking back at me, not at the barstools. Blood's coming out of his ear. They threw him down hard. He's not blinking. Shock.

Billy's voice, from a long distance: "That's all I've got."

I think of that scene from *Apocalypse Now* on the boat, when they suddenly go crazy and shoot that family. That's what happens now. I feel the explosions in the floor, barstools clattering to the ground, specks of red like schools of fish. Hearing's gone but for the deafening beating of my heart.

I move my head, just enough. Blue jeans, baggy, riding low, striped boxers. The fucker who opened fire.

There's no conscious decision made, no preparation. I drop him. My right leg comes up in a scissor kick, behind the knee, fucker goes down. I see the gun hit the wall behind me, but can't hear a thing. I imagine a satisfying clatter.

I'm up. The three other dudes stand by the door, aghast. Can't believe that white motherfucker dropped their boy. *Boys, I can't believe it either*.

Behind the bar, Billy's slumped over the cooler, green jersey spotted with red. He blinks, but I'm not sure if there's anything there.

I rush the brothers by the door. They're out ahead of me, into the wall of rain. Cold water streams across the street, up onto the sidewalk and neutral ground. They're gone.

Ah, but not the guy I left back in the bar. With his gun.

Before I realize I'm running, I'm halfway down the street. Rain blows into my eyes. I'm going to fall. I'm going to trip. The last thing I'll see through rain-washed eyes, black motherfucker with a gun.

Yet there's my car, water coming up to the rims—shit, I got this far, maybe I'll make it. I start to fumble for the keys.

Nah. I'll never make it.

The brothers on the porch. I take the stairs two at a time, and I'm up, dry, they're on either side of me rising slowly, eyes wide, mouths moving. Something registers behind me, and their hands dart into their waistbands.

Pieces brought up, aiming toward the bottom of the stairs.

I turn around.

There's just the one, inside the gate. Straw firmly in mouth. The dude lowers his gun. For the first time, he looks me in the eye. He smiles.

The current in the street is steady, rainwater halfway up to the knees. The man with the gun looks down, as if noticing the water for the first time, then slowly follows the current in the direction he came from. A wall of rain hits the street, and he vanishes into it.

TWO-STORY BRICK HOUSES

BY PATTY FRIEDMANN

Uptown

You only need two things to feel good at Newman School: Pappagallos that show your toe crack and a two-story brick house. Well, three things if you're Jewish. If you're Jewish, you have to go to Sunday school. I don't have any of those things, but I can fake the third one. Thirty-seven out of sixty-two kids in my class at Newman are Jewish, if you count Carolyn and Shira, and strangely enough, you don't think about them as being Jewish *because* they had bat mitzvahs. They also came from public school in seventh grade and are fat and don't care. It was Carolyn, who goes to a synagogue I've never heard of, who told me just to say that I go to Gates of Prayer. It's reform, but nobody's ever heard of it.

I keep working on my mother to buy me Pappagallos, but she says I get my shoes free and I should brag about it instead of mope. My great-grandfather owned the Imperial Shoe Store, which is on the corner of Bourbon and Canal Streets, and my grandfather gets such a deep discount that he buys all my shoes. Imperial is one of those stores that sells sturdy shoes like Stride Rites. Okay, but I don't understand why they waited until Capezios went out of style to get them in. I can have all the Capezios I want, now that I don't want them.

I don't think we're poor, but I can't really tell. We live in a house that's actually old and pretty, but it's wood and one-story so it doesn't even matter that my grandmother pays for us to have a maid. Well, she pays twenty-five dollars a week, but after a while Rena wanted a raise, and my grandmother said no, so my father pays her extra every week, taking it out of what he would spend on dry cleaning his suit. That's the way it is with my grandparents. My grandmother paid my tuition to Newman for kindergarten, and then she said she didn't feel like it anymore, so I've been on scholarship ever since. Which means my daddy has to reveal his income every year. Newman is very low-key about it, but my mother's not. I have to have very good grades. Which is pretty easy because this is more a school for rich kids than for smart kids, in spite of what the whole city thinks. I know for a fact that if your parents knew the admissions director when you were coming into kindergarten, she asked you which train was red and which one was black, and if you got it right, you were in. She came from a very old Jewish family and had nothing better to do than give admissions tests for Newman. She still does it.

There's a slumber party at Louise Silverman's house tonight, and I'm invited. I have been at this school for over ten years, and this is the first time I'm friends with all the snobbish girls. My mother is thrilled, and I am disgusted, but I'm also thrilled, to tell the truth. Louise lives on Octavia Street, and two of the other girls can actually walk to her house. Their houses look almost the same, and I think that's a message to me that if you want to be the right kind of person, then you should have that kind of house. Brick two-story. A plain rectangle. My mother probably thinks so too, but my father is the manager of a supermarket, and she knows crummy shoes and Rena's twenty-five dollars a week is probably her limit with her parents.

Louise and Meryl and both of the Lindas are failing Geometry. For a while, they took turns calling me up for homework help, then I started going over to their houses after school, and finally they quit pretending they could do anything without me. This is how I know people at Newman aren't smart. For Monday's homework we have to prove the congruence of the two triangles in a parallelogram. I'm headed over to Louise's early and we're going to work on it. She'll just hand it over to the other three. They won't be able to do it in Mrs. Walter's class when she comes at them, and they won't be able to do it on tests, and from what I've heard Mrs. Prescott will threaten them with public school, but at homework time they will think I'm giving them hope.

My mother has packed me my gold silk pajamas that my grandmother bought me on her last trip to Japan. "Those girls are going to be so jealous," she says. I think there's a chance she might be right, though I also think that even gold silk shoes from Japan would not hold up next to nice baby-blue leather Pappagallos.

I ask her to drop me off and not wait until someone opens the door. We have a 1956 Ford Fairlane sedan. I figure that if no one opens the door I can go ring another girl's bell. It is better than being seen in a 1956 Ford Fairlane sedan.

Louise grabs my arm at the door and pulls me in, which is as close as she comes to affection. "We'll do math right now," she says, and I think she must see that I'm excited, too, by an idea I've come up with on the way over. If Mrs. Silverman sees this little lesson I've made up for Louise, she will decide I am the best girl in all of Newman School and should be the only one Louise is friends with. She might tell all the other mothers, and then I'll be popular. These girls aren't like me. They definitely plan to grow up to be just like their mothers.

While I pull my math book out of my overnight bag, I ask

Louise to get me a couple of envelopes, please. She looks at me like I've asked her to get me cleaning supplies. This is not something she's ever found necessary. "Mama!" she hollers, and goes running upstairs. Her mother comes down to the kitchen and rummages in a drawer in the butler's pantry. These two-story brick houses fascinate me. They have rooms that make sense only for rich people who lived a hundred years ago, but they were actually built just ten years ago. I ask for scissors too. Louise's maid stands at the sink watching us with her arms folded. She's not doing anything but watching us. Her expression says she could do this geometry if someone asked her.

My wish comes true: Mrs. Silverman watches as I cut and fold and draw straight lines and prove beyond doubt the congruence of the triangles in a parallelogram. I even cut the envelope into the shape of a parallelogram despite the fact that a rectangle is already a sort of parallelogram, because I figure Louise and her mother aren't going to follow that extra piece of information. They are as delighted as if I've just guessed which card they've pulled from a deck. Mrs. Silverman kisses my cheek with red lips, and I leave the mark because no other girl is going to have a print to match Mrs. Silverman's tonight.

The maid is still standing at the sink around midnight when I pad into the kitchen to find a way not to cry. We are in our nightclothes, and everyone in her pink shortie pajamas has said how pretty mine are and has examined the little frog buttons closely so she can comment when I leave the room. Silk is so hot, and I don't want to have perspiration stains under my arms. They will show so easily. I don't feel sorry for myself. I really don't. I feel sorry for Carolyn, who of course is not here. I feel sorry for the maid. I feel sorry for everybody. I must look pitiful.

"What's a big old girl like you doing in baby nightclothes?" the maid says.

"They're from Japan," I say like a white person, and I suddenly don't feel so bad.

Louise is the one making the calls. They are calling Negro cab companies and sending taxis to Carolyn's house. "How you doin'?" she says, trying to sound colored. I think she sounds fifteen and stupid, but everyone else thinks it's hysterical and is laughing into a pillow. "Yeah, I just got off work, you could pick me up?" She rifles through the school directory. This is why she's flunking math. She can't even hold Carolyn's address in her head for two minutes. When she hangs up, they all start screeching with laughter.

"I thought you liked Negroes," I whisper. Though right now I hate her maid.

Louise looks around to see whether she does or not. She draws blank stares. We all took Civics last year and Mr. Ralph taught us to love President Kennedy, and now all the girls except me have giant hair rollers on their heads so they can look like Mrs. Kennedy in the morning. That is supposed to mean we like Negroes. I explain that to Louise, and she agrees. She has a picture of him in her room. Rena has one in her kitchen, but I've never told Louise that. President Kennedy is very good-looking, she says, but why am I asking about Negroes?

Because it's their cabs.

Oh, says Linda B., they're out anyway. We'll make Carolyn crazy. Remember Teal? I remember Teal. They called her all night every night until she was driven to public school in sixth grade.

And I think, I have a feeling *you* are going to be sitting in public school when Carolyn is up there in Trigonometry at

Newman. I'm having a good time. I'm inside my own head, but I like being in their company.

Linda B. is the one who makes the calls to Carolyn's house. She thinks she can do a voice deep enough to be a boy our age, and she asks for Carolyn. "Oh God, she used the F word and all kinds of Jewish words," Linda says, covering the receiver. "What's a shwotzer?"

"It's *schvartze*," I say, "and it's a derogatory word for Negroes." Then I realize they are going to think I'm Jewish the way Carolyn and Shira are, so I have to explain really fast that if they paid attention to the way words are derived they'd notice that there are people at school named Schwartz, and that means "black," so it's just a form of a German word. I don't mention that my father is from Germany, and that he's been secretly teaching me German since I was three years old. Well, talking to me in German. You don't *teach* a child. My mother doesn't know.

All the girls trip all over themselves telling me how smart I am. I think this is different from my pajamas. This is not something they are going to talk about differently when I leave the room. I am smart, and that fact is unassailably good, and in their presence I am better than they are no matter what subject comes up, as long as it isn't fashion.

When it seems that Carolyn has been tormented as close to going back to public school as is possible for one night, Linda R. says we need to play Secrets. Louise dims the lights, and we sit in a circle, and we drink Coke. There are eight of us, and we're going clockwise, and since we started with Meryl, I have three people ahead of me before I have to think up something to tell. I figure I'll decide on the basis of what they tell. My father likes to have what he calls private jokes with himself. I want to think up a private joke with myself. If

I can think of a secret that they think is something they can hold against me, but really is something I can use against them, it'll be a lot of fun.

Of course, Meryl has a crush on our English teacher and she had a dream last week that she went down to his French Quarter apartment and had sex with him. This is a complete lie. People don't have night dreams that everyone in the room has daydreams about, especially when nobody really wants to do anything more with that man than kiss him. I pick this apart in my head. It's a secret about *her*, and it's one people can use in the halls. Louise tells that Becca in her fourth period French class came right out in the girls' bathroom and said that her parents got a divorce because her mother was having an affair, not her father, even though it's always the father who fucks around. Becca is an atheist, and she doesn't care if she has any friends, but boys call her up anyway because she has huge breasts. She tells them no and goes out with Tulane boys. I'm not sure what to do with this for the purposes of tonight, but I am sure what to do with it for life in general. I'm going to quit pretending I'm anything but an atheist. My father hasn't said so, but I know he's one. He won't affiliate with a synagogue because he says synagogues in New Orleans are really just churches without crucifixes. I think he's just figured out that this God thing makes no sense. I know I have.

When it's my turn, something makes me tell that I speak German. It will be a private joke with myself. Linda B. says I have to say something, and I say, "*Du bist böse und hässlich,*" which means, *You are mean and ugly*, but I tell them it means, *You are smart and beautiful.* Linda says it sounds like the way Carolyn's mother talks, and everyone else chimes in, agreeing. Carolyn's mother throws in maybe one word that sounds sort of German, I tell them, and they mull that over for a while, ask me to say something else. I take it on as a parlor trick: They ask for *Boys think I'm sexy,* and I give them back, "*Männer denken dass Ich rieche wie Pferdescheisse,*" which means, *Boys think I smell like horse shit*. Linda wants to know how I know how to speak German when I've been sitting in Newman all these years with all of them, and Newman hasn't taught it to me. My father's from Germany, I tell them. No, he's not, they say. Nazis are from Germany. They start looking at me hard. My last name is Cooper. That's not a Jewish name. It's not a German name. It was Kuper until my father got to Ellis Island. I shouldn't have to explain this.

"I'm Jewish, for Chrissakes," I say, which I think is a pretty good joke, but they don't get it.

"How do we know you're not a Nazi?" Linda says.

"Because my grandmother was killed by the Nazis," I say. I want to go home.

They all get quiet for a moment. They all have grandmothers who are just like their mothers.

Finally, Louise, who is in my European History class and getting a B without cheating, says, "If the Nazis killed her, how can she be your grandmother when she was dead before you were born? I mean, the war ended in, what, 1945?"

"Because my father had a mother, and that's how you have a grandmother, no matter what," I say. I'm feeling better. Newman is a remarkable school. All of these girls will go on to college. Though some are going to take a detour through public school.

"Prove it," Louise says.

And I tell them, "There's a bundle of letters in my parents' bottom desk drawer." I can read every one. In German. Right up to the very end.

* * *

Mrs. Prescott has done the math for the mothers, and this six weeks is going to require As from all four of those girls just to get Ds. She's not sure any of them is what she calls Newman material. Meryl says that Newman material also has a lot to do with donations to the school, and her father is going to give five thousand dollars, and there's probably a secret formula that mixes grades with parents' contributions, so she's not worried. But she must have some kind of dignity problem, because she's not willing to come out of tenth grade with an F in Geometry, and that means I'm still going to have four friends at least until June. Meryl says we should have a slumber party at my house.

If people are going to come to my party, I want to have it, and I want to have it just the way they would. My mother won't have Rena spend the night, and when I think about it, I'm relieved but angry anyway. She also won't buy me shortie pajamas. So I cut the legs and sleeves off my silk pajamas and make very good hems in them, and there's not a thing my mother can do. There's also not a thing the other girls can say because the truth is that my pajamas are really better than theirs. At least I hope they are. My mother lets me have Coke. She doesn't know that Coke and Oreos are right while Pepsi and Hydrox are wrong. Daddy knows, and he's not telling. He doesn't think I should have to squirm through life. But there's no way to tell that to my mother because she likes to see me squirm. At least that's the way it looks to me.

When my very cute house is quiet, and we're all sitting around in my very cute living room, Linda R. looks at my parents' desk and says, "So, is that their desk?" As if it is a peculiar kind of furniture found only in some obscure foreign country. Which to most of them it might be. I haven't seen desks in most of their houses. Or bookshelves. I tell her yes. "So is that where you found the letters from the lady that got killed by the Nazis?"

I tell her yes.

Linda R. crawls right over to the desk and opens the bottom drawer. It's the drawer where we keep all our memorabilia. Very neatly. My baby book, my mother's baby book. A scrapbook of photos and an envelope of more photos. My mother's diploma and my father's honorable discharge from the U.S. Army, which he got four years and two months after he left Germany. And the packet of letters, which always lies nestled in the lower right-hand corner at the front. It's impossible to miss, and Linda doesn't miss it. She plucks it without the tenderness a person should afford these pages and pages of aerogramme paper, thin as onionskin. "Be careful with that," is all I can think to say.

She undoes the ribbon, and they cascade to the floor. I leap to take them before they can fall out of order. I have read them, but I've read them like a detective who doesn't want even fingerprints left behind. Linda pulls back, offended, as if I've called her a slob. "Hey, I just want you to read us one. Read it in *German*."

Of course, the one on the top of the stack is the last one, the most frantic one. My grandmother has seen the light now that it is too late. She is writing to my father in New York, sorry she didn't listen to him when he said they had to leave. My father has enlisted in the military to survive. *I think you know people on Park Avenue*, she says. *People on Park Avenue have money. I understand you can still buy a way to America. Please ask your friends for help. I don't know why I don't hear from you*. I read it in German. I translate without playing around.

"God, she didn't get it, did she?" Meryl says.

"Did your dad really know a lot of rich people?" Louise asks.

I don't say anything.

"Well, how come your father didn't just go over and *get* her?" Louise says. "I mean, just get on a plane or something? That's what I'd've done."

I tell her it was 1943. That ought to connote more than the fact that commercial air travel didn't exist, but it probably doesn't.

Louise says, "So what happened next?" She is far too excited.

"She fucking died in a concentration camp," I say. I fold the letter back and put it in its envelope and reassemble the packet of letters so it's impossible to tell they've been touched. I put them back in the drawer. I go to sleep hours before they have their fill of Coke and meanness.

Mrs. Prescott comes to take me out of Geometry class, and Mrs. Walter makes her wait until the end of the period; such is her power. I'm not bothered until she tells me she's taking me home. This is not something Mrs. Prescott would do; it's too generous. People who work at Newman are not generous because they would be destroyed by the children. She protects herself, saying nothing in the car, and when we approach my house and I see my grandparents' car and a police car, she doesn't do anything except say that someone will get me my homework. I have to walk in alone.

This morning, an hour before Geometry class, my father killed himself in his office.

He found a bag made of plastic in the store, put it tight over his head, and waited to die. The policeman has a manila envelope with some evidence in it that he wants me to look at. Everyone in the room is wide-eyed and dry-eyed, and I'm supposed to be that way too, but I bawl like a baby, and I can't look at stupid evidence, and I don't know who they think I am. I see Rena standing by the wall, and her eyes are wet and red. She loves my father. He always jokes with her, tries to use a Southern accent and says he's from the south of Germany. I go over and hug her because among Mrs. Prescott and my mother and Rena, she's the only hugging type I've seen today, even though she's tall and skinny. The policeman wants a sample of my handwriting. My mother tries to sound protective. "She doesn't need to give it to you," she says. "We've got a million samples all over the house."

Rena whispers to me that they have checked her handwriting too. Rena has very girlish writing. In fact, she writes like a fifth-grade girl. Which, if I think about it, is probably what she was when she quit school. I tell them I'll write anything they want if they will tell me what this is all about.

In the manila envelope is one of my father's mother's letters. It's the one I read at my party, but that doesn't mean anything because it was the one on top. Scotch-taped to it is a note. The note says, *Hitler didn't kill your mother. You killed your mother.*

I go over to the bottom drawer of the desk. Everyone follows me. I can't believe no one has looked. My mother knows about the letters. I pull the drawer open. Slowly, while my mother explains rapid-fire that this is where the letter came from, that it was in a packet, that she should have thought of this before. The packet of letters is gone. Well, the letters are gone, but the ribbon is lying on the bottom of the drawer, swirled around. And under it is a scrap of paper. I recognize it. It's torn from the pad we keep by the telephone in the kitchen. In the same handwriting as on the note attached to the letter, it says, *You're not so smart.*

SCARED RABBIT

BY TIM MCLOUGHLIN

Irish Channel

Okay, okay, so the mayor is looking to start a new anti-terrorist task force and he only wants the cream of the crop from law enforcement."

Tommy Mulligan had settled into his joke-telling stance, his back to the bar, elbows resting on the hammered copper surface. He faced his audience, seven or eight other cops and a few nurses, standing in a loose semicircle at the back of the crowded room. Thursday was nurses' night at the Swamp Room, and the place was packed. Nurses' night at a cop bar was always busy. Nurses' night at a cop bar in the Irish Channel was very busy. Nurses' night at the Swamp Room was a zoo.

"Which mayor?" someone asked.

"What?" Tommy said.

"Which mayor?"

"Doesn't matter."

"Not this bald prick."

"Better than Barthelemy," another said.

"So's bin Laden."

"Could it be Morial?" a nurse from Touro suggested.

"Screw him too. All the money in heaven for Comstat, but splits hairs about the goddamn raises."

"It don't matter which mayor," Tommy said, sensing he was losing his audience. "It's a joke. Let me tell the fuckin' joke."

Tommy had been hitting it heavy for the last hour, and his face was already flushed and sweaty. He'd reached that point in the evening where he thought he was the wittiest son of a bitch on God's green earth, and that was usually Lew Haman's cue to leave. But Lew wasn't going anywhere quite yet tonight. He sat silently next to Tommy, his back to the others, facing the bar in the rear, its rows of bottles decorated with casually tossed toy stethoscopes and white garters.

The Swamp Room had been a real bucket of blood when Lew was a kid, with a large scratched and smoke-yellowed Plexiglas panel in the floor. Beneath it two alligators were kept in a tank that, as he thought about it now as an adult for the first time, had to have been woefully small for them. His father would let him come in to watch them be fed, and more than the feeding itself he remembered the horrendous stench when the panel was lifted.

The space where the Plexiglas had been was covered with stone tile now, and sometimes used as an impromptu tiny dance floor. The whole bar had been rehabbed about twenty years ago, just long enough that it was beginning to look shabby again.

"*So he calls in two state troopers*," Tommy continued, "*two FBI agents, and two New Orleans detectives*."

It was the awful end to an awful night, and Haman was not in the mood to indulge his partner's humor. He drained his Jameson on the rocks and signaled the bartender silently to bring another. *Seventeen years*, he thought. *Three to go*. For the thousandth time lately he lamented joining the force so late in life. He'd come on an old man of thirty, and now he felt like a dinosaur at forty-seven, old even for a detective; and fuck that television *Law and Order* bullshit with fifty-five-year-olds running down gang-bangers in an alley.

Everybody knew that if you hadn't secured a desk job, you were an asshole to stay on past your early-, or at most mid-forties. You were an asshole or you were Lew Haman, with three years to go. Same thing, he decided.

"So the mayor takes all six guys, and he drives them upstate, somewhere in the woods, middle of fuckin' nowhere. He tells them 'Here's your first test. Go into the woods and find a rabbit. Bring it back out here.'"

They had been only fifteen minutes from going off-duty when they got the call. Lew had planned to go straight home after work, to skip the Swamp Room, the nurses, the drinking. He made such plans often, and rarely adhered to them, but you never knew. It might have happened tonight. Then the call came in.

Two uniforms had been driving along Magazine Street toward Jackson when a short, heavyset Hispanic woman stepped off the curb into traffic and waved them down. She told them that two kids had just robbed her on Constance Street. One held her face tightly scrunched in his hand while the other cut the shoulder strap on her bag with a large knife. The one holding her face pushed her backwards unexpectedly, and she fell. Then they ran off, laughing.

The uniforms loaded her into the back of their car and started cruising the side streets. Within a few minutes she began screaming and gesturing at a kid in a hoodie and ghetto-slung pants walking up Fourth Street toward Laurel.

"That's him," she said. "The one that pushed my face."

The uniforms jumped out and confronted the kid, and he reached one hand under his sweatshirt. One of the cops yelled, "Drop the knife!" then fired three times.

* * *

"So the first two guys to go in are the state troopers. They look at each other like—catch a rabbit, no fucking problem. *These are Troop D guys, country boys. They go into the woods and they come back out in about five minutes with a goddamned rabbit. Mayor tells 'em* good work *and he sends in the second team, the FBI guys."*

Ernie Lowell was about the nicest guy you could hope to meet. His nickname around the Sixth District was Reverend Ernie, a moniker bestowed upon him because he was always counseling fellow officers about staying on the straight-and-narrow, and avoiding the lure of drinking and dope, corruption, or ill-gotten pussy. He was married and had five children. To a lot of the other cops he seemed too good to be true, but Lew had always found him to be a sincere guy. He was a year younger than Lew, but had been smart enough to come on earlier, and was now in his twenty-fifth year, planning to retire in about six months. He'd never shown much interest in moving up in the ranks, and until tonight he had never, to Lew's knowledge, drawn his weapon from its holster, much less fired it at anyone.

Ernie's sergeant was the first to arrive after the shooting, and he relieved Ernie of his gun. The sergeant put Ernie, shaking and in shock, in the backseat. Ernie's partner told the story to the sergeant, and the mugging victim backed it up. There were no other witnesses on the street. No one but Ernie had seen a knife.

Lew and Tommy arrived next, and Lew dropped Tommy in front of the scene, then drove a few yards down the street until he could pull over to the curb. He walked back to Tommy and the sergeant. The kid in the hoodie was face down at their feet, the hood of his dark green sweatshirt still covering the back of his head. There was a thin stream of blood running from under the body, and the slightest beginning of a damp red stain on the back of the sweatshirt, as though one of Ernie's shots had almost, but not quite, gone through the body.

"What have we got?" Lew asked. The sergeant repeated Ernie's partner's story. Lew walked over to the partner and got it again from him, then spoke to the mugging victim, who also corroborated it.

"And you're sure this was one of the guys who robbed you?" Lew asked.

"That's him," she said, pointing to the body with her chin. "That's him."

Lew turned to leave.

"I think that's him," she said to his back.

"So the FBI guys, they take out an attaché case filled with all kinds of bells and whistles. First thing they do is divide the area into two sectors, and each one picks a sector. Then they disappear into the woods with global positioning equipment, sonar, and who the fuck knows what else. They're gone for about an hour, then they come back, and sure as shit they're carrying a rabbit."

Tommy and Lew stood over the body and compared notes as the ambulance arrived.

"Anybody else see the knife?" Tommy asked.

"No," Lew said. "Did you look at him yet?"

"Not yet," Tommy said. "Shame it's Reverend Ernie."

"I know."

"At least Ernie's black," Tommy said, and Lew looked at him. "You know, no media. Black cop, black perp, offsetting minorities."

"No yardage gain?"

"Yeah."

Lew looked over at Reverend Ernie in the backseat of the sergeant's car and nodded to him. Ernie looked confused, as though he didn't recognize him.

"So now he sends in the last team, the New Orleans detectives, you know. Old-time guys, polyester pants and skinny ties. They disappear into the woods and nobody hears a thing for about three hours."

The bartender returned and stood in front of Lew. Lew looked at his glass and saw that it was empty again. How many was that? The bartender rapped his knuckles sharply on the bar twice, indicating that the next round was on the house. He gestured broadly at the row of bottles behind him. "Make a wish."

Lew looked at him and smiled for the first time that day. *Make a wish.*

He wished that his hands didn't shake so much in the morning. He wished that he didn't hurt all the time, like there was an animal dying inside him. He wished that his daughter wasn't living in Algiers with a drug dealer who might or might not be a member of the gang Lew just got assigned to monitor. He wished that he wasn't having an affair with his doctor's receptionist. He wished his wife didn't know.

"Jameson," he said, still smiling. The bartender poured generously.

He wished he wasn't partnered with Tommy Mulligan. He wished he could still feel drunk when he drank, not just the dulling of pain. He wished he hadn't stopped off tonight, or that he hadn't had this last drink, or that he wouldn't have the ones that would follow. He wished that he wouldn't have to drive home tonight to Metarie as he did most nights, with his shield case open in his lap, badge and ID card readily visible for when he got pulled over. Mostly he wished he didn't have three years to go. Three years was too long. It was too damn long to be stuck with the likes of Tommy Mulligan, a bad drunk, and a loud, stupid braggart. A man who couldn't hold his tongue for three years. A man who would crack if pushed, even slightly.

He wished he didn't make decisions that were wrong; knowing they were wrong, feeling compelled to make them anyway.

He wished there hadn't been three men on the scene before he arrived today, and he wished there hadn't been three knives under the body when he'd turned it over. Three knives stupidly, amateurishly tossed, practically on top of one another. He wished he didn't feel the sickening weight of two of the knives in his left pocket. He had left the one that most closely resembled Ernie's description. He wished he had six months to go, like Ernie, instead of three years. Three years if he could even get Tommy Mulligan past a grand jury without stepping on his own dick.

The bartender replaced Lew's drink again as Tommy turned and winked at him.

"*So, after like three hours, there's suddenly all this fucking noise. Bang. Crash. Whap, whap, whap.*" Tommy emphasized every sound by pounding his hand—palm flat—on the bar. "*The two New Orleans boys come out of the woods, and they're carrying this deer. And the deer is like, all beat up. He's been worked over. So the deer looks at the mayor, and the deer says,*" and Tommy paused, savoring the moment. He was just telling a joke in a bar. Not a care in the world. He was beaming. "'*Okay, okay, I'm a rabbit.*'"

Lew raised his glass and let the laughter behind him blend in with the background bar din. It sounded distant, and somehow warm and cozy. Inviting. He wished he was there with everyone enjoying himself. He thought about where he'd toss the knives into the lake out at the West End tomorrow. He drank half his drink in a swallow and held the glass in front of him, looking through the amber fluid and ice at the bar mirror. Tommy Mulligan nudged him, hard, and some of the drink spilled from the glass and ran down his arm. He felt it inside his shirtsleeve.

"Get it?" Tommy said. "Do you get it? '*I'm a rabbit.*'"

"Sure," Lew said, feeling the cold liquid almost to his elbow. He continued to look through his trembling glass at the faraway party in the mirror.

"I get it," he said, "I'm a rabbit."

SCHEVOSKI

BY OLYMPIA VERNON

University District

For my brother, Ricky S. Vernon

She vomited on Magazine Street.

She stumbled in. The sign read, *Miss Mae's.* A bar. She and the other white girls, their angular faces melting and disobedient like a blade, a glacier. She and the other white girls, laughing, laughing and stumbling about on the corner of Magazine Street in Uptown New Orleans.

Yes, they laughed and stumbled about with their angular faces pointing eastward; everything about them—the whiteness of them collectively—caught the pupil of the eye and pinned it down. One of them, the girl on the edge of the crowd, stood dark-haired and falling apart; she spoke of her ex, the one who dumped her.

What was his name?

Schevoski, Schevoski was his name and she hated him now.

The tail end of her yellow hair stood away from her shoulders, parted in the middle; there was a strand in the corner of her mouth, her lips purred upward, as if she could not help but notice that she was the dying kind in the crowd; he had, indeed, dumped her, gone back to Russia or some other place where boys go when they're done with you.

Where had she met him?

At the university, at Tulane, where she'd turned the

corner of St. Charles and some other street she could not remember, now that she was drunk, now that she stood amidst the other Tulane girls with their Tulane bodies and wished, she wished she could evaporate.

Yes, now she remembered, she had turned the corner of Tulane and some other street and she wanted something to occur, something that girls her age wanted to happen without having to call out to it; *help me,* it whispered.

And there, Schevoski stood.

He had been pronouncing a singular word, like *beast*, and saw her, standing there before him; this is when he asked her: *Can you?* he asked in the beginning, but then, then when he saw how vulnerable she was, he said: *Say it, beast.*

Beast, she whispered. *Beast.*

How did he look to her now? Could she recall the drunken weave of his posture when she met him? It was that, that, that cooing sound he made, as if he were calling out to her, *Come here, there is something I need you to do.*

For no one *needed* her, not really.

Or was it that he had no face at all? Even when her friends asked her to describe the boy she'd come across at the corner of St. Charles and some other street, she could not remember—Napoleon, was it?—she could only say that he was from Russia and something had bitten her about the flesh.

He was invisible.

It was no wonder that because she had felt like this, that he was invisible, he wove around her a feeling of powerlessness. He had crept up behind her, just behind the ear, and let her go.

Now, now that she and the white girls stood near the edge of the jukebox at Miss Mae's, they, too, cooed, as

Schevoski had cooed, and lifted their angular faces upward; a water stain the shape of a guitar lay flat on the ceiling.

One of the girls whispered: *Look where he died.*

And they all laughed again when she whispered, *Look where he died,* all laughing and shouldering each other, as if they knew, inwardly, that this was Schevoski and that thing he called music; the *beast* was dead.

They looked at her, the broken-hearted girl who had driven them here, and yelled: *Look where he died, Look where he died. Schevoski. Schevoski is dead!*

Why had they been so cruel? the girl thought. Because she could not remember one street? One word? Because this water-stained guitar was his voice and mind? Why ever had she driven them here?

She leaned over the edge of the jukebox and vomited.

And the other white girls, the girls who had come to mock her in their drunkenness, shouted as she vomited: *Schevoski! Schevoski is dead!*

And she vomited and vomited, her index finger over the Bee Gees label of the jukebox, until her mouth grew immediate and she turned, held her stomach, and stumbled through the shouting girls and their exclamatory language, stumbled until she reached the wooden door of the bathroom, stumbled until everything she had eaten this morning came up.

Finally, her stomach was bare.

And the world seemed to spin around her and the water-stained guitar seemed to crawl upon the ceiling, follow her through the wooden door of this place and mock upon her the power of its language; *Schevoski is dead. And you are dead. You, beast.*

And the girls who she had driven here, the Tulane girls, as if they had suddenly become aware of their cruelty, took their fists and banged on the outer walls of the lavatory; they banged and their banging seemed to echo throughout Magazine Street and the city of New Orleans that there was a girl in the john and she was weak and her old man had dumped her and she brought us to this place so we could mock her, make her afraid, tear down these walls she had collapsed into and whatever it was she had left, we would take it. Everything would come true.

Her head spun inside the lavatory and the banging of the other girls from Tulane now began to bang inside her head and she could see them, each of them at once, their mouths open and childlike, swimming around in her heart and mind the torturous chaos of one's not knowing how vulnerable, how thin she is.

Just then, she thought of Schevoski, thought of how she'd met him, how cunning he was to have met her there on the corner of St. Charles and that street she could not remember—she wasn't the only one; now, now amidst the other girls from Tulane and the water-stained guitar, she remembered the photos of the other girls, the other exes, and the labels he had written underneath, all named after the streets on which he had met them—*Elba, Dupre, Willow, General Pershing, Eden*—and there, scribbled beneath her own name, *on the corner of St. Charles and . . .*

Now, now that these things had come to her, she looked up to where the water-stained guitar had been and did her own laughing. And the other girls from Tulane heard it, how powerful it was, and stepped away from the wooden door of the lavatory and stumbled, stumbled back to the abandoned jukebox, back to where the vomit had begun to swell.

Each of them noticed, one at a time and collectively, the image of the water-stained guitar: the *Schevoski is dead!* had now disappeared into the odorous air of Magazine and it was no matter, they were all dead, as the girl who'd brought them here was dead, as Schevoski was dead, like a blade, a glacier.

A beast.

ALGIERS

BY DAVID FULMER

Algiers

Valentin St. Cyr crossed to Algiers on the ferry. It was the end of a hot day in May of 1905, and the fading sun reached out to paint the sky in bloody streaks and spread little points of light over the river like early stardust. Every so often, the wake of a barge would traverse the surface. Then the water got quiet again.

The ferry moved unperturbed through the green shifting swirls. Valentin leaned on the stern railing as the profile of New Orleans retreated. It was good to get out of the city, especially out of Storyville, if only for one night. To get paid for it made it even better, even if he dropped a few dollars while he went about running off the card cheat.

What was the character's name again? McTier?

In any case, it was a Tuesday, and the red light district would be quiet. The Basin Street madams and the sporting women and their gentlemen callers could do without him for one night, and any problems would still be there when he got back.

Valentin spent a few moments patting his clothes in what must have looked like some sort of private genuflection. In fact, he was checking his weapons. The weight of his favored Iver Johnson revolver settled in the pocket of his light cotton suit jacket. His whalebone sap was lodged in the back pocket of his trousers, so that he could reach in with his right hand to swing it around with the force to roll up eyes and buckle knees. Finally, he kept a stiletto in a sheath strapped to his ankle, so it would be easy to grab if some rascal tried to drag him to the floor.

Not that he expected that sort of trouble tonight. He had handled cheapjack hustlers by the dozens. He wouldn't be walking into a rough back-of-town saloon to encounter a sport down on his luck and desperate for a good score, a rounder who thought he owned the place, or, worst of all, some low-down, no-good son of a bitch on a cocaine jag who saw things that weren't there, imagined everyone in the room was out to get him, and itched for an excuse to pull out his own weapon of choice and have at it.

There would be none of that tonight, or so said Valentin's employer, Mr. Tom Anderson. This McTier fellow was just another loud-mouthed, bullying sort, which meant he was most likely a coward, and would quail and run as soon as someone showed up to beat his hand—someone like Valentin St. Cyr. Sometimes all it took was a cold-eyed stare to get a sharp to pick up his loose change and crooked cards or dice and clear out. Other times, a fellow made his exit with his bloody forehead in his hands. And every now and then, nothing but a promise of deadly violence would do. So far, it hadn't gone any further than that.

Once the ferry docked, he stepped onto the pier and walked up the incline and through the narrow avenues of the little town until he found Evelina Street. When he arrived at the corner address, it was little more than a storefront that had been set up with a plank bar and some tables and chairs, not all of them matching. A ceiling fan creaked overhead and the floor was spread with dunes of sawdust that had gone dark with tobacco juice and spilled whiskey. The windows were open on two sides so the breezes off the river could carry away some of the smell. There was a trough in back that served as a toilet. It would take a hurricane to blow that stench away.

A Negro boy who was standing watch opened the door for Valentin, who tossed him a nickel and stepped over the threshold. Two working men leaned their elbows on the near end of the bar. Valentin stepped up and asked for Mr. Roy. The bartender, a tall and lank mulatto, pointed a finger toward the back of the room.

Settled behind the wooden table in the corner was Mr. Roy, a hugely fat man with broad African features and skin a mottled brown, as if he was suffering from some odd ailment. His hair was woolly and the whites of his eyes were a deep yellow, matching his large teeth. He wheezed on every breath and his body and clothes reeked of sweat.

Valentin had never seen him before and didn't know if he was a lawman, a criminal, or a nobody. Valentin didn't know much of anything, other than the fact that Anderson, "The King of Storyville," owed the owner of this rundown establishment a debt, and that Valentin was there to pay it off.

He took a seat across the table from Mr. Roy, who gasped lightly though his mouth as he regarded his visitor. The mulatto came creeping from behind the bar with a bottle and a clean glass, then made a quick retreat—making Valentin wonder if his reputation had arrived there ahead of him.

There was no point in exchanging niceties, so Mr. Roy got right to the point.

"The fellow's name is Eddie McTier," he said, heaving like a tugboat. "He's a guitar player and a gambler out of Georgia. He been in near every night. He busts in on every game, then cheats and takes all the money. Then he lies to cover it. When that don't work, he starts talking that he's fixing to pull his pistol. He must have took fifty dollars off my customers over here. Now no one wants to come around no more."

Valentin was noncommittal. He recognized the type, one of an army of tramps who preyed in places like Algiers, within spitting distance of New Orleans, where he wouldn't last a minute. That he was a guitar player signified nothing.

"Why don't you just put him out?" he inquired.

"I tried that," Mr. Roy huffed. "He just laughed in my face and spit on the floor, and then come right back in the next night. He says he ain't broke no law, and so he has a right. He also say he be carryin' some voodoo, 'count of playin' the blues and all, and so nobody want to cross him. Anyway, the gentleman owns the property wants him out for good. He's ruining business."

For a moment, Valentin thought Mr. Roy was making a joke. *What business would that be?* But the fat man's face was grave.

Valentin had seen this gambit before. If a fellow talked tough or bragged on his voodoo enough, people who should know better fall for the act. This McTier had everyone in the place believing he was a bad actor who wasn't going anywhere until he was good and ready.

Valentin poured an inch of whiskey in his glass and drank it down. "What time does he come around?"

"Soon as the sun goes down. So any time now."

Valentin picked up the bottle and the glass and nodded in the direction of the table in the other corner. "I'll sit over there. He and I'll play some cards. See if he tries to cheat on me."

"Oh, he will," Mr. Roy said.

"Then I'll have reason to put him out."

The fat man pursed his heavy lips. "Don't go gettin' yourself kilt over here."

"Don't plan to," Valentin said. "But if anything starts, you make sure everybody stays the hell out of the way."

He got up and moved to the table, so that he was for the moment hidden in shadow to everyone except the bartender and Mr. Roy, and only because they knew he was there. He drank one more short glass of whiskey. It was hot, and he wanted his wits about him.

Some minutes passed as the sun went all the way down over the river. Valentin let his thoughts wander until the boy who was standing guard stepped inside, rolled his eyes a certain way, then faded into the woodwork. Valentin smiled; the kid would himself make a decent rounder one day.

He heard Eddie McTier before he saw him. The windows were open all along the street side of the saloon and a raucous voice echoed from the next corner: jagged laughter, a blunt shout, and a couple raw curses. Valentin heard the thump of boots on the banquette and finished the liquor in his glass in one quick swallow. Then he leaned back a few inches from the table. The front door flapped rudely open and a short barrel of a black man pushed inside, dressed in brown trousers, a soiled white shirt, and a vest that had seen some dusty miles. A misshapen gray Stetson was cocked sideways on his head.

Eddie McTier stopped to glance around with a cunning sort of smile, almost a childish thing, as if pleased with himself and all he surveyed. He took the Kalamazoo guitar that was strapped on his back and set it in the corner next to the door. Then he let his oily eyes roam past Valentin, circle the saloon, and come back.

He stared into the corner, looking unsure. "Who the hell's that?" he asked the bartender.

The bartender swallowed.

McTier smacked a palm on the bar and said, "Twine! You hear me?"

"Fellow come over from New Orleans," Twine stuttered quickly. "He's lookin' for a game."

McTier peered at the man at the back table. "That right, friend?" he called.

Valentin didn't move or speak.

"You looking for a game or not?" McTier demanded.

Valentin leaned forward so that his face came out of the darkness and into the light. Without a word, he reached into the inside pocket of his jacket and produced a new deck of cards, which he tossed to the center of the table.

McTier peered at the faces as if looking for someone to let him in on the joke. All he got were averted eyes, so he started a slow stroll along the bar.

From the table in the opposite corner, Mr. Roy cleared his throat. "You ort to leave your pistol with Twine there."

McTier cocked his head toward Mr. Roy and then swiveled it to look at the bartender. Twine didn't make the slightest move.

"Let him hold onto it."

All three men turned to toward Valentin. McTier was the only one who spoke. "And what are you carryin' this evening, mister?" he asked.

"That ain't none of your business," Valentin said in an off-hand way.

There was another pause while Eddie McTier decided whether or not to take offense. It was as if an invisible artist had drawn invisible lines in the air, defining the two men and the cold drama that was being staged within those four clapboard walls. Twine stared between them, feeling sweat run from beneath his hair and down his forehead.

It took another few seconds for it to dawn on Eddie McTier that if he did anything except stand there, he'd be finished in Algiers and in New Orleans, for that matter. Meanwhile, Mr. Roy was idly imagining that he could have sold tickets to this event.

Valentin broke the silence. "Did you come to play cards or talk about firearms?"

McTier grinned with his gray, uneven teeth. He turned and called over his shoulder for Twine to bring him a pint and a glass. With a hitch of his shoulders, he pulled out the chair opposite the Creole and sat down.

"I come to play," he said.

Valentin nodded. "That's good," he said. "But, so you understand, you cheat and you're out."

McTier had been reaching for the deck. Now his lazy hand stopped in midair. He cocked a quizzical eyebrow. "What'd you say?"

"I said if you cheat, you're out. And you don't come around here anymore."

McTier let out a disbelieving little snicker. "Is that so? And who says if I cheat?"

"We'll let God be the witness," Valentin said, his mouth curving into a smile that his eyes didn't share.

McTier hiked his eyebrows and snatched up the deck with a brusque motion. "God, huh? You gonna need God if you play cards with me. 'Cause I got the devil on my side. I brought some voodoo from Georgia y'all ain't even *heard* of."

Valentin gave him a dubious look, as if suffering some boastful child. "Put your money on the table," he said. He reached into his own pocket, took out an envelope, opened it, and dumped out twenty gold dollars. He raised his eyes to meet McTier's. "And I mean *all* of it," he said.

McTier had three choices. He could get up out of the chair, leave, and never come back. He could play it straight and lose his poke. Or he could brazen it out and chop this Creole character into pieces.

While he waited for the guitar player to make up his mind, Valentin gazed past him toward the door, where two men in cheap suits and a young woman in a thin cotton dress had stopped to peer inside. They were whispering among themselves and the girl was staring as if she had never seen anything quite like him before. Once he caught her eye, her face broke into a smile that was shyly wicked.

Eddie McTier shifted his way into Valentin's line of vision and rapped his knuckles on the table. "That's it," he said. There was a small cylinder of gold coins in front of him that looked to be at least the equal of Valentin's own.

"That all of it?" Valentin asked.

"Every fucking dime," McTier replied with a snide curl of his lip.

Twine stepped up to the table with a pint bottle of amber liquor in one hand and a short glass in the other. He placed them at McTier's elbow and skipped away in a hurry.

McTier frowned at the bartender "How come everybody's so damn skittish today?" he said. "Y'all are actin' crazy."

Valentin pushed the deck of cards across the table. "You deal," he said.

McTier's face pinched with distrust. He watched Valentin for a second, then fanned a thumb through the deck. Satisfied it was clean, he broke it in half and began to shuffle. "What's your story, friend?" he inquired.

"No story," Valentin said. "Just passing through and looking for a game. What about you?"

"What, ain't nobody told you?"

"Told me what."

"I come from Georgia. Place called Happy Valley. I heard they like the blues in New Orleans. So I come over and I'm here to stay."

Valentin studied the sharp's face, feigning a vague interest, and watched his hands at the same time. McTier was playing it straight so far, but he was talking faster and faster, an old trick that was a variation on the magician's sleight of hand.

"I got me a woman back home in Thomson. Ain't but fifteen years old." He seemed to stumble for a moment. "Got me a child name of Willie. He's blind." Now he fell curiously silent for a few seconds, as if he had lost his way. Recovering, he poured his glass full and drank it halfway down. "But truth is, I got more women than I know what to do with," he crowed as his hands got busy again. "I found me this here young Ethiopian gal and brought her along. I left her over across the river."

"And what are you doing in Algiers?" Valentin asked.

McTier smiled and said, "Takin' your money, friend."

Valentin's face lightened suddenly and he grinned as if the guitar player had just told a good joke. The whispers at the door stopped and even Mr. Roy halted his wheezing for a few seconds.

"I say somethin' funny?" McTier asked.

"Deal," Valentin said.

"I'll deal all right," McTier said, and began snapping cards.

Valentin caught the move on the first hand and let it go. It was the same with the second and third, and McTier, looking giddy, drank some more as he watched the Creole's stack of coins shrink while his grew. A quarter-hour passed in this manner, and Mr. Roy, Twine, the two fellows at the bar, and the trio near the door were all looking at Valentin as if realizing that in fact he was a fool.

For Valentin, it was as easy as hooking a Mississippi catfish. Thinking he had a chump in his sights, and doing some showing off for the locals, McTier tried a more brazen ploy. This time the Creole's left hand came down with the force of a guillotine to grab the guitar player's wrist in an iron grip.

"What did I tell you?" Valentin's voice, though soft, rang out in a room that had suddenly gone dead quiet.

McTier tried to bluff his way out. "What the hell? Take your goddamn paw off me!"

Valentin shrugged and let go, then used the free hand to tear away the cuff of McTier's shirt, popping the link and revealing the card hidden there, an ace of spades. It would have come in handy on the next deal.

McTier lowered his forehead and his eyebrows dipped into a valley. He muttered something under his breath and a rank smell came off him. On the periphery of his vision, Valentin saw the two men standing in the doorway pull the girl back out onto the banquette as the rounders and Twine dropped from sight like ducks in a shooting gallery. Mr. Roy was too fat to move with any haste, so he just pushed his chair back into the corner as far as he could go, and watched.

McTier got to his feet, the torn cuff dangling. "This game's over," he said.

"Damn right," Valentin countered.

The guitar player jerked a thumb. "Door's right back there."

Valentin smiled dimly. "I ain't going anywhere."

"Then I'll take my money and leave."

Valentin shook his head slowly and said, "No, you won't."

A silence fell with a dark weight. From the corner, Mr.

Roy saw the way McTier's face changed. He had made his last threat and it hadn't worked. This time he had only two choices, to run away or stand and fight. Meanwhile, the Creole sat perfectly still, his hands on the table. Mr. Roy hadn't even seen him blink.

McTier let out a sudden raw growl as his hand went across his torso to the waist of his trousers. He snapped out a long-barreled Stevens Tip-Up .22 and brought it around at the same moment that Valentin rose abruptly, knocking back his own chair. The bark of the pistol shook the glasses behind the bar and the slug whistled past Valentin's temple so closely that he felt the wind as it *thunked* into a wall board behind his head.

In his arrogance, McTier had packed a single-shot revolver, never dreaming that he'd have to use it. It was a mistake, because now a second pistol cracked, and the guitar player stumbled back in two long strides, as if pulled by a rope. Both his hands came up and the .22 tumbled out of the right one. The hole in his chest was still smoking when his knees crumpled and he collapsed to the floor.

The last hollow echo died. Now flat on his back, McTier tried to raise himself, then collapsed back, coughed out a ragged breath, and went still as the blood from his chest welled and spread.

Mr. Roy let out a long, noisy wheeze. Three heads rose up from the cover of the bar and the two men and the young girl edged back into the doorway. The Negro boy who had so ably faded into the wall reappeared, his face cracking into a grin of amazement.

Twine leaned over the bar to stare down at the body. "Holy Jesus," he said.

Valentin lowered the pistol, laid it on the table, and sat back down. He picked up the pint, poured some of McTier's whiskey into his glass, and drank it down in a long, slow sip. He looked surprised and perhaps baffled, as if he had wandered in from outside.

Mr. Roy managed to push himself to his feet. "We can take care of it from here on."

Valentin, coming to his senses, understood. They would remove McTier's body and cover the shooting with the police, if they talked about it at all. He also understood that he needed to leave. "Give his guitar to someone who can use it," he said.

Mr. Roy nodded his heavy head.

Valentin walked across the dirty sawdust floor and out onto the banquette, where the young girl's dark round eyes locked on him with a sort of primitive wonder. She seemed to barely breath as he stepped past her and continued down Evelina Street without looking back. He arrived at the pier just in time to catch the last ferry.

PONY GIRL

BY LAURA LIPPMAN

Tremé

She was looking for trouble and she was definitely going to find it. What was the girl thinking when she got dressed this morning? When she decided—days, weeks, maybe even months ago—that this was how she wanted to go out on Mardi Gras day? And not just out, but all the way up to Claiborne Avenue and Ernie K. Doe's, where this kind of costume didn't *play*. There were skeletons and Mardi Gras Indians and baby dolls, but it wasn't a place where you saw a lot of people going for sexy or clever. That kind of thing was for back in the Quarter, maybe outside Café Brasil. It's hard to find a line to cross on Mardi Gras day, much less cross it, but this girl had gone and done it. In all my years—I was nineteen then, but a hard nineteen—I'd only seen one Mardi Gras sight more disturbing, and that was a white boy who took a magic marker, a thick one, and stuck it through a piercing in his earlobe. Nothing more to his costume than that, a magic marker through his ear, street clothes, and a wild gaze. Even in the middle of a crowd, people granted him some distance, let me tell you.

The Mardi Gras I'm talking about now, this was three years ago, the year that people were saying that customs *mattered*, that we had to hold tight to our traditions. Big Chief Tootie Montana was still alive then, and he had called for the skeletons and the baby dolls to make a showing, and there was a pretty good turnout. But it wasn't true old school, with the skeletons going to people's houses and waking up children in their beds, telling them to do their homework and listen to their mamas. Once upon a time, the skeletons were fierce, coming in with old bones from the butcher's shop, shaking the bloody hanks at sleeping children. Man, you do that to one of these kids today, he's likely to come up with a gun, blow the skeleton back into the grave. Legends lose their steam, like everything else. What scared people once won't scare them now.

Back to the girl. Everybody's eyes kept going back to that girl. She was long and slinky, in a champagne-colored body stocking. And if it had been just the body stocking, if she had decided to be Eve to some boy's Adam, glued a few leaves to the right parts, she wouldn't have been so . . . disrupting. Funny how that goes, how pretending to be naked can be less inflaming than dressing up like something that's not supposed to be sexy at all. No, this one, she had a pair of pointy ears high in her blond hair, which was pulled back in a ponytail. She had pale white-and-beige cowboy boots, the daintiest things you ever seen, and—this was what made me fear for her—a real tail of horsehair pinned to the end of her spine, swishing back and forth as she danced. *Swish. Swish. Swish.* And although she was skinny by my standards, she managed the trick of being skinny with curves, so that tail jutted out just so. *Swish. Swish. Swish.* I watched her, and I watched all the other men watching her, and I did not see how anyone could keep her safe if she stayed there, dancing into the night.

Back in school, when they lectured us on the straight-and-narrow, they told us that rape is a crime of violence. They told us that a woman isn't looking for something just because she goes out in high heels and a bustier and a skirt that barely covers her. Or in a champagne-colored body stocking with a tail affixed. They told us that rape has nothing to do with sex. But sitting in Ernie K. Doe's, drinking a Heineken, I couldn't help but wonder if rape *started* as sex and then moved to violence when sex was denied. *Look at me, look at me, look at me,* the tail seemed to sing as it twitched back and forth. Yet Pony Girl's downcast eyes, refusing to make eye contact even with her dancing partner, a plump cowgirl in a big red hat, sent a different message. *Don't touch me, don't touch me, don't touch me.* You do that to a dog with a steak, he bites you, and nobody says it's the dog's fault.

Yeah, I wanted her as much as anyone there. But I feared for her even more than I wanted her, saw where the night was going and wished I could protect her. Where she was from, she was probably used to getting away with such behavior. Maybe she would get away with it here, too, if only because she was such an obvious outsider. Not a capital-T tourist, not some college girl from Tallahassee or Birmingham who had gotten tired of showing her titties on Bourbon Street and needed a new thrill. But a tourist of sorts, the kind of girl who was so full of herself that she thought she always controlled things. She was counting on folks to be rational, which was a pretty big count on Mardi Gras day. People do odd things, especially when they's masked.

I saw a man I knew only as Big Roy cross the threshold. Like most of us, he hadn't bothered with a costume, but he could have come as a frog without much trouble. He had the face for it—pop eyes, broad, flat mouth. Big Roy was almost as wide as he was tall, but he wasn't fat. I saw him looking at Pony Girl long and hard, and I decided I had to make my move. At worst, I was out for myself, trying to get close to her. But I was being a gentleman, too, looking out for her. You can be both. I know what was in my heart that day and, while it wasn't all over pure, it was something better than most men would have offered her.

"Who you s'posed to be?" I asked after dancing awhile with her and her friend. I made a point of making it a three-some, of joining them, as opposed to trying to separate them from one another. That put them at ease, made them like me.

"A horse," she said. "Duh."

"Just any horse? Or a certain one?"

She smiled. "In fact, I *am* a particular horse. I'm Misty of Chincoteague."

"Misty of where?"

"It's an island off Virginia." She was shouting in my ear, her breath warm and moist. "There are wild ponies, and every summer the volunteer firemen herd them together and cross them over to the mainland, where they're auctioned off."

"That where you from?"

"Chincoteague?"

"Virginia."

"My family is from the Eastern Shore of Maryland. But I'm from here. I go to Tulane."

The reference to college should have made me feel a little out of my league, or was supposed to, but somehow it made me feel bolder. "Going to college don't you make you *from* somewhere, any more than a cat born in an oven can call itself a biscuit."

"I love it here," she said, throwing open her arms. Her breasts were small, but they were there, round little handfuls. "I'm never going to leave."

"Ernie K. Doe's?" I asked, as if I didn't know what she meant.

"Yes," she said, playing along. "I'm going to live here forever. I'm going to dance until I drop dead, like the girl in the red shoes."

"Red shoes? You wearing cowboy boots."

She and her friend laughed, and I knew it was at my expense, but it wasn't a mean laughter. Not yet. They danced and they danced, and I began to think that she had been telling a literal truth, that she planned to dance until she expired. I offered her cool drinks, beers and sodas, but she shook her head; I asked if she wanted to go for a walk, but she just twirled away from me. To be truthful, she was wearing me out. But I was scared to leave her side because whenever I glanced in the corner, there was Big Roy, his pop eyes fixed on her, almost yellow in the dying light. I may have been a skinny nineteen-year-old in blue jeans and a Sean John T-shirt—this was back when Sean John was at its height—but I was her self-appointed knight. And even though she acted as if she didn't need me, I knew she did.

Eventually she started to tire, fanning her face with her hands, overheated from the dancing and, I think, all those eyes trained on her. That Mardi Gras was cool and overcast, and even with the crush of bodies in Ernie K. Doe's, it wasn't particularly warm. But her cheeks were bright red, rosy, and there were patches of sweat forming on her leotard—two little stripes beneath her barely-there breasts, a dot below her tail and who knows where else.

Was she stupid and innocent, or stupid and knowing? That is, did she realize the effect she was having and think she could control it, or did she honestly not know? In my heart of hearts, I knew she was not an innocent girl, but I wanted to see her that way because that can be excused.

Seeing her steps slow, anticipating that she would need a drink now, Big Roy pressed up, dancing in a way that only a feared man could get away with, a sad little hopping affair. Not all black men can dance, but the ones who can't usually know better than to try. Yet no one in this crowd would dare make fun of Big Roy, no matter how silly he looked.

Except her. She spun away, made a face at her cowgirl, pressing her lips together as if it was all she could do to keep from laughing. Big Roy's face was stormy. He moved again, placing himself in her path, and she laughed out loud this time. Grabbing her cowgirl's hand, she trotted to the bar and bought her own Heineken.

"Dyke," Big Roy said, his eyes fixed on her tail.

"Yeah," I said, hoping that agreement would calm him, that he would shake off the encounter. Myself, I didn't get that vibe from her at all. She and Cowgirl were tight, but they weren't like *that,* I didn't think.

When Pony Girl and Cowgirl exited the bar, doing a little skipping step, Big Roy wasn't too far behind. So I left, followed Big Roy as he followed those girls, wandering under the freeway, as if the whole thing were just a party put on for them. These girls were so full of themselves that they didn't even stop and pay respect to the Big Chiefs they passed, just breezed by as if they saw such men every day. The farther they walked, the more I worried. Big Roy was all but stalking them, but they never looked back, never seemed to have noticed. And Big Roy was so fixed on them that I didn't have to worry about him turning around and spotting me. Even so, I darted from strut to strut, keeping them in my sights. Night was falling.

They reached a car, a pale blue sedan—theirs, I guess—

and it was only when I watched them trying to get into it that I began to think that the beers they had drunk had hit them awfully hard and fast. They weren't big girls, after all, and they hadn't eaten anything that I had seen. They giggled and stumbled, Cowgirl dropping her keys—Pony Girl didn't have no place to keep keys—their movements wavy and slow. The pavement around the car was filthy with litter, but that didn't stop Pony Girl from going down on her knees to look for the keys, sticking her tail high in the air. Even at that moment, I thought she had to know how enticing that tail was, how it called attention to itself.

It was then that Big Roy jumped on her. I don't know what he was thinking. Maybe he assumed Cowgirl would run off, screaming for help—and wouldn't find none for a while, because it took some time for screams to register on Mardi Gras day, to tell the difference between pleasure and fear. Maybe he thought rape could turn to sex, that if he just got started with Pony Girl, she'd like it. Maybe he meant to hurt them both, so it's hard to be sorry for what happened to him. I guess the best answer is that he wasn't thinking. This girl had made him angry, disrespected him, and he wanted some satisfaction for that.

But whatever Big Roy intended, I'm sure it played different in his head from what happened. Cowgirl jumped on his back, riding him, screaming and pulling at his hair. Pony Girl rolled away, bringing up those tiny boots and thrusting them at just the spot, so he was left gasping on all fours. They tell women to go for the eyes if they's fighting, not to count on hitting that sweet spot, but if you can get it, nothing's better. The girls had all the advantage they needed, all they had to do was find those keys and get out of there.

Instead, the girls attacked him again, rushing him, crazy

bitches. They didn't know the man they were dealing with, the things he'd done just because he could. Yet Big Roy went down like one of those inflatable clowns you box with, except he never popped back up. He went down and . . . I've never quite figured out what I saw just then, other than blood. Was there a knife? I tell you, I like to think so. If there wasn't a knife, I don't want to contemplate how they did what they did to Big Roy. Truth be told, I turned my face away after seeing that first spurt of blood geyser into the air, the way they pressed their faces and mouths toward it like greedy children, as if it were a fire hydrant being opened on a hot day. I crouched down and prayed that they wouldn't see me, but I could still hear them. They laughed the whole time, a happy squealing sound. Again I thought of little kids playing, only this time at a party, whacking at one of those papier-mâché things. A piñata, that's what you call it. They took Big Roy apart as if he were a piñata.

Their laughter and the other sounds died away, and I dared to look again. Chests heaving, they were standing over what looked like a bloody mound of clothes. They seemed quite pleased with themselves. To my amazement, Pony Girl peeled her leotard off then and there, so she was wearing nothing but the tights and the boots. She appeared to be starting on them as well, when she yelled out, in my direction: "What are you looking at?"

Behind the highway's strut, praying I couldn't be seen, I didn't say anything.

"Is this what you wanted to see?" She opened her arms a little, did a shimmying dance so her breasts bounced, and Cowgirl laughed. I stayed in my crouch, calculating how hard it would be to get back to where the crowds were, where I would be safe. I could outrun them easy. But if they got in the car and came after me, I wouldn't have much advantage.

The girls waited, as if they expected someone to come out and congratulate them. When I didn't emerge, they went through Big Roy's pockets, took the cash from his wallet. Once the body—if you could call it that—was picked clean of what little it had, Pony Girl popped the trunk of the car. She stripped the rest of the way, so she was briefly naked, a ghostly glow in the twilight. She stuffed her clothes, even her ears and her tail, in a garbage bag, then slipped on jeans, a T-shirt, and a pair of running shoes. Cowgirl didn't get all the way naked, but she put her red hat in the garbage bag, swapped her full skirt for a pair of shorts. They drove off, but not at all in a hurry. They drove with great deliberation, right over Big Roy's body—and right past me, waving as they went.

I suppose they's smart. I suppose they watch those television shows, know they need to get rid of every little scrap of clothing, that there's no saving anything, not even those pretty boots, if they don't want the crime to be traced back to them. I suppose they've done this before, or at least had planned it careful-like, given how prepared they were. I think they've done it since then, at least once or twice. At least, I've noticed the little stories in the *Times-Picayune* this year and last—a black man found dead on Mardi Gras day, pockets turned out. But the newspaper is scanty with the details of how the man got dead. Not shot, they say. A suspicious death, they say. But they don't say whether it was a beating or a cutting or a hot shot or what. Makes me think they don't know how to describe what's happened to these men. Don't know how, or don't feel it would be proper, given that people might be eating while they's reading.

Just like that, it's become another legend, a story that

people tell to scare the little ones, like the skeletons showing up at the foot of your bed and saying you have to do your homework and mind your parents. There are these girls, white devils, go dancing on Mardi Gras, looking for black men to rob and kill. The way most people tell the story, the girls go out dressed as demons or witches, but if you think about it, that wouldn't play, would it? A man's not going to follow a demon or a witch into the night. But he might be lured into a dark place by a fairy princess, or a cat—or a Cowgirl and her slinky Pony Girl, with a swatch of horsehair pinned to the tailbone.

THE BATTLING PRIESTS OF CORPUS CHRISTI

BY JERVEY TERVALON

Seventh Ward

> *As each one has received a gift, use it to serve one another as good stewards of God's varied grace.*
>
> 1 Peter 4:10

Some priests you know what they're up to before they open their mouths. Father Murphy acted so righteous you'd believe his sermons were spun gold, but he really didn't need to say a word, I already knew all about him. He hated Negroes, and if they made the mistake of coming to his church and sat in the colored section, the last two pews of Sacred Heart, like they were supposed to, he would berate them for being so brazen and uppity as to actually attend Mass. Colored people needed to make novenas, and I don't think the Lord makes a distinction between white people and everybody else, so we had to put up with this heartless man who must have thought wearing a collar excused him of having to treat Negroes with a hint of kindness, Christian or otherwise. He still had a swollen face and the shadow of a black eye he had received almost a month ago from Father Fitzpatrick, but obviously you can't beat the hate or hell out of someone. It doesn't work no matter how good it might feel to try, and Father Fitzpatrick had done his brutal best.

I looked as white as anyone at Sacred Heart, but I didn't pretend to be anything other than Negro. I assumed I'd receive a special dispensation from him, I'd be spared the vicious race baiting that he'd become notorious for, but before he began his sermon he pointed at the last two pews to the few Negroes who were there and shouted, "You people are not welcome, but you still come!" Then he looked directly at me, red-faced and breathing heavily; but it didn't seem as though he knew who I was; he didn't seem to recognize me as the daughter of John Carol, his friend, drinking partner, and fellow Irishman. I couldn't imagine him saying to me during Mass, *Helen, move to the back of the church. Don't make me embarrass you,* but after hearing the venom in his voice I wasn't sure. I sat there stone-faced and could only breathe easily when Mass ended and the pews emptied.

Once away from the pulpit, outside on the steps, he presented himself with reserve and dignity as though his heart wasn't as black as night. It was odd to me that this man who was kind to me as a child had changed so much as to hate so blindly. Or maybe I had never noticed it before because to him I was John Carol's daughter, and not the daughter of a colored woman. He had overlooked that because he thought of me as he wanted to think of me, a pretty little Irish girl. When I grew into a woman, that had changed too, and I began to receive letters from him that I could never show my father.

I waited for most of the crowd to disperse before I approached Father Murphy.

"What brings you here to Sacred Heart, Helen, novenas to St. Jude?"

"Yes, Father, but I wonder if I may have a minute of your time."

"Well, I'm busy," he said snappishly.

"It'll only take a minute."

At first I thought he'd turn me down, and I have to

admit I was surprised by the frown on his face, but that passed. He looked at me and smiled as though this was the first time he'd truly noticed me, and I was uncomfortable because of it; just as I was uncomfortable about the letters he had sent me.

"Walk with me," he directed.

For an older man, he moved quickly and I could barely keep up. He led me to the rectory, unlocked it, turned and waved impatiently for me to enter. I followed him along the dim hall watching his narrow shoulders, wondering if I had made a mistake.

He opened another door and there was a young priest behind a desk typing.

"Please leave," Father Murphy said, and the priest moved quickly out of the room. When we were alone, he pointed to a very large leather chair. Then he pulled another chair close to it and sat down next to me.

"What can I do for you, Helen? Are you finally responding to the letters I've been sending you?" he asked with a stupidly coy smile.

I paused for a moment, trying not to show how afraid I was as I looked for the right words.

"It's about Father Fitzpatrick."

His face suddenly drained of its ruddiness. He leaned forward until he was so close to my face that I could see his nose hairs.

"What about him? Did you find him lying drunk in his own filth in a gutter? He's a disgrace to himself and to the Church, and to associate with him proves that you have no self-respect. To the world you consort with niggers like he does. They don't see you as a colored woman. They see you as a white woman who's an embarrassment to her race."

I stood ready to walk out on him and slam the door hard enough to shatter the frosted glass window.

Father Murphy sighed, and took my hand. "I apologize for that. Please don't tell your father. He needn't be reminded how bad my temper is."

I refused to respond with words; instead I glared, wanting very much to slap him across the face. Maybe he didn't respect me because I was colored, but I did respect myself and I refused to be insulted by any man, and I didn't think he was much of a man.

"I never understood you, Helen. You're a beautiful young woman; you could marry well, but you lower yourself. You could live a good life and leave New Orleans and no one would ever have to know that you're a Negro. You must realize you have friends who want to help you better yourself."

"I'm not here for my benefit. The situation with Father Fitzpatrick is out of hand. Negroes are enraged and won't stand for drunken louts disrespecting and sometimes threatening them because they come to Sacred Heart to make a novena."

"I encourage anyone to come to our church—the Germans, the Italians—but I draw the line at Negroes. One can't be open-minded about what is unnatural. These blacks need to know their place."

I sighed deeply and tried to remain civil, though my blood boiled and I could feel my face flush with anger.

"Knowing one's place may be important, but Father Fitzpatrick came to Sacred Heart to talk things out and you insulted him, and then you were both rolling in the street. That can't go on; someone is going to get killed."

Father Murphy abruptly shouted, "You defend that fool, Fitzpatrick! He can go to hell! What is done is done. I will deal with him. What about you? Why do you keep company with such a man? You need to ask yourself why you live as though you are colored; you have a choice. You can turn your back on those people and trash like Fitzpatrick and live with dignity. I've talked to your father about this and he refuses to say more than you've made your decision and that you're stubborn. If you were under my roof I wouldn't allow you to degrade yourself associating with those who are obviously your inferiors. You aren't the same as the common Negro any more than I am."

Furious words burst from my mouth: "The English think you Irish are dogs. I'm not interested in your opinion of the colored, as I'm sure you're not interested in the English's opinion of you. My father came here to find his fortune and he did; he took up with a colored woman who loved me as he does. I am as colored as she was, and I'm proud of that."

"You're young," he said with an odd smile. "Your sentiments are admirable. It would be good if this could be worked out."

The anger was gone from his voice, and then Father Murphy moved his hand down to my thigh.

"Helen, I can give you far more than your father. I can help you if you're kind to me. Why won't you respond to my letters?"

I let his hand stay there for a second, paralyzed by the suddenness of it.

"Be kind to me, Helen," he said with a smile that was more a leer, and he moved his hand higher up my thigh.

I reached for the lamp on the coffee table before I knew what I was going to do. He realized it, but he was a split second too late. I caught him flush on the side of the head. He dropped with the heaviness of someone dead; I stood over him for a moment, wondering what to do next.

* * *

"My God, Helen, did you kill him?" Father Fitzpatrick asked in horror.

He was a good-looking, tall, and well-built man with hair black as a crow's feathers. He did have bad teeth, due mostly to his habit of getting into fistfights. Father Fitzpatrick insisted that we call him Billy and never Father unless he was in the church, and even then he looked pained when someone did.

He was seated on the steps of a very clean but small shotgun house that served as the temporary rectory of the Corpus Christi Church while the parishioners raised the money to build the real rectory. I stood in the shade fanning myself with a street car schedule.

"No, Billy, he moaned . . . and before I ran from the office, I saw him try to stand."

"Good. He deserves to die, but not by you."

"It's not good. My temper has gotten me nothing but trouble. My father wants to send me to Baton Rouge."

"Listen to him. You must know how vindictive Murphy can be. He can do most anything without remorse. He has no conscience, but he does have all the conviction of a man who speaks with the authority of Jesus Christ himself. If I see him on the street it's unbearable. He mocks the priesthood and demeans it; and it's shameful that no one will stand up to him."

"So *you* must? No matter how awful Murphy is, you can't think that beating him in the street will solve anything. Aren't you afraid of losing your church or being defrocked?"

He laughed. "This from a woman who just bashed a man in the head. God knows the truth but waits. I trust in the Lord to guide and protect me. Or least to help me sober up before Mass."

"Must you make light of everything?"

He shrugged. "Why are you afraid of Baton Rouge? It's a fine town."

"I won't go to Baton Rouge. My father wants me to stay with relatives who I can't tolerate."

"Why can't you tolerate them? From what I hear, they eat and dance in Baton Rouge just like they do here."

"They drink and argue constantly. They have no culture."

He poured himself another whiskey and laughed. "Sometimes I forget how haughty you are."

"I am not haughty," I said, and waved goodbye to him as I rushed to catch the trolley. I couldn't help but like Father Fitzpatrick. He was a kind and worldly man who was ill-suited for the priesthood, and largely lived his life as though he wasn't part of it. I knew that he frequented bars and gambling dens, and it was rumored that he had more than one female admirer, but he had a good heart and made sure that those who had need in the Seventh Ward were tended to, and that the Creoles and Negroes were treated with the same respect as the whites. The rumors that Father Fitzpatrick was on the way out of town were very hard to ignore, but until the day they ran him out of town, his rage at Murphy would be uncontrollable. It was only a matter of time before he'd get a couple too many whiskeys in him and walk the few blocks to Sacred Heart to bust Murphy's eye once again, and this time Murphy would most certainly be ready for him.

When I arrived home on Gravier she was already on the porch, fanning herself with her hat. Even from a distance she looked tall and imposing, an iron rail of a woman, black as night and fiercer than a lioness.

"Your father asked me to escort you to Baton Rouge. He explained to me his thinking and I agree with him. He has very good reasons for you to go."

"Yes, Aunt Odie, he does, or so I've been hearing for the last few days."

"Have you gotten threats?"

"Threats? Not yet. I can't say that I expect threats."

"Child, think. You assaulted the kind of man who has the means and the temperament to hurt you."

"What do you suggest?"

"Listen to your father. If you don't go to Baton Rouge, you need to leave this house and move in with him for a time."

"I can't do that. This is my mother's house and I promised her I wouldn't become a child tethered to his ankle."

"Well, if you're not going to Baton Rouge, I will stay with you until this situation is resolved. Murphy holds sway with those drunken countrymen of his. Those Irish thugs drove the colored off the docks. They want to chase us out of town and they will certainly hurt you if given a chance."

I always listened to Aunt Odie, but of course she didn't necessarily feel the same sort of obligation to listen to me. If she thought I needed watching, I would be watched. I was a woman with some means and I did have a mind equal to a man's, and though I loved my father, sometimes it seemed I was still that child wrapped around his ankle.

I was preparing to stew a rabbit that evening and my hands were bloody with it, when I heard someone rattling the screen. I supposed it might have been Aunt Odie, who had gone to the market for lemons. I called out to her, but she didn't respond. I turned to the door and saw a redhaired white man standing there, rubbing his hands together with a brutal look on his face.

"You know why I'm here," he said with vicious pleasure.

"Get out of my house!" I shouted at him.

"I will teach you a lesson."

"Damnit, I said get out of here!"

He ignored me and took a step forward, pulling at his belt. I retreated to the kitchen, hoping to get my hands on a knife before he reached me.

Then I heard Aunt Odie's voice.

"Stop!" She had a knife in one hand and an open jar in the other filled with what looked to be water.

The big redhaired man didn't seem impressed. He pulled a blackjack from his pocket and started toward her while keeping an eye on me.

"Run home now, before something bad happens to you," Odie said, as if she were talking to a child.

"Nigger woman, don't order me."

Aunt Odie tossed the contents of the jar into his face and he screamed and smashed against the wall and the door before stumbling outside, begging for water for his eyes.

"Lye," she said as she locked the door. "It's as good as a bullet or a knife."

I was in Baton Rouge when I heard about Father Fitzpatrick; that he never made it home the night before from the Napoleon House, the bar he frequented in the French Quarter.

We were sure that he was dead, beaten to death by one of Murphy's hooligans and tossed into the river. I wasn't surprised, though I was grief-stricken. My father insisted that I stay in Baton Rouge, but I was nearly losing my mind with my relatives.

I spent weeks at my aunt's bakery, sweat blinding my eyes, roasting while the bread baked. My unhappiness was too much for words; I didn't want to drown in my sweat in a town without culture, without my friends and loved ones. I was finished with Baton Rouge; my time in exile was done. I had to return to New Orleans with or without my father's permission. My mother hadn't raised me to be a coward, living in fear, in seclusion. I had to know what happened to Father Fitzpatrick.

Rumors continued to roil that the colored would be attacked if they tried to enter Sacred Heart, and worse. I wanted one last conversation with Father Murphy, one that he wouldn't recover from, but that wasn't to happen. I can't say I was unhappy when I heard that Murphy was found beaten to death in the rectory, but the bitterness in my heart would last as long as my memory of Father Fitzpatrick.

OPEN MIKE

BY JAMES NOLAN

French Quarter

There must be hundreds of kids who have wound up dead in the French Quarter. Eva Pierce was just one of them. Everywhere you walk in the neighborhood you see fliers about them taped to lampposts: *Information Wanted* or *$5,000 Reward*. And below is a blurry snapshot of some scruffy young person. After Eva's body was discovered, bundled inside a blue Tommy Hilfiger comforter floating in Bayou St. John, the girl's mother moved down here from Idaho or Iowa or Ohio—however you pronounce it—and blanketed the Quarter with those signs. She even printed her daughter's last poem on the flier, but no dice. The fifteen hours between when Eva was last seen and when her body was found in the bayou remained a blank.

That's when the mother rang me. I'm listed in the Yellow Pages: *Off-Duty Homicide Detective: Dead or Alive, Inc.*

Mrs. Pierce met me under the bingo board at Fiorella's restaurant at the French Market. It wasn't my suggestion. I hadn't been to the market since I was a kid, when my daddy used to take me on Saturday mornings to squabble with his wop relatives while we loaded up at a discount on their fruits and vegetables. On my daddy's side I'm related to everyone who ever sold a pastry, an eggplant, or a bottle of dago red in the Quarter, and on my mother's side to everyone who ever ran the numbers, pimped girls, or took a kickback. I peeked inside the rotting old market, but sure didn't see any Italians or tomatoes. Now it's just Chinese selling knock-off sunglasses to tourists.

Mrs. Pierce was short and round as a cannoli, with a stiff gray bouffant and a complexion like powdered sugar. With those cat's-eye bifocals, she looked like someone who might be playing bingo at Fiorella's. But when she opened her mouth . . . *Twilight Zone*. Mrs. Pierce said it wasn't drugs or sex that did her daughter in, but—get this—poetry.

"And the police aren't doing anything," she said with a flat Midwestern whine that made me want to go suck a lemon.

"Look, lady, I'm a cop—Lieutenant Vincent Panarello, Sixth District—and the police have more trouble than they can handle in New Orleans. They don't pay us much . . . I got a wife and three kids in Terrytown, so that's why I moonlight as a detective."

"My daughter loved moonlight."

"I bet."

"She read her own original poetry every Tuesday night at that rodent-infested bar on Esplanade Avenue called the Dragon's Den." She was twisting the wrapper from her straw into a noose.

"Yeah, that used to be Ruby Red's in my day. A college joint, the floor all covered with sawdust and peanut shells." I didn't tell her how drunk I used to get there in high school with a fake ID. While I was going to night school at Tulane, Ruby Red's was where I met my first wife Janice, may she rest in peace.

"Well, the place has gone beatniky." Mrs. Pierce leaned forward, her eyes watering. "And do you know what I think, Lieutenant Panarello?'

"Shoot."

"I think one of those poets murdered my daughter. One of those characters who read at the open mike. And that's where I want you to start. To listen for clues when the poets read. Eventually one of them will give himself away."

"Listening to the perms will cost you extra." And so will the French Quarter, but I'd already averaged that in when I quoted her my fee.

"I'll meet you there Tuesday at 9 p.m. It's above that Thai restaurant. Just go through the alley—"

"I know how to get up there." I could have climbed those worn wooden steps next to the crumbling brick wall in my sleep. That's where I first kissed Janice. Funny, but she also wrote poems she read to me on the sagging wrought-iron balcony. The life I really wanted was the one I had planned with her. The life I settled for is the one I got.

Mrs. Pierce handed me a picture of her daughter, a list of her friends, and a check. I eyed the amount. Local bank.

"What your daughter do for a living?" I pushed back my chair, antsy to blow Fiorella's. I could already smell the fried chicken grease on my clothes.

"Why, she was a poet and interpretive dancer."

"Interpretive dancer. Gotcha."

I studied the photo. Eva was about twenty-four, pretty, with skin as pale and powdery as a moth's wing. But she was dressed in a ratty red sweater over a pink print dress over black sweatpants. Her dyed black hair was hanging in two stringy hanks of pigtail like a cocker spaniel's ears. Who would want to kill her, I wondered, except the fashion police?

When I got down to the station I pulled the report. Eva was last seen at Molly's bar on Decatur Street at 4 a.m. on a Tuesday, where she told her roommate, Pogo Lamont, that she was going home to feed their one-eyed dog named Welfare. They lived on Ursulines at Bourbon, upper slave quarter, uptown side. She never made it home. After an anonymous 911 tip, her body was hoisted out of the bayou at 7 p.m. the next evening. One clean shot through the temple, real professional. No forced sexual entry. Her purse was lying open on the grassy bank, surrounded by a gaggle of ducks trying to get at the bag of stale popcorn inside. A cell phone and twenty-five dollars were tucked in the bag, so the motive wasn't robbery. Also inside the purse were a red lipstick, a flea collar, a black notebook filled with poems, two 10 mg. Valiums, an Ohio picture ID, a plastic straw that tested positive for cocaine residue, and a worn-out restraining order against Brack Self, a bartender and "performance artist" who turned out to have been locked up the whole time in Tampa for beating on his present girlfriend. That, and an Egyptian scarab, a petrified dung beetle supposed to be a symbol of immortality.

Which didn't seem to have worked for Eva Pierce, poet and stripper.

I made it to the Dragon's Den on a sticky Tuesday evening, with a woolly sky trapping humidity inside the city like a soggy blanket. It had been trying to rain for two weeks. The air was always just about to clear but never did, as if old Mother Nature were working on her orgasm. I carried an umbrella, expecting a downpour. The place was right next to the river, and hadn't seen a drop of paint since I last walked in the door thirty years ago, with all my hair and a young man's cocky swagger. A whistle was moaning as a freight train clacked along the nearby tracks, and the huge live oak out front shrouded the crumbling façade in a tangle of shadows.

An old rickshaw was parked outside, where an elfin creature with orange hair sat scribbling in a notebook. He shot me a look through thick black plastic glasses, and then went back to writing.

Guess I'd found the poets.

I slapped a black beret on my head as I headed through the clammy alley, the bricks so decrepit that ferns were sprouting from the walls. I needed to blend in with the artsy crowd here, so I wore a blousy purple shirt and tight black pants, and carried a paperback by some poet I'd had to read at night school called Oscar Wilde. A wizened old Chinese guy was squatting over a tub of vegetables in the patio, and the air smelled like spices. Something was sizzling in the kitchen. I felt like I was in Hong Kong looking for my Shanghai Lil.

Except for the Far East decor, the bar upstairs hadn't changed that much. A small stage and dance floor had been added at the center, and the tables were low, surrounded by pillows on the floor. Is that where poets eat, I wondered, on the floor?

"I'll have something light and refreshing, with a twist of lime," I lisped to the two-ton Oriental gal behind the bar, waving my pinky. A biker type in a leather cowboy hat was observing me from across the bar.

"You a cop?" he yelled.

"Why no," I said, batting my eyelashes, holding up the lavender book so he could read the cover. "I've come for the poultry."

"Hey, Miss Ping," he shouted to the bartender, "give Lieutenant Girlfriend here a wine spritzer on my tab."

Just as I lurched forward to knock this asshole's block off, in walked Mrs. Pierce with that orange-haired garden gnome from out front.

"Here you go, Lieutenant Girlfriend," Miss Ping said, setting down the drink.

"Lieutenant," Mrs. Pierce said, "this was Eva's roommate, Pogo Lamont."

"Lieutenant Girlfriend," Pogo cackled, extending his hand.

"Come on, son, I want to talk to you on the balcony," I said, grabbing him by the shoulder.

"Unhand me this instant!" the little creep cried out.

"Watch out," grunted the joker in the leather cowboy hat. "Lieutenant Girlfriend's already hitting on the chicken." Miss Ping barked a throaty laugh.

The kid followed me onto the balcony, which was pitching precariously away from the building. I steadied myself as if stepping onto a boat, not trusting the rusted iron-lace railing to keep all 250 pounds of me from rolling off.

"Okay, you know why I'm here," I said, plunking down my drink on a wobbly table. "Who's this Brack Self character that Eva took out a peace bond against?"

"Oh, that snarling beast," Pogo said, curling up like a cat into a chair. "A former beau who used his fists to make a point. Black and blue weren't Eva's most becoming colors."

"She liked it rough, huh?"

"Oooh, Lieutenant Girlfriend," Pogo squealed.

"Say, you little—" Play it cool, I thought. This is just a job.

"She met him here at the open mike when the poetry series started. That first night he got so wasted he just unzipped, whipped it out, and pissed sitting right at a table. While I was performing, I might add. Now that, honey, is what I call literary criticism. Eva mopped it up, and never stopped. And ended up mothering him."

"How long they together?"

"Until the third occasion she summoned the police."

He couldn't have killed her from a jail cell in Tampa. Maybe he had friends.

"How long you been coming here?"

"Since I was a boy. When Mother couldn't find a babysitter, she'd haul me here when it was Ruby Red's—"

"I used to come here then, too. Who was your mom?"

"Lily."

"Lily Lamont?" She was the fancy-pants Uptown debutante who used to cause scenes whenever I was here with Janice. In those days the port was right across the train tracks from the Quarter, and Lily Lamont was usually being held upright between a couple of Greek or Latino sailors. Once I swung open the door to the can to find her on her knees giving one of them a blow job while a rat looked on from the urinal. That's when I stopped bringing Janice to this dump.

"Did you know Mother?" Pogo squirmed in his seat.

"Only by sight." So this was the stunted offspring of one of those Ruby Red nights. If Janice were still here, we'd have children his age.

"Your mother still alive?" I asked.

"If you care to call it that. She's secluded inside her Xanadu on Pirate's Alley."

I softened to the little creep. He told me that as a kid, his mother would often show up at their apartment on Dumaine with a strange man and they'd lock themselves inside her room for three days with a case of bourbon. Now Pogo lived on a trust fund from the Lamonts, which paid the rent on the apartment. He was finishing a book of poems dedicated to his mother titled *The Monster Cave*.

"Where did Eva strip?"

"At Les Girls on Iberville. She gave it up soon after she

moved in with me. You see, I paid for everything. Because Eva was my teacher and muse."

"She ever bring any guys home from there?"

"Not guys. Other strippers sometimes."

"So she swung both ways?"

"Oooh, Lieutenant Girlfriend." Pogo nudged my leg with his foot. "Do you?"

I heard some ranting and raving from inside the bar, and edged my way in to listen. The place was packed, with a permanent cloud of cigarette smoke hovering in the spotlight. First up was Millicent Tripplet, an obese woman with ruby lipstick, who recited a poem about how oppressed she felt when she was being fucked by a certain guy, and how depressed she felt when she wasn't. That got a howl of appreciation. Then a rapper named Pawnshop took the stage, coked out of his gourd, to blow the trumpet and rap about how all the bitches and ho's weren't down with his skinny black ass in the baggy jumpsuit. His rhymes were catchy but the rhythm was a snooze. Then came a comic from the racetrack who sounded like my Uncle Dominic; next up was some nerd in a plaid sports coat who read a sonnet about peat moss and death; and then some anorexic lady dressed all in lilac who choked up in the middle and had to sit down. I couldn't figure out what her poem was about. I think her pooch died.

One thing I clocked: The better the poet, the shorter the spiel. The worst ones droned on forever. I gave Mrs. Pierce an empty shrug, as if to say, *No clues here, lady*. Then she took the stage, hands folded, looking like a Methodist Sunday school teacher. She held up the flier and announced that she would read the last poem her daughter ever wrote:

I've always known you
though we haven't met.
I know how your name tastes
though I've never said it.
You linger on the last step
of stairs I never descend.
I stand with my address book
on a landing to which you never
climb, and every day we stop
just short of each other.

I invoke you to appear,
to kiss childhood back
into my skeptical mouth,
rain into this parched air.
I invoke you at the sudden angle
of smoke, secrets, and zippers,
at the hour when earlobes,
skin along inner thighs,
a smooth chest is tenderest,
love unfolding like a hammock
to fit whatever is nearest.
I invoke your breath's fur
on my neck, your curve of lips,
the blue seaweed of your hair where
we'll weave a nest of lost mornings.

The words sent a chill down my spine. It was as if Eva had been waiting for her murderer. Had a date with death. All I could see was Janice, her face bent over a glowing red candle holder, her straight blond hair swaying as she read poems to me. I had to rush out onto the balcony where I could sit alone and be twenty again, if only for a moment, and remember what a love so fragile felt like.

Finally it was raining, coming down in torrents, the oak branches and curlicues of iron lace dripping fat, dirty tears. *Drip drop, drip drop*. What was that Irma Thomas song we were always listening to in those days? *"It's raining so hard, it brings back memories."* An ambulance raced past, its flashing red lights hellish on the slick street. And I had to endure it all over again, her body dragged from the driver's seat of our crumpled red Chevy. She had been coming home with a birthday surprise for me, and the MacKenzie cake box was soaked with her blood. I never thought I'd be sitting again with Janice on the balcony at Ruby Red's, listening to the rain.

I began to haunt the Quarter for the first time in years, trying to get a handle on Eva's world. Mostly she hung out in what they used to call Little Sicily, around the French Market and lower Decatur Street, where my daddy grew up. Like all the Sicilians in this town, his family had lived over their corner grocery store, Angelo's Superette at Decatur and Governor Nicholls. My only relative left in the neighborhood was Aunt Olivia, a butch little old maid who used to run a laundromat with her mama on Dauphine Street. She owned half the Quarter, and my Uncle Dominic, who hadn't worn anything but pajamas for the past twenty years, owned the other half. When I was young everyone was always going, *Oh, jeez, you got family in the Quarter, you should visit them.* But like my mama always said, "Me, I don't go by them dagos none. They just as soon stick a knife in your back."

The neighborhood was a different place now, and I couldn't understand what anyone down here did to make a living. You hardly saw any grocery stores or dry cleaners or fruit vendors or florists or printing offices or notions stores. Mostly the shops were Pakistani joints selling Mardi Gras masks made in China. Even the criminals were candy-assed, just a bunch of two-bit drug dealers and purse snatchers, nothing like the outfit my mama's family used to run. In those days, if a girl didn't cough up to her pimp, she got a Saturday-night makeover with acid splashed in her face. The girls used to roll the sailors right and left, slipping mickeys in their drinks or switchblades between their ribs. Now I walked around at night unarmed with a couple hundred bucks in my pocket. The streets were filled with gutter punks, their mangy mutts, and older kids playing dress-up. These kids thought they were being *bad bad bad.* They'd snort their little powders and do their little humpety-hump on somebody's futon. Then they'd ride their bikes and eat their vegetables, just like their mamas told them. They even recycled.

I figured with all these Pollyannas floating around, older predators were bound to be lurking in the shadows, dying to take a bite out of this innocent flesh. So the first place I hit was where Eva used to strip, Les Girls de Paree on Iberville between Royal and Chartres. This block of seedy dives was the real thing, the way the whole Quarter used to look when I was coming up. The Vieux Carré Commission must have preserved it as a historical diorama. A hulking bozo with a mullet haircut held the doors open onto the pulsing red lights of a dark pit belting out bump-and-grind. Inside, Les Girls smelled like dirty drawers in a hamper. Or to put it less delicately, like ass.

Some skanky brunette with zits on her behind was rubbing her crotch on an aluminum pole and jiggling her store-bought titties. You'd have to be pretty desperate to throw a boner for a rancid slice of luncheon meat like that. Only two old guys were sitting in the shadows, and I couldn't figure out how this joint sucked in any bucks. Finally, Mullet-head waltzed over to ask what I wanted.

"I want to talk about Eva Pierce."

"Miss Ivonne," he called out, eyeballing me up and down, "copper here."

This over-the-hill fluffball with champagne hair clopped over to my table. I couldn't take my eyes off her lips. "What can I do for you, officer?"

"Eva Pierce" is all I said. Her lips were pink and puffed out like Vienna Sausages. They must have kept a vat of collagen under the bar.

"I've been waiting for this little bereavement call," she said, sliding into a chair. "I'm still broke-up about Eva. She didn't belong here, and I was glad to see her leave. All she ever did was write poetry and sip 7-Up. But she sure attracted the chicken-hawks."

"Anyone in particular?"

"I don't rat out my customers."

"Eva liked it rough, and swung both ways, right?"

"Where you hear that, babe?" She yanked a Vantage from inside her bra and lipped it.

"Her roommate Pogo."

"Me and his momma used to have the best damn time." she shrieked, pounding the table. "But don't ever cross that woman. No siree."

"You know Lily Lamont?"

She slit her eyes at me. "You sure get around for a cop."

"Some people pay me to."

"Look, officer," she said, shooting a stream of smoke toward the ceiling through those lips, "Eva went home with a couple of the girls here, but they just wanted somebody's shoulder to cry on. Eva was a mommy, not a dyke. She took care of stray animals and people. Like that Brack creature and poor Pogo. She was like Dorothy in the goddamn *Wizard of Oz*. All she ever talked about was that farm in Ohio."

"So who'd want to kill her?"

"You got me," she said. "Maybe the wicked witch with her flying monkeys. Or the blue guy."

"The blue guy?"

Miss Yvonne stifled a laugh. "Buffed-up psycho used to come in here, hair and beard dyed cobalt-blue. He wore a cat-o'-nine-tails around his neck. Sure took a liking to Eva, but I run him off."

I was walking back down Chartres Street, thinking about Janice, when I heard a dog leash rattling behind me.

"Oh, Lieutenant Girlfriend." It was Pogo walking this dust mop named Welfare, now squatting at the curb. I hadn't seen Pogo since last Tuesday at the Dragon's Den. I was becoming a regular at the open mike, and starting to get a kick out of it. It was like a cross between a gong show and the observation room on Acutely Disturbed at DePaul's.

"Been meaning to ask you," I said. "Eva go to the movies a lot?"

"Never," he said, picking up a dog turd between two fingers with a plastic baggie. "She preferred to star in her own epic drama."

"So why was she carrying popcorn the night she died?"

He stopped. "Popcorn? I never thought about that. Maybe she swung by the Cloister after she said goodnight at Molly's. Sometimes the bartender there hands out bags of popcorn. Just before dawn."

I smiled. The Cloister. A few doors down Decatur from Molly's.

Pogo put the plastic baggie in his pocket. Who would've ever thought that one day the Quarter would be filled with rich people walking around with dog turds in their pockets? The dagos moved to Kenner just in time.

"Ever see Eva around a man with a blue beard? Blue hair and beard. And a whip?"

"Oh, him."

"She date him?"

"He followed her to the open mike from Les Girls. She wouldn't have anything to do with him. Now we have to listen to his poetry."

"His perms any good?"

Pogo pulled out the baggie of dog mess and waved it in my face. "See you at the open mike, Lieutenant Girlfriend."

If the garage rock band at the Cloister banged out one more song, I thought my skull would pop. I nursed several Seven and Sevens while I jotted down random thoughts in my notebook, hoping Swamp Gas would finally run out of steam. The crowd was twentysomethings dressed in black with all the hardware in Home Depot dangling off their mugs. I wondered if they got snared in each other's rings and things when they got down to business and had to use a wire cutter to separate themselves. Nobody seemed to be having a particularly good time. Janice and I'd had more fun eating thirty-five-cent plates of red beans and rice at Buster Holmes. A steady stream of couples was going in and out of the bathrooms in back, but not for any lovey-dovey. They were wiping their noses and clenching their jaws when they walked out. That explained the coke residue on the straw in Eva's purse.

Finally I was getting somewhere.

Swamp Gas petered out at about 5:00 in the morning. I was getting ready to leave when I spotted this geezer with a snowy white pompadour hobbling around in his bathrobe and slippers. When he turned around, I had to laugh.

"Hey, Uncle Dominic, it's me, Vinnie. Chetta's boy." I hadn't see the old guy since my daddy's funeral.

"Vinnie, let me get a look at you." He cuffed my head and patted my cheeks. "Not a day goes by I don't think of my sweet little sister. How she making?"

"Same old, same old." Mama was still fuming about how Uncle Dominic had gypped her on the inheritance. *He stuck a knife in my back,* she growled whenever his name came up.

"Remind her she still owes me three hundred bucks for property taxes the year she sold out."

"What you doing here at this hour," I asked, swiveling my hips, "getting down with the girlies?" His robe was covered with lint balls.

"Just checking on my investment. Got six, seven other buildings to see this morning. You?" he asked, swiveling his own hips. "Thought you was married. You just like your papa."

"Here on a murder case. Know this young lady?" I flipped out the picture of Eva and he fished glasses from his robe pocket. "Killed the night of March 28."

"Let me think," he said, staring at the snapshot. "Yeah, yeah, I seen her here that morning. Last time I come in to check on my investment. Around this time. I axed her what she was writing down in her little book, and she says, 'A perm.' Looked like a bunny with them funny pigtails."

"She leave alone?"

"Yeah, yeah. No, wait—" He slapped his forehead.

"Madonna, how could I forget? She left with that *pazzo* what got the blue beard."

Blue Beard.

Bingo.

Then somebody handed me some popcorn still warm in the bag.

The next morning I radioed Blue Beard's description in to the Eighth District station in the Quarter, and rang Pogo, Miss Ivonne, Miss Ping, and Uncle Dominic to ask them to contact me the minute they spotted him. Uncle Dominic told me he wanted a cut of the reward, and lost interest fast when I told him there wasn't any. But both he and Miss Ivonne promised to make a few phone calls to help locate Blue Beard. Mrs. Pierce sputtered "God bless you" when I reported that I was zeroing in on the killer.

Where the hell could he be? It wasn't like a man with blue hair could hide just anywhere, even in the French Quarter.

That afternoon I got a staticky message on my cell phone.

Lily Lamont.

A husky, spaced-out voice said she needed to talk with me in person. That evening. She left an address that at first she couldn't remember right.

My heels echoed on the flagstones in deserted Pirate's Alley like the approaching footsteps in those radio plays my daddy used to listen to. A mist had rolled in from the river, wrapping St. Louis Cathedral in fog, and I squinted to make out the address under the halo of a streetlamp. I pictured Lily Lamont blowzy and toothless now, passed out on a filthy mattress cradling an empty bourbon bottle.

Nothing could have prepared me for what I found.

After I was buzzed in, I mounted a curved mahogany staircase that swept me up into a cavernous Creole ballroom under a spidery bronze chandelier. In a zebra-upholstered throne, there sat a mummified lady with white hair pulled back tight from her porcelain face, buttering a slice of raisin-bread toast.

"I'm famished," Lily Lamont said, taking a bite. "Would you care for some toast and tea? That's all I ever, *ever* eat."

I shook my head. Perched in the zebra chair next to hers was a bulky goon with a body like a boxer's gone to seed. He was caressing the top of his shiny bald head, several shades paler than his face.

"I don't believe we've ever formally met, Lieutenant Panarello," she said. Her bones, thin as chopsticks, were swallowed by a red silk kimono fastened by a dragon brooch.

"Not face-to-face." What was I supposed to do, tell this lady I saw her on her knees in a men's room thirty years ago?

"And this is my associate, Lucas," she said, gesturing to Baldie.

I nodded, taking a seat in an elaborately carved bishop's chair under an alabaster lamp of entwined snakes.

"Nice place," I said. The floor-to-ceiling windows were draped with damask swags. Outside, shadows from the extended arms of a spotlit Jesus loomed over the cathedral garden.

"I bought this house last year from your uncle, Dominic Zuppardo." Her sharp little teeth gnawed on the toast like a rat's. "At a pretty penny. Actually, I paid him twice as much as the sale price we registered. That helped with my property assessment and his capital gains taxes. Smart man."

Bet Uncle Dominic is kissing her butt now, I thought. So that's who tipped her off to my investigation.

"Met your friend Miss Ivonne," I said, since we were having a family reunion. "Place where Eva Pierce used to strip."

"How is Ivonne?" Lily asked with a tight smile. "I set her up with that club. I've never been in it, of course." Her frail shoulders shuddered.

Ditto, I thought. Miss Ivonne probably called her, too.

"Look, I won't beat around the bush," Lily Lamont said, brushing toast crumbs from her fingertips. "I want you to call off your investigation into Eva Pierce's death. The killer is probably in Timbuktu by now. Questioning all of these people is silly."

"But I know who did it. A guy with blue hair and beard."

"Have you ever seen him?" Her enormous hazel eyes studied me slyly over the gold rim of an ornate teacup.

"No, but he used to come to the open mike at the Dragon's Den all the time to read his lousy perms."

Baldie winced. Then a shit-eating grin spread across his face. Why the hell would he care about Blue Beard's poems?

Unless he wrote them.

"Do you have children, lieutenant?" Lily's voice was filling with church choirs.

"Three. A boy at De la Salle, a girl at Mount Carmel, and another girl starting out at Loyola University next year." That was why I moonlighted—to pay all those tuitions. The older girl worked at a pizza parlor after school to save up for Loyola. Her dad, you see, was a New Orleans cop.

"And wouldn't you do anything to help your children?"

"Anything short of—"

"Eva Pierce was a horrible influence on my son." Lily swayed like a cobra as she mouthed the words in a slow, woozy monotone. "She turned him against me. You should read the venomous words about me she inspired him to pen. She was just using him."

"Maybe he liked being used," I said, locking eyes with Pogo's mother. "Maybe it's all he's ever known."

"Here, this is for you." Her long indigo fingernail flicked an ivory envelope across the coffee table. "It's a check for $25,000. Eva's mother hired you to investigate. I'm hiring you to stop the investigation." She arched a penciled eyebrow. "Simple."

I stood up. "Can I used the john?"

"Lucas will show you the way."

I studied the rolls of skin on the back of Baldie's head as I followed him down a long corridor, trying to picture him with blue hair and beard. The smartest thugs know the best disguise is something attention-getting but dispensable. And who would testify against Lily and this hitman? My uncle? Miss Ivonne? Trust-fund Pogo? The whole Quarter owed Lily Lamont a favor.

In the bathroom I tore open the envelope with an Egyptian scarab embossed on the flap: 25,000 smackers, made out to cash. I folded the check into my wallet. It was five times what Mrs. Pierce was paying me. I splashed water on my face and took a long look in the mirror. The jowly, unshaven mug of my daddy stared back at me, the face of three generations of Italian shopkeepers who worked like hell and never managed to get ahead. *What, you crazy or something?* they screamed at me. *You want your daughter to graduate from college? Take the damn dough and run, Vinnie.*

I picked up the plush blue bath towel folded next to the mirror. Underneath was a syringe, a packet of white powder, and a silver iced-tea spoon.

I rang Mrs. Pierce as soon as I'd escaped the junkie fog in Pirate's Alley.

"Look, lady," I told her, "the investigation is off. Your

daughter just got mixed up with the wrong crowd, that's all. Blue Beard is probably unidentifiable by now. He could be anywhere. I can't, in good conscience, waste any more of your money." All true.

Mrs. Pierce started sobbing and then hung up. She'd been right. It wasn't sex or drugs that got her daughter killed, but poetry. Me, I was never so glad to drive home to Terrytown, to the wife and life that I've got.

I didn't make it back to the Dragon's Den until one sweltering August night later that year. The air smelled of river sludge and the façade was shimmering in the heat like a mirage made of shadows and memories. The old Chinese guy was still hanging over his tub of vegetables in the patio. He shot me a thumbs-up as I mounted the stairs, mopping my face with a handkerchief.

Every step was an effort.

"Look what the cat drug in," Miss Ping said, setting me up with my Seven and Seven.

"Where's that sign-up sheet for the open mike?" I asked her. She pushed a clipboard toward me. With a shaky hand I scrawled *Vinnie P.*, third name on the list. I couldn't believe what I was about to do. It seemed like jerking off in public. So I sat on the balcony to calm myself down and go over what I'd written.

"Hey, honey, what you doing in the den with the TV off?" my wife had asked me. "You sick?"

"Writing a report." I'd swatted her away.

What I'd been writing for two weeks wasn't exactly a report but some buried feelings—poems, I guess you'd call them. I couldn't sleep or concentrate, and had even thought of going to Saturday confession, but then nixed that dumb-cluck idea. I couldn't tell the Father who would marry my kids and christen my grandbabies that I, a cop, was the accessory to a murder. Those poets that I'd listen to during the open mike, something like this was eating them up, too. Their girlfriends left them or their parents never loved them or they felt lonely and empty—I don't know—they just needed to spill their guts and be heard. By anyone. Just *heard*. They didn't tell it straight but in a symbolic way, you know, twisting it up enough so that it wouldn't be only their story but everybody's. So that's what I'd been writing: what happened to me investigating Eva Pierce's murder. And with Janice. Where it all went wrong and how I wound up feeling the way I did, as old, corrupt, and dirty as this French Quarter.

I had to get it off my chest.

Pogo stuck his face into the balcony, eyes popping out at the sight of me.

"She's a vile bitch," he hissed, biting his lip. Then he waved me inside.

Only about ten of the usual suspects were sprawled around the room. The first two poets went on forever. I was so wound up I couldn't concentrate on a word they said.

Finally, the clown with the leather cowboy hat held up the clipboard.

"And here, ladies and gentlemen," he announced, "is a rising star in the Quarter poetry scene. A man of the law who will grace us with his debut reading. He came to bust us, and now he's one of us. Put your hands together to welcome Lieutenant Girlfriend."

Everyone clapped like crazy as I stepped onto the stage feeling like a horse's ass. Pogo was jumping up and down, waving his arms like a cheerleader. I shuffled through the pages to get them in order. My voice caught as I started to speak.

Miss Ping plinked an ice cube into a glass. The air conditioner coughed.

Then a huge gray rat scurried across the room, stopped in the middle of the floor to take in the audience, and disappeared under the stage I was standing on.

Everyone jumped to their feet.

"Okay, you assholes, sit down," I said, adjusting the mike. "That rat has to wait its turn just like all us other poets. This is called 'Janice and Eva Swap Lipsticks in the Changing Room to Hell.' I bet you lunkheads aren't going to get it, but here goes."

ALL I COULD DO WAS CRY

BY KALAMU YA SALAAM

Lower Ninth Ward

Even though her mouth was empty, Rita savored the crunchy flavor of animal cookies, old-time animal cookies made with real vanilla. Her son laid out in a casket and here she was thinking about snacks. But that was because animal cookies were Sammy's favorite.

When he was small, Rita would gallop the shapes up Sammy's little round stomach, moving the crisply baked dough in bounding leaps. Usually the miniature animals ended up between Sammy's laughing lips.

His fat cheeks dimpled with a grin, Sammy would squirm in Rita's lap, turn and clap his small hands in glee as he chomped down on the golden tan figures. Sometimes he'd cry out in mock pain when a bear would take a really hard jump and end up bounding over his head into Rita's mouth. Animal crackers and funerals.

Now little Gloria, twenty-three-and-a-half months old, sat in Rita's lap. Tyronne sat silently next to her. Gloria squirmed briefly. Without really hearing a word he said, Rita patiently endured Pastor White droning on and on. Out of the corner of her eye, Rita stole a glance at Sammy's corpse laying in the coffin. Absorbing that awful stillness, Rita's instinct took over: She protectively hugged Gloria, bowed her dark face into the well-oiled coiffure of her daughter's carefully cornrowed hair, and planted a silent kiss deep between the black, thick, kinky rows.

Rita was beginning to doubt life was worth living, worth sacrificing and saving . . . for what, to have children who get shot down? What sense did it make to be a mother and outlive your children?

Two deacons moved forward and flanked the coffin. Like passing through a room where the television is on but no one is watching and the sound is off, Rita was aware the men were there to lower the coffin lid, but she really paid no attention to the dark-suited sentinels. Rita had long ago said goodbye and there was no need to drag this out. The elder of the church-appointed guardians efficiently closed the blue velvet–trimmed coffin lid. Someone two rows to the rear of Rita uttered a soft but audible, "Oh, my Lord." The lamentation cut clearly through the reverent silence that had settled on the small congregation. This was the end of the wake but only the beginning of a very long and sleepless night.

Friends and acquaintances shuffled slowly, very slowly, out of the sanctuary into the small vestibule where people lined up to script their condolences in one of Sammy's school notebooks that had been set out on a podium. There was a pencil sitting in the middle of the book. A few people had signed in ballpoint pen, but most signatures (some were written in large block letters, others in an indecipherable cursive) were scripted with the pencil's soft lead and seemed to fade immediately upon writing.

Rita looked up. *No, that couldn't be,* she thought to herself. That couldn't be Paul "Snowflake" Moore darkening the sanctity of her sorrow. Rita instantly shifted the sleeping weight of Gloria from her shoulder. Wordlessly, she handed Gloria to Tyronne. Tyronne had already seen Snowflake and knew a confrontation was in the making. In one seamless motion, as soon as Tyronne received Gloria into his large hands, he spun on his heels and handed Gloria to the first older woman he saw. By the time he turned back to Rita, she was already in Snowflake's face.

"Get out of here!" Rita hissed between tightly clenched teeth. "You the—"

"I just come to pay my respects. I ain't come to cause no trouble."

"You don't respect nobody."

By now the packed anteroom crackled with dread. The woman who had taken Gloria scurried back into the sanctuary; just a few months ago she had witnessed a fight break out at a funeral.

Tyronne rushed behind Rita, who was oblivious to her backup towering above her. With the arrogance of power, Snowflake stoically stood his ground and impassively peered at Rita and Tyronne. The tension increased.

"Get out!" Rita screamed, and pushed Snowflake hard in his chest. Snowflake glowered. She was fortunate that this was a wake, that Sammy was her son and might even be related to him, fortunate that a lot of people were standing there watching, but most of all, fortunate that none of Snowflake's usual retinue was surrounding him, because then Snowflake would have been bound, at the very least, to slap her down. As it was, Snowflake's hand instinctively went to his .38 derringer, snug but ready in the waist-pocket of his vest.

The confrontation escalated so fast the onlookers barely had time to breathe in and out; a few of the younger men were in fact holding their breath. Surely Snowflake wasn't going to accept being pushed around without doing something in retaliation.

Tyronne quickly stepped between the antagonists. "She's upset, you understand. Please, leave her be. We appreciate your concern but it would be better, man, if you would leave." Tyronne stared unflinchingly into the depths of Snowflake's emotionless eyes. Snowflake stared back and pulled an empty hand out of his vest pocket.

Everybody except Tyronne, Snowflake, and Rita prematurely relaxed and let out a relieved breath.

"I said get out!" Rita screamed a second time. The deacon who had closed the coffin lid ran to the phone to dial 911. Half the people who had been standing around now quickly moved out, some exiting the front door, others retreating back into the sanctuary. Rita reached around Tyronne in another attempt to shove Snowflake toward the door.

The rest happened so quickly only Tyronne and Snowflake saw it all. Tyronne took a swift half-step to his right to cut off Rita, who was charging around him. He leaned backward briefly, pushing against her with his shoulders.

Snowflake's left hand leapt with lizard rapidity to knock away Rita's outstretched right arm, and in the process was detained by Tyronne's right hand that gripped with a viselike strength and was surprisingly unyielding.

An onlooker moaned, "Oh, Lordy, no!"

"Get out!" Rita's vehement command overpowered the onlooker's exclamation.

Snowflake's right hand had already come up with his gun at the ready. Tyronne stepped in so close to Snowflake that if he pulled the trigger there was no telling what direction the slug would travel: upward into the ceiling, upward into Tyronne's chest, or upward into Snowflake's jaw.

"He got a gun," some young male voice blurted at the

same time Rita was reaching to get around Tyronne so she could sink her nails into Snowflake's smoothly groomed face. Snowflake pushed his right forearm against Tyronne's chest, attempting to back him up and simultaneously free his left arm, which Tyronne held secure at the wrist. As is often the case in impromptu street fights, the peacemaker in the middle was the person in the most danger.

"Young man, please. Has there not been enough shooting and death?" the pastor asked in a calm but insistent voice, as he rushed through trying to get to where Rita, Tyronne, and Snowflake were locked in a tug-of-war.

Rita spit at Snowflake. She missed his face but a glob stuck to the top of his left shoulder. Some older lady fainted but no one paid her any mind because she was too far away from the focal point of the fight. The minister smothered Rita in his protective arms.

"Can't you see this woman is grieving over her son?"

When Reverend White grabbed Rita, Tyronne bear-hugged Snowflake and spoke slowly and carefully into Snowflake's ear: "I'm begging you, man. Please don't shoot my wife. She's so upset she ain't got no idea what she's doing. You can understand her only son is dead and she thinks you had something to do with it. You got the gun. If you got to shoot somebody, shoot me. But please don't shoot my wife."

Snowflake's gun was pinned between the two men.

"Will everyone please either leave out the front door or join me in the sanctuary where we will pray for sister Rita?" Reverend White picked Rita up and dragged her out of immediate danger. Supporting her with firm grips under her arms, two ushers grabbed the woman who had briefly fainted and spirited her out into the welcome chill of the night air.

The whole scene had been acted out so quickly, it

seemed like a blur of simultaneous motion. Within ninety-five seconds, Snowflake and Tyronne were alone in the forlorn vestibule.

"Thank you," Tyronne said as he stepped back half a step, reached into his lapel pocket, pulled out a white handkerchief, and gently dabbed Rita's spittle off Snowflake's cashmere jacket. "Thank you."

It sounded so, so insane, but that was all Tyronne could think to say to the man standing in the receiving area of the church holding a loaded gun gleaming beneath the chandelier lights. From inside the sanctuary, the Twenty-third Psalm seeped through the swinging doors. Reverend White led and the assembled congregation responded with a tremulous sincerity.

"*. . . Yeh, though I walk through . . .*"

"Yeah, what up?"

Rita almost dropped the phone. It was Snowflake. She quietly hung up. So it was just like she thought. Snowflake was behind it all.

Here it was, two weeks after the funeral, and only now had Rita finally been able to summon the strength to clean out Sammy's closet.

When she pulled the closet door open, Sammy's scent assaulted her. She buckled at the knees and had to grab the door frame with one hand and push hard against the knob with the other just to keep from falling. It was like Sammy was hiding in the closet and had come charging out when she opened it.

Rita started to close the closet door. She couldn't stand any more. Her intruding into Sammy's life had already gotten him killed. She blacked out momentarily.

When she recovered consciousness, she was stooped on one knee inside the closet door. This was as close to a breakdown as she had allowed herself to come.

Fueling her weakness was the indescribable mantle of guilt that refused to lift. She had taken the money out of Sammy's backpack because she wanted to talk him into stopping. He did. His death stopped everything. And the money, well, four thousand dollars barely paid for the funeral.

Rita heard some sound behind her, turned to look over her shoulder, and saw Tyronne standing in the doorway, his brow deeply furrowed.

"I'm all right. I was just going to clean out his closet and . . ." How do you explain to a man that a mother knows how her child smells, that you could identify his clothes blindfolded, that opening this closet door was like finding the secret place your child's death had not yet visited, the place where the child was still overpoweringly present? How does a mother tell a stepfather that the smell of dirty clothes piled on a closet floor knocked you to your knees?

"If you want me to help, I'll be in the front room," Tyronne said softly. Then, after waiting a few moments and hearing no response to his offer, he turned and left the room even more quietly than he had entered.

Tyronne was trying so hard to be helpful and patient and considerate. But Rita knew the details, and the ultimate impact of all of this was way beyond his understanding. So much of Rita's reality was based on events she would never reveal to Tyronne, such as the fact that Sammy's father was Silas Moore, Snowflake's oldest brother, and that she and Snowflake knew each other in ways that were hard to explain.

* * *

"Stand up, baby, show this boy what a woman look like."

"Silas, I don't have any cloth— Silas, I'm naked."

"I know you naked. This my little brother. He ain't nothing but ten years old and he ain't never even seen no pussy."

"I done seen it before."

"Yeah, when?"

"Joanne showed me her thing."

"Who you talking 'bout?"

"Joanne dat live 'cross the hall."

And Silas had laughed at Paul. "Bo-Bo, that ain't no pussy. Bet she ain't even got no hair on it good yet. How old that girl is?"

"She eight and it's still pussy, it just girl pussy."

"Yeah, well, I'm talking 'bout real pussy. I'm talking 'bout a woman's pussy. Rita, stand up and show this boy what a woman's pussy look like."

"Sil, I don't want to."

"Do it for me, baby."

"She ain't got to show me nuthin', I done seen pussy befo'."

"Rita, I said stand up."

As Rita recalled standing up that day with Silas, she turned around to see if Tyronne was still there looking at her, but he was gone. Rita lowered herself into a sitting position in the closet doorway and another wave of memories flooded over her.

When she was seventeen, the fact that twenty-two-year-old Silas "Silky Sil" Moore considered her a woman filled her with pride. Sil was the biggest player in the courtyard. He always had money—had a big car and could have any woman he wanted, and he wanted Rita.

"Why you like me?"

"Look here, Rita, let me give you some good advice. When you hit a streak a good luck, don't question why. Just ride it long as it last, and when the luck leave you, get up off it and be thankful you got what you did."

"You saying you gon' leave me?"

"Naw, baby, I'm saying life is like the weather—it's always changing. Sooner or later, everything gon' change."

"I ain't gon' never stop lovin' you."

"Now, nah, girl, you can't say that. Don't be judging tomorrow by what's happening today. Suppose I take to liking another girl? Would you still love me?"

"As long as it was liking and not loving, what I care? My love for you ain't got nothing to do with you liking or not liking somebody else."

"You don't sound like no seventeen-year-old. That's one of the reasons I likes you."

"Yeah, and what's another reason?"

"Come here, I can show you better than I can tell you."

Rita could see her silly little seventeen-year-old self trying to act so womanish, and really doing nothing but being a stone fool for a man who was just using her.

No matter how hard she tried, Rita could never forget that day. Sil had pulled her close and kissed her. As her tongue flickered into his mouth, he sucked it hard, almost to the point of hurting her, and then released her.

Sil unbuckled his pants and let them drop at his feet. He slid his shorts down and sat on the side of his bed. "You want a mouthful of this?" he said, while guiding her hand to his erect penis.

Rita knelt quickly and started to give him head—she knew he liked the way she did it. She practiced doing it, sucking on a banana sometimes for five minutes straight without stopping, strengthening her jaw muscles. And other times she would chew five sticks of gum at a time, over and over, and over and over, and over, building up her stamina.

Some of the girls said they didn't like it but they had to do it to keep a man, but Rita liked it. She liked feeling him in her mouth and liked the soft, slightly salty taste of his sperm. As with most of the girls she grew up around, Rita knew there were only two ways out for most women: one was to hitch your wagon to a man on the move and the other was to luck up and get a good job if somebody put in a good word for you, or somebody who was related to you got you on somewhere. There generally wasn't no other way out, and usually finding a good job, when all you had was, at best, a public high school diploma, was harder than finding a good man. At least every young girl had a body and most of them could attract a man for a good six or seven years after they made eighteen. There wasn't nothing they taught you in high school that lasted that long.

"Wait a minute, baby. Go close the door, this is something for just me and you."

When Rita turned away from Sil's dick and made her first move toward the door, she saw little Paul standing there wide-eyed. She never said a word to him, just closed the door in his face.

How could she tell Tyronne about all of that?

By the time Rita discovered she was pregnant, she and Sil had already broken up. Her turn was over and it was time for another high school cutie to hang on Sil. And when Samuel was born, Sil was in prison. Rita didn't even bother trying to contact him. You ride it till it's through, and when it's over you let it go.

Rita snapped back to the present and began pulling clothes, boxes, and whatnot out of the closet, setting them on the floor beside her in three distinct piles. One pile was clothes she would give away. One pile was stuff she would throw away, sneakers, two old pairs of underwear, stuff like that, and a third pile—well, not really a pile, just a couple of things—a third stack was memorabilia she would keep. Sammy's drawing notebooks mainly and a neat stack of comic books he liked to read. Rita didn't know why she felt it important to keep the short stack of comic books, but somehow these things reminded her of Sammy more than even his picture on the bedroom dresser.

Rita lovingly looked through Sammy's notebooks. He had two that were full and one only partially complete. The partially complete one had the best drawings and also had a phone number written on the inside cover.

She had noticed the number immediately, because, unlike everything else in the notebook, it was written in ink and underlined.

Maybe this number held the key to who killed him. Rita believed it was Snowflake but she had no proof.

"Girl, he like you. Look how he looking at you."

"LaToya, I got a baby already. Less he ready to be a daddy and a lover, I don't even want to hear nothing."

"Girl, he kinda cute. I wish he would look at me like that."

"Yeah. Whatever."

"What you mean, 'whatever'? That man got a job. He a security guard."

"Yeah, and since he got a job, he probably got a woman."

Rita and LaToya went up to the window together to cash their Shoney's paychecks. LaToya kept eyeing Tyronne. He was kind of built, too. LaToya cashed her check first and stepped away while Rita cashed hers.

When they got outside, LaToya burst out laughing.

"Girl, what's so funny?"

"You gon' see."

"No, tell me now. What up?"

"You gon' see, when he call you."

"When who call me?"

"Tyronne."

"Tyronne who? What you talking about?"

"I'm talking about that security guard in the bank who had them juicy lips."

"Call me . . . What you talking about? He don't even know me."

"Well, he got your number."

"How he got my number?"

"'Cause while you was cashing your check, I told him that you liked him but you was shy and that you told me to give him your number."

"No, you didn't."

"586-8540. Rita Deslonde."

"Oh, you wrong for that," Rita said, and chased LaToya a quarter of the way down the block.

Now, as she held Tyronne's revolver in her hand, Rita had to smile as she thought back to how they had gotten together. He had called. He had asked for a date, and Rita decided he was all right when he didn't hesitate about taking her and her eleven-year-old son Samuel to the Audubon Zoo.

What she liked most about Tyronne was the way he talked to her about his life and his experiences—not just his dreams but also his fears.

"So, Tyronne, I can't believe you don't have a girlfriend already."

"Believe it or not, it's true."

"How come?"

"I guess 'cause a lot of girls think I'm kind of square or something."

"Well, after what all I done seen, square seems kind of nice to me."

"We'll see."

Rita smiled, thinking about just how square Tyronne actually was. He wasn't much of a lover. He would roll on top of her and be through almost as soon as they got started. But that was okay, she could teach him how to take his time.

She also had to teach him how to get high. He said he never like smoking "that stuff" all that much. With him around, a nickel bag lasted a long time. They might smoke once a week or so. Gradually, Rita just gave it up, unless she was under a lot of stress.

The only thing they ever fought about was keeping a gun in the house. Rita knew having a weapon went hand in hand with being a security guard, but she just didn't like the idea of one in the house with a child who was always snooping into everything. Finally, Tyronne hit on the idea of keeping the gun in a lock box. She had a key and Tyronne had a key. Rita could live with that.

Rita slid Tyronne's gun into her purse, closed the box, covered it back up with clothing, and slid the second dresser drawer fully closed. Then she turned around in the dim bedroom. It would soon be dusk. She had no words to tell Tyronne about Sammy, about his father—well, she had told him that Sammy was the result of a brief fling when she was seventeen years old and that she had never told the man that he was the boy's father. That was true. However, Rita hadn't told Tyronne that Silas Moore was the father, or that Silas was in prison. Nor, of course, had she told Tyronne that

Snowflake was Silas's baby brother. New Orleans was such a small town, all the poor people knew each other, or knew somebody who knew some . . .

Her past wasn't pretty and there was no way she wanted to share the foolishness of her youth with Tyronne. He wouldn't be able to deal with it. It would haunt him. He was a good man but . . . well, it would hurt him too much to hear certain details of her life. Plus, he had no way of understanding some things. Rita remembered a conversation about a news show on Channel 4.

"Well, goddamn, look at that. That girl can't be no more than sixteen or seventeen and she caught up in a drug ring."

"Tee, when it's all around you—"

"It was all around me when I grew up. But I mean, she's a girl . . ."

"Well, the drug dealer is probably her pimp. But sometimes it ain't even about being no prostitute or nothing. Those girls just be starved for affection and those guys give them dresses and jewelry and stuff and they think they're in love."

"Yeah, and after they get pre—"

"You mean like I got pregnant with Sammy?"

The question hung in the air for a long time.

After about a minute of silence, Tyronne spoke up: "So, I guess you're telling me you're like that girl."

"No, I'm telling you I understand what that girl is going through and I don't think you do. I think you see the condition she's in only from the outside, and me, I feel the condition she's in on the *inside.*"

"I guess I'm thinking of how we used to mess over them young girls in Vietnam and it's hard for me to imagine them growing up and coming out okay after all that stuff . . ."

"Well, if you live, you grow up. You got no choice about that. As for it being okay, who's to say what's okay?"

After another long pause, Tyronne looked at Rita. "Baby, there's a whole lot I don't know, but I know you're okay and I love you."

Tyronne's love was disarming and sometimes uncomfortable. He was so honest about his own shortcomings and so accepting of hers. Rita used to wish she could start her life over with Tyronne, wish she had met him when she was fourteen instead of meeting Roger, wish she had gone with him in high school instead of Sherman and Bekay, wish she had waited for Tyronne to father Sammy. But what was the use of wishing? Life was what it was, not what you wished it to be. She should just count her blessings and feel lucky she and Tyronne had eventually hooked up.

The whole time they were discussing the girl on Channel 4, Rita had been standing next to the chair where Tyronne liked to sit while watching television. She bent and kissed him lovingly. "I love you back, Tee, with everything I got. I love you too."

Everything I got, Rita thought to herself. The rub was, there were things she no longer had because they had been taken from her. Rita wished she had those missing things so that she could love Tyronne with everything, just like he loved her. But that was only a wish. The reality was both more complex and much more repulsive.

Clearly, Tyronne had never been molested as a child, so he still had some innocence in his loving. Rita had no innocence left. To Rita, the fierce reality of her childhood was unsparing and unforgiving. Rita was certain if Tyronne knew all the sad and sordid things that had happened to her and all the silly and stupid things that she had done to herself, no matter how much he loved her, he would probably leave her. Everything in Rita's life told her, no matter what they said or how much they loved you, men didn't tolerate their women making too many mistakes and indiscretions, especially if sex was involved. Tyronne was a man and, deep down, was probably no different.

Plus, Tyronne was nice and good-hearted, the very kind of man who always has a hard time dealing with people who fuck up over and over again. Tyronne got upset if she threw a Coke cup out the car window. Rita could imagine what would happen if he knew about some of the other things she had thrown out the windows of her life.

He believed that most people were basically good and a few people were evil-minded. Rita knew that everybody could go either way, it just depended on the circumstances and what they felt their chances were of getting what they wanted versus getting caught.

Rita paused briefly in the doorway and hoped everything would be all right for Tyronne. He deserved good things. He was a good man.

Even though he had killed as a soldier, Rita could tell, from the way Tee talked about his 'Nam experiences, that he would never kill anyone in cold blood nor would he understand being a cold-blooded killer, and that's why right now she couldn't share with Tyronne that she had decided she was going to kill Snowflake.

She wasn't going to talk about it and she wasn't going to think about it. She wasn't even going to cook up no scheme about how she was going to do it. She was just going to do it.

Some things are best never said, Rita thought to herself as she passed through the front room. *It's bad enough we act on some of the evil thoughts and fucked-up desires we have, we don't have to talk about them;* or, at least, that's how she rationalized walking out the door past Tyronne without telling him anything other than, "Tee, I got to get some air. Walk around some. I'll be back."

Tyronne looked at her. He ached to comfort her but knew her well enough to recognize that there were areas of her life she refused to allow him to touch. All he could do was wait, helplessly wait, until she was ready to open to him. "Rita, be careful."

"I'm just going for a little walk." If she stopped to say any more she might not do it. She had to do it now, while the smell of Sammy was still in her nose and the fuck-ups of the past were lingering in her consciousness.

Twelve blocks later, Rita stood in the gloaming looking at Snowflake's house across the street. Lights were on. A Jeep was in the driveway and a fancy car was parked out front. She knew he was home.

Should she go knock on the door? Should she just stand and wait? Was it safe to just stand on the sidewalk? Maybe he was checking her out right now.

Sheltered by the darkening dusk, Rita simply waited for something to happen. A light shower began. She'd had the presence of mind to bring an umbrella and she raised it above her head. She stood in the rain for twenty-eight minutes, her eyes fastened to Snowflake's house. Then she saw the door open. He was standing on the porch locking the door.

Rita quickly dashed across the street, holding the umbrella in her left hand and reaching into her dangling purse to pull out the revolver with her right. She had no plan. She was just going to flat-out kill him.

They almost bumped into each other as Snowflake ran toward his BMW. Snowflake had seen the woman running across the street in the rain but had paid her no mind until she was right on top of him.

"Paul Moore, this is for Samuel Deslonde." *Bam.* The first shot caught him square in the chest. He had no time to react. The force of the bullet hurled him over the hood of his car. Rita stood over Snowflake and shot him twice more. *Bam. Bam.* Once in his right side and the other in the back of his right shoulder. He slid off the car, a bleeding heap of inert flesh in the street.

The rain was falling steadily. Rita froze momentarily. Not sure what to do now, she looked around. A few people near the corner were standing under a sweetshop awning, looking at her. She put the warm pistol back in her purse and swiftly walked away. No one said anything to her as she passed.

Rita took the long way home and did not stop until she was standing, wet and distraught but dry-eyed, in their living room. When she came in, Tyronne rose slowly. He had Gloria in his arms, she was sleeping. He gently set her down in the chair and rushed silently over to Rita.

He quickly surveyed her from head to toe, wiped her damp hair back from her face, and gathered her up in a huge embrace.

"Tee, I—"

"Shhhh, shhhhh. Don't say nothing, baby. Whatever it is, we'll deal with it. I don't care. We'll deal with it."

"I shot Snowflake."

There were so many questions he wanted to ask her. Had anyone seen her? Did anyone follow her? Had it been on the street or in a bar, or where? She had probably used his gun, which meant he could take the rap if it came down to that. Say he did it. Gloria needed a mama more than a daddy. Besides, probably wasn't nothing going to happen. The cops never spent too much time looking for who shot a known drug dealer. No matter what happened, they would deal with it.

Tyronne hugged her tighter. "I don't care. All I care about is you back here with me. Whatever happens, we'll deal with it. Together."

Rita buried her face in Tyronne's shoulder and did something she had not done since she was fifteen and had a train pulled on her at a party. After that gang rape she had cried. She cried and she cried. And she cried.

It felt good. Rita cried for twelve long minutes, tears rolling out of her eyes big as Cuff. When she finished, Tyronne was still holding her and whispering into her ear, "No matter what happens, we gon' deal with it. We gon' deal with it."

What started out as tears of pain were now tears of gratitude. Nobody had ever loved her like this before. Nobody. All Rita could do was cry.

THERE SHALL YOUR HEART BE ALSO

BY BARBARA HAMBLY

The Swamp

"Kentucky Williams owns a *Bible?*" Benjamin January cast a doubtful glance catty-corner across the trampled muck of the Broadhorn Saloon's yard to the shabby building's open back door. The Broadhorn was a substantial building for this part of New Orleans, a neighborhood known quite accurately as the Swamp. Constructed of the lumber from dismantled flatboats, it stood a story-and-a-half tall and boasted not only porches but a privy, though the four whores who worked out of it did so in a line of sheds that straggled away into the trees of the true swamp—the *cipriѐre*—beyond. Under the brilliant winter sunlight the bullet-pocked planks and unspeakably puddled weeds looked every bit as grimy and rough-hewn as the establishment's proprietress, who a few moments before had bellowed out the back door for January to come in: She needed his services.

"Last night some suck-arse bastard tried to steal my Bible!" she shouted at January.

"In many ways that's the most surprising element of last night's fracas," remarked January's friend and fellow musician Hannibal Sefton, fishing in the pocket of his dilapidated frock-coat for a bottle of opium-laced sherry. "It was her uncle's—another surprise, since I'd always assumed that, like the Athenian hero Erechtheus, she was birthed from the earth itself. It's in no way a remarkable volume: printed in Philadelphia thirty or forty years ago by a Bible society. The frontier was flooded with them when families started taking up lands in the Mississippi and Alabama territories."

He had risen from the bottom step of the ladder he was sitting on when January emerged from the trees. January had reason to approach the Broadhorn cautiously: Even at 9:30 on a Tuesday morning there were men drunk enough to take violent exception to a man of January's color appearing in the vicinity of white men's chosen watering holes. January stayed away from the Swamp when he could. Only Hannibal's note had brought him that morning.

"I thought myself something might have been hidden in it," Hannibal went on, as they crossed the goo of the yard to the saloon's rear door. "Pages cut out to make a hollow, or something of the kind. I can't imagine anyone in the Broadhorn ever *opened* the book. But that doesn't appear to be the case. For whatever reason, the thief was prepared to do murder to get it."

January paused on the saloon's sagging rear porch, trying to see into the impenetrable gloom within. Born a slave, one of the first things he'd learned in early childhood was that there was "buckra territory"—in his case, the front part of his master's house—where a black child would be thrashed for setting foot. Even after his mulatto mother had been freed and they'd gone to live in New Orleans, he'd still been forbidden to use the front entrance of the house her white protector had given her.

In the Swamp, it was as much as a black man's life was worth to go into a saloon patronized by the white crews of the flatboats and keelboats that came down the river with their cargoes of furs, pigs, and corn. The black prostitutes would be tolerated in most saloons in that insalubrious district that sprawled from the upper end of Girod Street along the back of the town to the canal and the cemeteries. But the only black who was truly able to come and go freely in the Broadhorn was Delly, a sweet-tempered, simpleminded girl of seventeen whose buck teeth, skewed jaw, and prominent facial moles had relegated her to the role of washing cups and doing as much cleaning up as the Broadhorn ever got.

It was Delly who lay on the narrow bed in Kentucky Williams's room behind the bar. Williams yelled, "Git the hell in here, Ben, what you doin', wipin' your goddamn feet?" and January followed her voice into that tiny cubicle, which appeared to do duty as the Broadhorn's storeroom as well. Williams sat at the foot of the bed, a big-boned white woman wearing what the black whores called a *good-time dress*, a faded calico mother-hubbard whose front was splashed and blotted now with crusted brown blood. One sleeve was torn and a makeshift bandage, also spotted from a seeping wound underneath, ringed her right forearm. "Gimme your dope, Hannibal," she added more quietly, holding out her uninjured hand, and Hannibal passed over his bottle of opium-laced sherry without a word.

The girl Delly lay quietly on the bed, her face wrapped in several bar rags and what looked like somebody else's torn-up mother-hubbard bound around her chest and shoulder.

"Dumb bitch tried to pull him off me," growled Williams to January, gently holding the bottle to Delly's lips. "Can you swallow a little of this, honey? Easy . . . not too much . . . that's my good girl." She patted Delly's hand encouragingly. "Didn't think I could goddamn take care of myself." She took the cigar out of her mouth for a gulp of the sherry, then passed the bottle back to Hannibal. "How bad's she hurt, Ben? She be all right?"

Hannibal's note had said, *Bring your kit,* so January had brought the battered leather case of probes, forceps, fleams, and scalpels that his mentor in New Orleans had given him back in 1817, when he'd left to study medicine in Paris—little realizing at that time how useless it was for a black man to attempt to practice medicine on whites, even in that land of *liberté, egalité,* etc. Oddly enough, in the two years since his return to New Orleans in 1833, he'd found himself acquiring a clientele after all: unfortunately, all of it among the poorest class of freed (or runaway) slaves, who couldn't afford the mainly light-complected physicians patronized by the better-off free colored artisans.

January had long ago resigned himself to the fact that he was going to be playing piano for his living the rest of his life.

In addition to the tools of his one-time trade, he'd brought vials of camphor and opium, and bundles of herbs recommended by his voodoo-priestess sister and various "root doctors"—freed and slave—in the countryside. One of these he held out to Hannibal.

"Can you get some boiling water from the Turkey Buzzard, and steep about a quarter of this in it?"

The Turkey Buzzard stood about a hundred feet from the Broadhorn, and combined the usual Swamp amenities of bar-room, gambling parlor, and bordello with about a dozen beds for hire in three or four chambers, qualifying it as a hotel. It boasted a kitchen of sorts, and a dining room that served up grits, beans, and whatever mules might have given up the ghost the previous day—occasionally varied if an alligator happened to get too far from the canal at a time when the patrons were sober enough to hit it.

"Did you put anything on this, Mrs. Williams?" January asked, gingerly beginning to unwrap the bandages on Delly's face.

"Like what?" The proprietress pulled her snarly light-brown hair back into a knot on her nape. "My daddy said duck shit an' cobwebs was good for cuts, but I was god-damned if I'd go huntin' for a duck in the middle of the night. 'Sides, that was just for little cuts, not a big hack like he gave her. There's ducks down at the turnin' basin by the cemetery, though, if you need—"

"My teachers swore by brandy." January flinched a little as the bandages stuck, then came away from the split mess of brow and cheek. Though crusted almost shut with blood, Delly's brown eyes blinked up at him unharmed.

"You mean brandy-brandy?" asked Williams doubtfully. "Or the tonsil varnish me an' Railspike make out of tobacco juice an' red pepper?"

"Brandy-brandy, if you've got it."

Williams fished in a broken goods box under the bed. "You want Lemercier or Saint-Valbert?"

Stifling the urge to inquire how bottles of France's finest had wound up in the back room of a New Orleans bucket shop, January asked instead, "What happened here?" as he took the bottle and gently began to clean the wounds with its contents. "And how do you know the thief was trying to steal your uncle's Bible? What happened to the thief, by the way?"

"Absquatulated, the pusillanimous fuckard." Williams perched back on the bed at his side and took a thoughtful swig of the Lemercier. "Lit out of here like I'd stuck a burnin' fuse up his arse. I marked him good, though. And I know he was tryin' to steal my Bible 'cause he come in here an' tried to buy it yesterday afternoon."

"*Buy* it?"

"Yeah. I thought it was queer." She took the cigar from her mouth and blew a thoughtful cloud, lashless blue eyes narrowing in their tangle of lines and crusted paint. January would have guessed the saloonkeeper's age at forty or so—his own—had he not known how quickly the harsh life of the riverfront dives aged a woman: She was probably a decade younger than she looked, and unlikely to live a decade longer.

"This po'-faced jasper comes in here yesterday afternoon, just as I got the doors open. Asks for rum an' stands here *sippin'* at it—who wants to *taste* it, fer God's sake?" She took another gulp of the Lemercier, and passed it back to January to daub on the long knife rake that slashed across Delly's right pectoral and down the side of her breast. Delly herself lay listening, jaw gritted hard, her eyeballs drifting now and then from the opium. January guessed she wasn't used to it, from the way one swallow seemed to have dulled the pain.

On the other hand, of course, Hannibal's favored brand was quadruple-strength Black Drop that would knock out a horse.

Now Delly whispered, "You said he was a ringer, ma'am."

"That I did, honey." Williams squeezed the girl's hand again. "That I did. He was dressed rough, like most of the hard cases that come in here—plug hat, Conestoga boots—but he wore it like he didn't want to touch the insides of his clothes with his body. His hands was clean, too. You could tell he hadn't never done hard work with 'em, not like haulin' on a line or pole-walkin' a boat up a bayou. His hair, too, clean an' cut short, an' he had one of them sissy little beards, just around his mouth. Well, he coulda been a gambler, an' it wasn't none of my laundry to wash." She shrugged. "But then he starts an argument with the next man who comes in—

Snag-Face Rawlin, that was—pushin' on about somethin' in the Bible, like who was the first King of Israel or somethin' like that. Next thing I know, he asks me, do I have a Bible to settle the question? Snag-Face is sayin', *Oh, hell, what's it matter?* But this stranger just won't quit, an' wants to settle the question—"

"Herod," whispered Delly through teeth clenched against the pain, as January quickly cleaned out the wound on her chest with the hot herbal wash Hannibal brought in. "Was Herod the first king of Israel?"

"That was it. He pushed a bet onto Snag-Face—fifty cents Herod was. And when I guess Herod wasn't, he said all damn an' blast, an' would I sell him the Bible so's he wouldn't make that kind of fool mistake again? I said no, it was my uncle's Bible. He offered me five dollars for it, and when I said no, he offered me ten."

January's eyebrows shot up. Cheaply printed evangelical Bibles could be purchased for twenty-five cents, new.

Williams ground out her cigar under her heel. "So I figured, when my door creaks open in the dead of night an' some plug-ugly with a handkerchief tied over his face holds a gun on me an' says, *Gimme the Bible*, I'm guessin' it was the same po'-faced bastard with the sissy beard."

January finished tying off the stitches and took from his satchel clean rags for a bandage. "I think I'd like a look at this Bible."

"There," said January, and flipped the pages at random in four or five places till he found what he sought.

Hannibal leaned around his shoulder and read: *And the greater house he cieled with fir tree, which he overlaid with fine gold . . .* He glanced at January inquiringly.

"Not at the words. Under them."

Hannibal leaned close to the page, squinting in the strong morning sunlight. They'd carried the book out to the porch and rested it on the rail. Around them, in sheds and shanties and tents, the Swamp was waking up, as usual with a hangover. "Are those pencil dots?" asked Hannibal after a moment. "Under each letter?"

"Not just pencil dots." January took a magnifying lens from his instrument case and held it above the page. "That page has been marked two or three times—sometimes in pencil, once with a pin. Look back in Genesis, you'll see some of the pages have been marked that way four and six times, sometimes for as much as a dozen lines down the column. Always starting at the top of the page . . ."

Hannibal's mobile eyebrows shot up in enlightenment. "Someone was using it for a book code."

"That's right. And instead of doing the sensible thing one would do with a Bible—citing book, chapter, verse, and then letter-count—our code-makers simply treated it as an ordinary book, starting at the top of the page: page 394, 101st letter, or whatever it was. Which meant that both the sender and the receiver had to have the same edition of the Bible, which would have been easy if they'd originally bought them together in the same shop in Philadelphia. What did you say your uncle's name was, Mrs. Williams?"

"Walter." The proprietress scratched under one uncorseted breast. "Walter Buling. My daddy had a farm below Natchez. Uncle Walter came there in 1825, sick as a horse with the consumption. That's where he died."

"Walter Buling." January nodded slowly, and turned to the back of the book. Where pages are sometimes inserted to make up odd-numbered signatures, only a single, ragged, yellowed edge remained. "When I was eleven years old," he said, "in 1806, New Orleans was clapped under martial law for a number of weeks by the governor of the Louisiana Territory, a gentleman named Major-General James Wilkinson."

"Wilkinson!" exclaimed Williams. "Gentleman my arse—wasn't he the skunk who swindled all them folks out of Texas land grants about ten years ago?"

"He was indeed," January replied. "He'd earlier been twice court-martialed for botching invasions of Canada and Spanish Florida during the war with England in 1812, and died in disgrace in Mexico shortly after the Texas debacle. But in 1806, while governor of the Territory, he teamed up with former Vice President Aaron Burr, allegedly to conquer Mexico, to separate the Southern states from the North, to loot all the banks in New Orleans in the confusion, and to form an empire that Burr would then rule from New Orleans, presumably with the help of Wilkinson's American troops.

"Now, my mother still swears that Wilkinson was playing a double game and taking money from the Spanish viceroy of Mexico—then as now, she knew everyone in town. In any case, Wilkinson sold Burr out, testified against him in court, and was protected by Thomas Jefferson for the rest of his life as a result. Who was paying whom how much back in 1806 I have no idea, but I do remember that Walter Buling of Natchez was one of Wilkinson's lieutenants."

"So you think Buling lifted some money in the confusion?" Hannibal thumbed the onion-skin pages, peering through the glass at the lines of pinpricks and dots, the occasional notes in the margin: *e-45, t-67, a-103* . . . "Either a Spanish payoff or from one of the New Orleans banks . . . ?"

"In partnership with a Confederate who either died or

was taken out of the game somehow. The Confederate's coded directions to the money is probably what's in our friend's hands—and I'd guess our friend has only recently learned that the books containing the key were Bibles owned by Buling and the Confederate."

"How would he find out?"

"Probably the same way you did," said Hannibal. "The Confederate may very well have been our friend's uncle or father, the same way Buling was related to you."

January nodded. "However he found it out, he *did* find it out. But since Buling counted the letters as if the Bible were an ordinary book—from the top of the page, rather than by chapter and verse—our friend needs to have the identical edition to decode them. Obviously he doesn't: his relative's Bible having disappeared in the intervening years, leaving only the coded message itself. So all he could do was trace Buling's."

Williams scowled, and she rubbed gingerly at the bandages January had put on her arm. "That means he'll be back, don't it?"

"If he's come this far, I think it definitely means he'll be back."

Her eyes narrowed, cold as a wild pig's. "Thinks he can go cuttin' up Delly an' whoever gets in his way . . . I'll be ready for him when he comes back . . ."

"It will probably be with Confederates of his own," pointed out Hannibal. "*Bella, horrida bella, et Thybrim multo spumantem sanguine cerno . . .*"

"Oh, I think we can deal with our friend without causing the river to run red with blood." January picked up the Bible and thumbed again to the torn-out page at the back. "And if we're lucky, compensate poor Delly for her injuries as well."

* * *

It didn't take January long to locate the culprit. It was all a question of knowing who to ask. The Carnival season was in full swing, and he and Hannibal were playing that night at a ball in one of the great American mansions that lined St. Charles Avenue, upriver from the old French town. In between sets of marches and quadrilles, waltzes and schottisches, January made it his business to nod smiling greetings to every one of the dozen or so physicians who attended, men with whom he'd worked at the Charity Hospital during the summer epidemics of cholera and yellow fever. These greetings led to soft-voiced chats and a little friendly joshing about his "winter job" from white men who hadn't the slightest idea what it was like to be denied work because of the color of their skin. From this, January deftly steered the conversation to inquiries about a thin-faced white man with a Vandyke beard, probably at a hotel, who'd called in a physician's services that morning for knife wounds . . .

By the end of the evening he knew that the man who'd knifed Delly—and who'd been cut in return by Kentucky Williams—was Matthew Porter of St. Louis. St. Louis, January recalled, being the city from which Major-General Wilkinson had governed the Louisiana Territory in 1806.

Since January was a law-abiding soul, even when the laws included Black Codes that forbade him among other things to smoke cigars in public, the following morning he consulted the City Guard, in the person of his friend Lieutenant Abishag Shaw. He suspected it would do him no good and his suspicion was rapidly confirmed.

"Iff'n you want me to, I'll speak to Captain Tremouille about it," offered Lieutenant Shaw, scratching his verminous hair. "But I'll tell you right now what he'll say: that we got too few men—'specially now in Carnival season—to go chasin' after a white man who'll just say he never knifed no nigger gal in his life. No jury in town's gonna convict him of it on the word of a Salt River man-eater like Kentucky Williams anyways."

His due to law and order paid, January then took a long walk into the genuine swamp beyond the Swamp, the *ciprière:* the maze of small bayous, impenetrable tangles of palmetto and hackberry, tall silent groves of cypress and magnolia that lay between New Orleans and the lake. Few white men came here. Even now, in the winter with the ground mostly dry, it was easy to become lost, even for January who'd been raised with a slave-child's awareness of the invisible geography of landmarks, paths, rendezvous points. In the summer it was a nightmarish jungle of standing water, gators, snakes, and mosquitoes that would swarm a man like a living brown blanket.

He wasn't sure if there was still a runaway slave village somewhere west of Bayou St. John, but as he quartered the squishy ground he would occasionally see fish lines in the bayous, or red flannel juju-bags hanging from the trees. He was just beginning to wonder if he'd have to abandon his quest and return to town—he would be playing at a subscription ball at the Théâtre d'Orléans that night—when he turned his head and saw, standing in the deep oyster grass across a murky little bayou, the one man in New Orleans taller than his own 6'3" height: massive, African-black like himself, clothed in rags with only a muscular stump where his left arm had been.

Cut-Arm, king of the runaways of the *ciprière.*

"You not wanderin' around out here lookin' for anybody, Music-Master, are you?"

"It just so happens," said January, "that I am."

* * *

Cut-Arm's dark eyes narrowed with fury when January spoke of what had happened to Delly, who like most freed slaves in town had some passing acquaintance with the runaways in the *ciprière*. When January spoke of how he intended to get his revenge, the big runaway's teeth showed white in a savage grin. "That's good," he rumbled. "Maybe not so good as seein' his blood, but it'll take a lot longer, and I think he'll suffer more."

Thus it was that January was loitering on the brick banquette of Rue Chartres opposite the Strangers Hotel at 10:00 the next morning when a man who fit the description of Matthew Porter emerged from its doors: tallish, well-dressed, his brown Vandyke beard newly barbered, and his right arm in a sling. January's guess was confirmed a few minutes later when, as Cut-Arm had promised, one of the hotel's maids came across the street to him and whispered, "He just left. It's all clear."

January had taken the precaution of dressing that morning in the simple but respectable dark clothing that could have passed him as either a free workman or an upper servant. Nobody gave him a glance as the woman brought him to one of the smaller guest rooms on the second floor. He'd gambled that Porter would be too cautious of pickpockets to take the coded message—whatever it was—with him when he went out, and a few minutes' search of the trunk yielded it, tucked between pages 102 and 103 of an almanac that was in turn nestled among Porter's shirts.

It was, as January had suspected, the end leaf torn out of the back of Kentucky Williams's Bible, covered with neatly inscribed numbers. In his own memorandum book he made a note of the number of lines (thirty-two), the approximate number of characters per line (between forty-seven and fifty-four), and the width of all margins. "Meet me tomorrow," he said to the maid, handing her a dollar, "at the same place, at the same time as today, bringing me this paper." He slipped it back into the almanac. "You make a note of what two pages it's between when you take it out—he may move it, and I don't want him to guess it's been messed with. I'll give you another piece of paper, just like it, to put back in its place. You think you can do that?"

"Shoot." She grinned. "For two dollars I'd swap out the whole damn almanac one page at a time. Cheap bastard didn't give me no tip, not even a dime, when I brought him up a bath last night, and pinched my tit into the bargain. You know how heavy it is, luggin' all that hot water? What is it?" she asked hopefully. "You put a juju on the new piece of paper?"

"In a manner of speaking," said January.

Returning to the room he rented from his widowed mother on Rue Dauphine, he carefully tore one of the front blank pages from Kentucky Williams's Bible, meticulously matching the irregularities of the ragged remains of the torn page in the back. It took him a little experimentation with watering ink to achieve the faded hue of the original. While his various samples were drying, he set to work with the Bible to code a new message, using for good measure as many of the letters as had been in the original's first three lines, which he'd taken the precaution of copying.

"My guess is, those are all that Porter read, if he even read that far," he said to Hannibal that night, when he walked out to the Broadhorn to check on his two patients. "If anything sticks in a man's mind out of a mass of numbers like that, it'll only be the first few. Which is the reason, of course, for a code in the first place."

"Did you figure out what them first lines said?" Delly asked, her brown eyes round in the grimy lamplight of her attic cubicle. "Does it say where the treasure's hid?"

"It does." January tied up the clean dressing, gently tugged the girl's ragged nightdress back into place. "The first three lines—and, I suspect, the rest of the coded text—are names, clearly invented. Jack Falstaff is one; Montague Capulet is another. Beside each name is the name of a bank."

Delly frowned at this prosaic anticlimax—she'd clearly expected paces counted from Death-Head Oak and Skull Rock.

But a slow grin spread over Hannibal's thin face. "Where Uncle Water Buling cached whatever he could make off with under Wilkinson's nose, in the confusion of Burr's projected invasion. How many of those banks are still in operation, do you suppose? Private banks come and go like waterfront cafés."

"Which would be why Uncle Walter spread the funds out among so many. The first on the list is the Bank of New York, and that's still in operation. So Kentucky will get at least a little money out of it."

"Which she'll probably drink up within a week," sighed Hannibal. "I would, anyway. It does seem a waste."

Screams resounded from the yard below, followed by shots and the crash of a body being heaved out the Broadhorn's back door. Both men and Delly tilted their heads toward the window to ascertain that it was only a fight between six or seven customers, clawing and gouging in the mud of the yard while Kentucky Williams roared curses at them from the porch.

"It does," January agreed. "But if we do more than take a reasonable sum for services rendered, on the grounds that as upstanding citizens we deserve the money more than she does, how does that make us different from the man who slashed up Delly with a knife?"

The next morning, January took delivery of the code paper, and spent until early afternoon closeted up with the Bible, deciphering names. "I'd like to get this back to the saloon before it opens," he said to Hannibal, who had put in an appearance—at a far earlier hour than was usual for him to be about—to assist. "The doctor I talked to said Porter's wounds weren't deep. He should be able to use his arm by this evening. It would be a shame if the book isn't there when he makes his next attempt."

Right on schedule, that evening, while January was again changing Delly's dressings, a tumult of shouting and two shots resounded from the saloon below, followed a moment later by Hannibal's arrival at the top of the ladder.

"He's downstairs," gasped the fiddler, panting from just the climb. "Done up as a preacher in the most ridiculous wig and false whiskers you've ever seen."

"Who got shot?" January asked, scrambling down the ladder after Hannibal, crossing to the porch at a run.

"Nobody—but Porter went down with what I assume to be chicken blood all over him like an Indian massacre."

They sprang up the porch steps and peered through the Broadhorn's back door in time to see a tallish, thin man in the shabby black suit of an impoverished minister lying, gasping theatrically, on the floor among a half-dozen kneeling ruffians. His hands and gray-whiskered face were covered with gore in the saloon's dim lamplight.

"I'm dying! Oh, I'm dying! For the love of God, is there a Bible in this house?"

As Williams promptly fetched the Holy Writ from where January had stowed it earlier under the bar, Hannibal and January traded disbelieving glances. "I've seen better acting at Christmas pantomimes," Hannibal whispered.

The allegedly dying alleged preacher clutched the volume to his ensanguined chest and sobbed, "Bless you, my daughter—"

And with a crash, the lights went out.

"Two accomplices," reported Hannibal softly, as he and January stepped aside to let three blundering forms spring through the door between them and sprint away across the yard.

Inside the saloon, men were crashing around and cursing; a moment later a match flared, and someone exclaimed, "Fuck me, where'd that preacher go?"

"Not badly done, though," added the fiddler, as he and January strolled back to the ladder. "Kentucky's promised us each ten percent of whatever we can retrieve from those bank accounts, and twenty percent for Delly, which is very generous of her. I'll write to the Bank of New York tomorrow. I suspect that our friend Mr. Porter's in for a very frustrating few months, writing to banks that no longer exist about accounts whose names he doesn't have right."

"Oh, I didn't substitute names," said January. "A man who considered it his right to carve up a saloonkeeper and a completely innocent black girl—who's going to be scarred for the rest of her life—deserves more than a little frustration. No, I wrote up a very elaborate treasure map leading to an island in the middle of the swamps below Villahermosa in the south of Mexico; a friend of mine in Paris who'd been a doctor in the French Navy under Napoleon told me about it. He said nine-tenths of their men came down with fever there and most of them died. A *land wrought by Satan,* he said, *to punish sinners.*"

Hannibal's eyes widened. "Do you think he'll go?"

"He will if he wants the four hundred and fifty thousand dollars in Spanish gold I said was buried there."

"Considering the amount of money he'll have to borrow to finance an expedition," mused Hannibal, "and the time it will take, and the gnawing anxiety of knowing there's a treasure just waiting for him . . ."

"If he's willing to seek it," said January gently. "Which we know, from his actions, that he is. *Where your treasure is*—wholly imaginary, in this case—*there shall your heart be also* . . . and for Mr. Porter, almost certainly his fever-ridden bones as well."

Hannibal paused, his hand on the rungs of the ladder. "For such a thoroughly nice man, Ben, you can be a complete son of a bitch."

"Thank you," said January. "I have my moments. Now let's start writing those letters to the banks, and see how much of the real treasure is left to collect."

PART II

LIFE IN ATLANTIS

MUDDY POND

BY MAUREEN TAN

Village de l'Est

On the Wednesday after the levee failed and flooded New Orleans East, sixty-eight-year-old Sonny Vien waded into chest-deep water to rescue the Virgin Mary.

The two-foot-tall statue was at the far corner of the house, near where the front yard met the side yard. It was sheltered by a stone grotto that Sonny had built and surrounded by a garden that his wife, Tam, had planted. Climbing red roses framed the grotto and tiny white flowers formed a carpet at the Virgin's feet. In a perfect blending of New Orleans tradition and Vietnamese-Catholic belief, they had positioned the grotto so that the Virgin's back was to the house while her delicate Asian features and outstretched arms were directed toward the not-too-distant levee.

For thirty years, the blue paint of the statue's gown had faded, the brass cross at the grotto's peak had weathered, and the garden had flourished. For all that time, the sainted Virgin—not the statue, but the mother of Jesus it represented—had remained vigilant, holding back the dangerous water of the canal and protecting the snug white house on Calais Street.

And then the Virgin failed, Sonny thought bitterly as he navigated through the foul water toward the cross that was now the only thing marking the location of the grotto. She'd failed to protect Tam from the cancer that so unexpectedly took her life. Then she'd failed to protect the house—to protect Village de l'Est and, in fact, the whole of New Orleans—from the catastrophe that was Hurricane Katrina.

If it had been up to him, the statue would have remained where it was. Failed and submerged. But Tam would have judged that a sacrilege. And with her less than six months in the grave, Sonny's actions were most often guided by what he thought she would have wanted. That was why he'd ignored Mayor Nagin's evacuation order and ridden out the hurricane rather than leaving their three Siamese cats to fend for themselves. And that was why he had left behind the security of his windowless second-floor attic.

Wearing the same worn T-shirt and faded khaki shorts he'd had on when he'd first retreated from the flood, Sonny had gone back downstairs. He'd already ventured into the flooded first floor several times before, intent on retrieving a few more photos, gathering a little more food, fetching a couple more blankets. So as he'd waded once again through the knee-deep water, he averted his eyes from the sight of his favorite chair soaked beyond repair, looked quickly past the darkly stained wallpaper curling away from the walls, tried not to think about the rugs beneath his feet. But he couldn't ignore the smell—the odor of rotting food, wet paper, decomposing wood, and mildew that the stagnant water seemed to bind together.

The smell had followed him as he pushed open the water-swollen side door, then stepped onto a tiny porch. As he made his way gingerly down a trio of steps linking the porch to the driveway, a Vietnamese proverb sprang, unbidden, into his mind. He spoke it aloud before leaving the last step, tipping his head as he listened to the way the flowing syllables of his native tongue echoed off the unnatural silence beyond his kitchen door. A silence that—at least today—had been unbroken except for birdsong and the occasional racket of low-flying helicopters.

"*An co di truoc. Loi nuoc theo sau.*" ("When having a party, go first. When walking in the water, go after.")

Sonny had smiled—a tired, twisted smile—as he considered the uselessness of the proverb's wisdom. Then he went first and alone into the tepid water, using his wiry 5'2" frame to estimate its depth. About four feet, Sonny decided, knowing that he was one of the lucky ones.

Though he hadn't anticipated the flooding, he'd been cautious enough to follow a New Orleans maxim. As Katrina made landfall, he'd taken his old shotgun—rather than an axe—with him into his attic. He hadn't needed it. But in the hours after storm-driven water overtopped the nearby levee, he'd heard shotgun fire echoing in the distance. And he feared that in the lower-lying areas surrounding Village de l'Est, people trapped by rising water in their windowless attics were blasting holes in their roofs to escape deathtraps.

Another helicopter flew overhead, its clatter magnified as the sound bounced off the swamped houses below. It was on its way, Sonny was certain, to pluck unfortunates from their rooftops. To rescue people whose lives were endangered. But because that did not describe Sonny's situation, it didn't occur to him to signal for help. He didn't need rescuing. As others had evacuated, he'd prepared. He had food and water, the company of his cats, a battery-powered radio, and a dry attic. No matter if it took a week or two or even three, Sonny knew that eventually the water would recede. Then his neighbors would return.

Ta ve ta tam ao ta. Du trong du duc ao nha van hon. That's what generations of Vietnamese had advised each other. ("Let's go home and bathe in our own pond. Clear or muddy, it's the water of our pond.")

Now *that* proverb, Sonny thought, was appropriate to the present situation. War and governments might have compelled the immigrants of Village de l'Est to abandon their homeland. But a big storm? An unexpected flood? Sonny shook his head. That would not keep a *Viet Kieu*—a Vietnamese living in the land of golden landscapes—away from home for very long. He was certain that most would return to the muddy pond that was now Village de l'Est. And they would rebuild.

In the meantime, he would wait. And rescue the statue. For Tam.

The day was hot and humid, so Sonny moved slowly through the water, conserving his energy, using his sandaled feet to feel his way along the path that led to the statue. The flagstones paralleled the driveway for a dozen feet, then rounded a corner into the front yard. From there, the path curved outward until it reached the center of the yard, then curved back until ending at the grotto. No need for American efficiency in this route, Tam had insisted as Sonny laid the stones. And then she'd filled the shallow half-moon between path and house with delicate shrubs, colorful flowers, fragrant herbs, and interesting objects.

Now all that beauty was submerged, replaced by debris and rainbow slicks of chemicals floating on the muddy water. The carefully placed objects and lush growth had become nothing more than hidden hazards. For the first time, Sonny wished the route to the grotto was more direct.

At a place where the arc of the path took it closest to the street, something caught Sonny's ankles, sending him plunging into the water. For a heartbeat or two, he panicked, certain that he'd encountered a cottonmouth. That its curved fangs would soon plunge into his ankle, delivering its lethal poison.

Urgently, Sonny kicked himself free of the tangle, flailing his arms wildly as he scrambled back onto his feet. That was when the section of flexible drainage hose, dislodged by his movements, drifted to the surface. Still sputtering and coughing, Sonny cursed the hose, cursed his pounding heart and his irrational fear. Though he'd admitted it to few besides Tam, snakes terrified him. Especially vipers. He ran his hands over his face and his crew-cut gray hair, slicking away the worst of the water. And then he stood quietly, concentrating on his breathing as he struggled to regain his sense of calm.

Deliberately—almost defiantly—he ignored one of the customs he'd had since childhood. Though Tam would have disapproved, he did not pray to the Virgin for courage. Instead, he lifted his chin, turned his back on the grotto, and focused his attention on the ruined landscape.

Debris was everywhere. The screeching wind that had twisted signs and toppled trees had also shattered windows and torn away whole sections of houses. Power lines hung like thick, twisted vines, dangling down into the water, no longer sparking as they had when Katrina swept inland. Only the roofs of a few drowned cars made it possible to separate street from front yards.

One of those cars, Sonny saw, belonged to his neighbor on the corner.

The car was a distinctive color. Blackberry, its owner, Charlie Pham, had informed him just a week earlier. The presence of the expensive car in front of Sonny's modest house puzzled him. No doubt the five members of the Pham family would have evacuated New Orleans in their minivan. But why, Sonny wondered, wasn't the new Cadillac parked in the relative security of Charlie Pham's brick garage? Sonny pondered this briefly, then shrugged, confident that there was some simple explanation.

His wandering gaze moved on, taking in the flood-ravaged houses of neighbors and friends. Abruptly, he looked back in the direction of the grotto, grateful that Tam had not lived long enough to see another home—another community—devastated and abandoned. They had been little more than children when they'd fled the Communists, abandoning their village in the North for the safety of South Vietnam. Then, when Saigon fell, they'd left Vietnam behind forever. And they'd come to America. Where their lives had been blessed.

Until now.

Once again, Sonny felt a stab of anger toward the Virgin. He used that feeling to push aside his fear and waded forward again. As he neared the grotto, he made an even greater effort to stay on the path as tangles of thorn-laden rose tendrils broke the water's surface all around him—reminding him that he'd left Tam's roses untended and untrimmed for a long time.

Sonny considered the possibility that the flooding was punishment for his neglect. But in the space of a few steps, he dismissed the idea as superstition and turned his attention to the task confronting him. He elbowed aside debris that had collected in front of the grotto, then firmly closed his eyes and mouth, held his breath, and plunged into the water. His fingers slipped over the smooth, rounded stones that lined the grotto's interior. Then they encountered the statue. He wrapped his arms around the Virgin, reminded himself to use his knees rather than his back to bear the weight, and hefted the statue upward, out of the water.

It was heavier than he remembered.

He hugged the statue tightly against his chest, staggering beneath the weight, and moved back along the path. By the time he reached the place where he'd bumped into the hose, he was breathless from exertion. And he knew that he'd have to rest before carrying the statue the remaining distance into the house. But it felt like failure—and, though he hated to admit it, a lot like sacrilege—to drop the Virgin back into the muddy water. So, now more tired than cautious, Sonny left the path and headed for a nearer goal—Charlie Pham's Cadillac.

The flooding had caused him to misjudge the car's location. But it was still closer than the side porch. Struggling to maintain his balance and his hold on the statue as he stepped off the curb, Sonny waded forward into the street. He ignored the water that crept up his shoulders and tried to ignore his growing dread. Maybe the car had simply broken down and been left where it stalled. Heading away from Charlie's house.

But heading where?

With his last bit of strength, Sonny hefted the Virgin onto the roof, laying her on her back. The rigid blue folds of her cast-stone robe scraped the pretty dark purplish paint of Charlie's pride-and-joy as Sonny pushed the statue into a secure position. Then he finally admitted to himself that only a catastrophe—and nothing so small as an approaching hurricane—could have prompted Charlie to leave his new car in the middle of the road.

Free of the statue's weight, Sonny almost bounced as he walked in the deep water around the car, seeking an explanation for why his friend had abandoned his Cadillac.

Just as he noticed that the driver's door was open, Sonny also saw the top of a human head. It bobbed a few inches above the water, in the V where the door hinged to the car's frame. The bald dome with its distinctive, monklike fringe of longish dark hair was definitely Charlie's.

Sonny's first thought was that Charlie was the victim of an unsuccessful carjacking. Or a robbery gone wrong. Periodically, the streets of Village de l'Est spawned violent gangs—gangs encouraged by the Vietnamese immigrants' reluctance to call the police. Before Katrina, neighborhood gossip had centered on just such a group. A few greedy, alienated young men intent on victimizing their own people. Charlie, Sonny suspected, would be an obvious target. Everyone in Village de l'Est knew that he owned a jewelry store on Alcee Fortier Boulevard, the heart of the Vietnamese business—and tourist—district.

Sonny moved reluctantly toward the body.

When he fought beside American GIs in Vietnam, death had been familiar and unavoidable. But decades in America had conditioned Sonny to leaving death to others. And now, thanks to Katrina, the roads were impassable, the phones didn't work, and the police . . . Sonny shrugged. No doubt the low-lying Versailles District Police Station was also underwater. And anyway, the NOPD would be too busy with the problems of the living to worry about the welfare of the dead.

There is no one else to rely on, Sonny told himself.

So he took a deep breath and went down into the water again, this time deliberately opening his eyes. Trying to peer through the muddy water. He sought the dark shape of Charlie's body, used eyes and hands to discover that Charlie's legs—clothed in loose-fitting jeans—were caught beneath the car door. Sonny freed the body, let it float to the surface, came up beside it, and gulped air. Charlie was face down in the water, and Sonny scanned the length of his friend's back, seeing nothing that indicated how his friend had died. Comforted by that, he rolled Charlie over. Briefly and against his will, Sonny recoiled at the sight of the distorted, waterlogged features. But he could see there were no marks of violence on the front of Charlie's body either.

Almost relieved, Sonny considered a more natural cause of death.

For a moment, he ignored the body floating beside him and looked carefully around. Noticed, for the first time, a few leafy branches jutting from the water not too far from the front of the car. He glanced upward at the canopy of trees shading Calais Street. Easy enough, now that he knew what to look for, to spot a splintery wound on a storm-battered magnolia. To guess that the thickest part of that fallen limb was now underwater, blocking the street. Blocking the car.

Obviously, he reasoned, Charlie had been driving away from his house in the hours just before Katrina made landfall. Too late, really, to be evacuating if the wind had already grown strong enough to tear away tree limbs. Sonny wondered now if the older van had failed mechanically. Stranding not just Charlie, but his entire family. Delayed for some unknown reason, they would have hurriedly piled into the Cadillac with the storm breaking all around them. Then, still within sight of their home, a tree limb had crashed to the pavement, blocking their way. Charlie was middle-aged, extremely fit, and one of the most determined people Sonny knew. Instead of turning around and taking the slightly longer route to Michoud Boulevard and Chef Menteur Highway, Charlie would likely have hurried from his car, intent on pulling the branch out of his way.

Suddenly, Sonny found significance in the power lines dangling in the water. The city's electricity was still on when Katrina made landfall. If Charlie hadn't noticed a live wire making contact with the wet ground nearby or if a power line tore loose just as he stepped from the car . . .

Charlie would have been electrocuted.

And if there were passengers . . .

Now Sonny was imagining a car full of victims. People he cared about. Charlie's five-year-old twins, Magdalene and Michael. Agnes, who was three and nearly as tall as her brother and sister. They would have been strapped into their car seats. And Nga. A kind woman who had moved in with her son-in-law after his wife died. To help with the children.

Maybe she'd tried to help Charlie during the storm.

Sonny's stomach twisted with dread as he pictured all of those bodies inside the car. Or floating somewhere nearby. Bloated after days in the water. He shook his head, thinking that this was too much to ask of any man. That nothing—not even the war—had prepared him to face this horror alone.

That's when Sonny began praying to the Virgin again. Not to the statue on the roof of the car, but to the sainted ancestor who had once been a flesh-and-blood woman. A woman who had remained quietly and steadfastly brave in the most horrific of circumstances.

"Please, give me courage," he said aloud.

Then, without giving himself an opportunity to lose his nerve, he went below the water again.

He couldn't see well enough to search the car from the outside. So Sonny crawled into the front seat, felt around for a body in the passenger seat. No one. He left the car, stood long enough to drag in another lungful of humid air, then resumed. Quickly, he ran his hand along its frame and located the rear door handle. Locked. So he went in again through the open driver's side door, struggling to hold his breath as he leaned between the bucket seats. Real leather, Charlie had told him—not really bragging, simply pleased. Sonny kept his eyes open, seeking small shadows, his outstretched arms moving through the water that filled the rear compartment, bracing himself for the moment he would feel a small body.

He found nothing. After thanking the Blessed Virgin for his courage, Sonny decided that Nga and the children must have evacuated in the van after all. Maybe only Charlie had been delayed. The jewelry store he owned was no more than two miles away. It was possible that Charlie had spent too much time securing the store, then foolishly returned home for one last look or to fetch one last possession. That was when fate must have dealt him an unexpected and lethal blow.

It took Sonny only a moment to decide that he owed it to his friend—to his friend's family—to secure the body until it could be claimed and properly buried. It took a little longer to figure out how, exactly, that could be done. In the end, he decided to return Charlie to the Pham house. There, he would find some dry place to lay the body, say a final prayer for his friend, and then turn his back. Walk away. Return to his own high-and-dry attic—to the now almost irrelevant task of moving the statue—until the water receded and civilization returned to Village de l'Est. Then he would contact the authorities and make sure that Charlie's family was notified and his body taken care of.

It didn't seem like enough, but that was all he could think to do.

He grabbed a handful of Charlie's sodden shirt, ignored the unnatural coolness of the flesh below the fabric, and waded down the center of Calais Street, towing the body behind him. He guided it up the front walk that led to the Phams' big white house with its wraparound porch and pretty green shutters. Once on the porch, Sonny was left standing in water that was little more than calf deep. His friend's body, no longer anchored by Sonny's grip or buoyed by several feet of water, rested on the porch floor with the water nearly covering it.

The door was locked, but Sonny knew to tip back one of the terra cotta lions to retrieve the extra key. He unlocked the door, bent back down to take hold of Charlie, and dragged him inside. Left him stretched out on the tiled foyer floor as, more from habit than necessity, Sonny closed the door behind them. Time spent in his own devastated home had prepared him for the sight of Charlie's. Except for the children's toys floating in the water.

Almost angrily, he grabbed Charlie's shirt again, grunting just a little as he slid the sodden weight across the foyer and into the flooded living room.

He heard Nga gasp as he came through the entryway. Heard her gasp and then let out a sound that lay somewhere between a sob and an abruptly muffled wail. With his eyes, Sonny searched for the source of the painful sound, saw her sitting halfway up the staircase to the second floor, illuminated by the light coming in through a broken window.

She was dressed, as was her custom, in a traditional *ao dai.* Her flowing black trousers were topped by a fitted gray-and-white patterned overdress whose long front and back panels were slit to the thigh. Sonny recalled how Tam—who was short and round—had always been good-naturedly jealous of Nga's beauty. But now Nga's large brown eyes and bow-shaped lips were stretched wide with shock. Her long, glossy hair—which Sonny had never seen except wrapped tightly in a bun—was caught in a limp braid. And there was nothing graceful in the way she moved down the stairs.

She hauled herself into a standing position, then leaned a slim shoulder against the wall as one of her delicate hands dragged reluctantly along the railing. When she drew closer, Sonny could see that there were dark circles beneath her eyes. And that her right cheek was bruised and swollen.

When she reached the body, Nga took Sonny's outstretched hand and used it briefly for support as she knelt in the water beside her son-in-law. She ran her hand lightly over Charlie's face, then sketched a cross in the center of his forehead with her fingers.

"I knew," she murmured in Vietnamese, her eyes still on Charlie. "He was a good father, a dutiful son-in-law. When he didn't come back, I knew that he had to be dead. Or terribly injured." Then she switched to English as she looked up at Sonny. "Where did you find him?"

Her voice remained calm despite the anguish that touched her face. Though she and Sonny usually conversed in Vietnamese, Sonny understood that concentrating on an adopted language—no matter how well she spoke it—made it easier for Nga to control her emotions.

He matched the language and tried to match her calm. Despite his desire to find out why she was still in New Orleans, he quickly explained what he'd seen and how he thought Charlie had died.

"It would have been a quick death," he said finally, hoping to give her some comfort.

To his surprise, Nga had another concern altogether.

"Which direction was the car facing?" she asked.

Though Sonny wondered if shock had compelled her to focus on such a triviality, he answered her question.

"Then he didn't make it to the store," Nga said flatly. At that, her voice broke, and she pressed her hand to her mouth again. But even as she muffled a sob, her eyes widened and Sonny saw something he interpreted as relief touch her features. "Unless . . ."

She scrambled to her feet.

"We must search the car," she said, her voice suddenly stronger. "You told me where you found it, but perhaps the floodwater turned the car around. Maybe Charlie was *returning* from the store."

Almost before she finished speaking, Sonny was shaking his head against such foolish hope. But, suddenly energetic, Nga ignored his reaction, abandoning her son-in-law's body to rush through the foyer to the front door. She made it as far as the porch steps before Sonny was able to catch up with her. He grabbed her wrist, stopped her from plunging forward into the deeper water.

"Let me go!" she cried.

Sonny ignored her attempts to pull free, ignored the small fist pummeling his chest.

"Stop it, Nga!" he demanded, fearful that grief had driven her to madness. "Charlie is dead. Now you must think about the children. Are they upstairs?"

Abruptly, she stopped struggling and, for a moment, stared at him. As if surprised by his question. Then she spoke.

"They are gone. Held for ransom. They took them on Sunday."

At that, Sonny released Nga's trapped wrist, and he knew that his face reflected his shock.

Absentmindedly, she rubbed her arm as she continued speaking, seemingly oblivious to the water soaking her slacks and lapping above the hem of her dress.

"The children were already in their car seats. Waiting to leave. Charlie and I were in the house, grabbing just a few more things. We came outside in time to see two men in our van, backing it out of the driveway. And another in a car in front of the house. All wearing masks. The man driving the car shouted at us in Vietnamese. 'Stay by the phone! No police or the children die!'

"Magdalene and Michael and little Agnes were crying, screaming in the backseat. Charlie begged the men to please, please give the children back. That he would pay now. Whatever they asked."

Nga stopped speaking, stared out in the direction of the street. In the direction, Sonny suspected, that the kidnappers had taken. He watched as she pressed her eyes shut long enough to trap the tears that threatened her cheeks.

"It was hot," she murmured in Vietnamese. "So I'd left the motor running, the air-conditioning on to keep the children cool. If I'd just kept the key in my pocket . . ."

"You couldn't have known," he replied in Vietnamese, shaking his head. "Blame them, not yourself." And then he asked in English: "What did you and Charlie do?"

Nga took a deep breath, let out a trembling sigh, then spoke again: "We waited for hours, until after dark. And I was certain that they had already killed the children. But Charlie said no, that such a gang wanted money, not the attention of the police. So if they murdered—" Nga shook her head, as if to push the thought away. "Charlie told me that the waiting was just to make sure we would pay without hesitating. He said they must have planned this, that the evacuation just gave them an opportunity—a time when we would be vulnerable and the police would be too busy to help."

"And then the kidnappers phoned," Sonny said, his tone making it a statement. "And Charlie went out into the storm, trying to get to the store."

Nga nodded.

"They told him to empty the safe at the store, to bring all the money and jewelry back to the house. They promised to come for it the next day. If the ransom was enough, he would get his children back."

But like so many in New Orleans, Sonny thought, the kidnappers hadn't anticipated the strength of the hurricane. Or the depth of the flooding.

"Have they returned?"

She nodded, briefly touching the bruise on her cheek with a trembling hand. And Sonny cursed himself for noticing at such an inappropriate moment that the nails on her long and graceful fingers were painted a delicate pink.

"Not on Monday," she said, "but yesterday. Just before sunset. Long after I judged my entire family dead. Only one man came. He pounded on the door until I opened it and asked for the money and jewelry from the store. That's when I told him that I thought the storm had killed Charlie. I begged him to return my grandchildren."

"How did he get here?" Sonny asked. "Did he walk? Was his clothing wet?"

She nodded. And Sonny thought to himself that the kidnappers could not be too far away.

"He demanded the combination for the safe," Nga continued. "He said that they would go themselves to get what was owed them. I swear, I would have given it to him had I known it. But the store is Charlie's business, not mine. When I told him that, he struck me. Called me a useless old woman. Then he said that everyone knew the Phams were wealthy and that we'd installed an alarm on our house to protect our valuables. I told him it was just for protection, for me and the children. Nothing more. But he didn't believe me. He gave me a day to gather up my valuables. And then . . ."

Nga's face crumpled and tears began streaming down her cheeks. Sonny opened his arms to her and she pushed her face into his shoulder, sobbing out the rest of the story.

"He said that they would bring the children back with them before sunset. That they would drown them in front of me if what I had to offer was not enough."

Sonny held her, letting her cry, knowing that her natural reserve would soon have her straightening in his arms, stepping away from him. And when that happened . . . He shook his head just a little, pushing away another stab of sorrow.

A moment later, she did just what he'd expected. And then she walked past him, back through the foyer.

Sonny followed her, saw her hesitate as she caught sight of Charlie's body, then watched her straighten her spine and lift her chin. She walked to the base of the staircase. Kept her back to Sonny as she shook her head, laughed a little. It was a sound untouched by humor.

"These . . . thugs would be disappointed to know that Charlie grew up more American than Vietnamese. He believes . . . *believed* . . . in banks. That's where our money is kept. And most of the jewelry we own is in a safe deposit box. But still, there were a few things around the house." She glanced over her shoulder at Sonny. "Shall I show you what I have?"

Sonny nodded, then watched as she walked back up the carpeted stairs. Just past the landing, Nga bent to pick up a bundle tucked in the shadow of a step. Sonny saw that it was a lace-trimmed pillowcase.

"I gathered up everything that those men might value," she said as she came back down the stairs, then opened the bag for him to peer inside. "Credit cards. Bracelets, watches, rings. A few gold coins. All the cash I could find. Almost five hundred dollars. I have a key to the neighbor's house, so I even went there, too. Looking for valuables they'd left behind. I found a few things."

Sonny imagined adding every bit of cash and jewelry he had to her bag and knew it would still not be enough for men who were willing to steal children. Though he said nothing, Nga sensed his doubt. Or perhaps she read it in his expression.

Panic pinched her voice, making it shrill. "Then what shall I do?"

Sonny murmured another prayer to the Virgin. For courage. And for a return of skills he thought he'd never use again. Not in America, where there was no war.

"We will wait for them to come," he said finally. "And we will get the children back." *Or we will all die in the attempt*, he thought.

Hours later, the men came back.

For much of that time, Sonny had been waiting in the shelter of a collapsed carport opposite the Phams' front yard. He'd been sitting above the water on a section of crossbeam, but when he saw the men approaching, he slipped into the water.

There were three of them, just as Nga had said. Two moved through the deep water on either side of a raft created from a section of privacy fence. Another walked behind. They were bare-chested, golden-skinned, and muscular. Despite the masks they wore, it was easy to see that they were young men. A tattoo of a sinuous green dragon curled around each man's upper right arm.

The Pham children were sitting at the raft's center, bound together shoulder-to-shoulder with duct tape. Facing outward. More duct tape covered their mouths. Above the tape, their eyes were terrified. It would take little effort, Sonny realized, to tip the raft and send the bundle of children tumbling into the water. Where they would certainly drown.

The children shared the raft with three handguns.

The procession stopped in front of the house, in front of the porch. Sonny watched as the two flanking men abandoned their positions and went up the steps. Two of the handguns went with them. They shouted loudly and waved the guns in Nga's direction when she came to the door.

Maximum intimidation, Sonny thought.

One of the men pointed at the raft, clearly threatening.

Nga nodded, looking nervous, but did just as she and Sonny had agreed. She gestured for them to come inside. To view the valuables she'd collected.

"Keep them inside for as long as possible," Sonny had instructed her, silently admiring her courage when she'd immediately agreed. They had spread the ransom across the dining room table, then gotten rid of the pillowcase so that gathering up the money and jewelry would be less convenient for the kidnappers.

Nga had added to the plan: "There's a wall safe upstairs. I'll put half of the money back into it. When they demand more, I'll reluctantly tell them about it. Then I'll take them upstairs. After that, they can wait as I search the house for the extra jewelry I've just remembered."

"Smart," Sonny'd said, and then he'd grinned at her. "Be

sure to move slowly, old woman. That way you'll give an old man the time that he needs."

Now, as he slipped quietly into the water, Sonny murmured another prayer to the Virgin. He apologized to her for previous transgressions, then asked her to intervene on his behalf. To ask the Lord's forgiveness for what he was about to do.

"*Ban cung sinh dao tac,*" he said finally. ("Necessity knows no laws.") And he hoped that the old adage was respected in heaven, too.

Then he made sure his grasp was firm around the razor-sharp filleting knife he'd taken from his tackle box when he'd briefly returned to his little house. And he moved forward, only his nose and eyes above the water's surface, the top of his head camouflaged by a small, leafy branch. When he'd tested it, Nga had assured him that it looked as if the branch were merely floating loose on the water.

Sonny had already checked his route, knew exactly where the obstacles lay between him and the porch. He moved forward quickly, detouring when he needed to, half-swimming, half-gliding through the water. Recalling how he'd once crossed rivers in just this way, intent on an enemy.

The man who'd been left behind was entertaining himself by terrorizing the children. He had retrieved his gun and, with his free hand, was leaning on the raft, pushing it downward against the water's pressure, then releasing it abruptly. He was laughing at the children's muffled cries.

Sonny emerged from the water directly behind him. He wrapped one arm around the young man's shoulders as he slid the blade firmly across his throat. Just as he'd been taught back in Vietnam. Then he held the body for a moment, waiting for it to hang limp before lowering it slowly into the water.

The gun sank before he could retrieve it, but that didn't matter.

He smiled at the children and touched his fingers to his lips. But he left them taped up and gagged. Impossible to trust ones so young to the silence that was essential to saving their lives. He pushed the raft back down the street, moving as quickly as he could, finally beaching it on his own tiny side porch.

He took the children up into the attic.

"Stay here," he said in Vietnamese, and then again in English. "Your grandmother and I will be back soon."

He tossed them a package of cookies, then wedged the attic door shut from the outside so that they couldn't follow him. They would die slowly, he knew, if he did not succeed. If he did not return.

He went back to the Pham house.

Just inside the living room, he stood on his tiptoes to reach past the ornate façade at the top of a mahogany display case. His shotgun, fetched from his attic hours earlier, was exactly where he'd placed it. Ready to use.

He followed the angry voices. And the high-pitched wavering voice of a woman. One who Sonny knew was far too brave to be as panicked as she sounded. He crept up the stairs, now too busy concentrating to be praying. Then he swung around the corner into the master bedroom.

Nga had backed away from the men, left them standing before the small wall safe. When she saw Sonny, she dove for cover behind the bed. Just as they'd agreed.

"Drop your weapons," Sonny said in Vietnamese, making the effort to keep his voice low and absolutely steady. "Or you're dead men."

The two did as he said, turning to face his shotgun.

Impossible to read the expressions on the faces beneath the masks. But Sonny didn't much care what they thought. He marched them down the stairs at gunpoint. Into the water of the first floor. Past the place where Charlie's body had been before he and Nga dragged it up to the second floor, placed it in the bathtub, gently wrapped it with a sheet.

He showed them to the front door.

"Your friend is dead," he said. "But I was able to take back the children without killing you. Say your prayers tonight and thank God and the Virgin for your worthless lives."

Sonny stood on the porch, gun leveled in their direction, watching as they waded out into the deeper water.

Nga had come downstairs, too, and stood just behind him.

"The children are safe," he murmured.

"*Kam ouen,*" she replied quietly. ("Thank you.")

Sonny would have smiled, but just then one of the men stopped moving. He turned to face the porch, and his friend followed his lead.

"As long as the water is high," he shouted, "we own Village de l'Est! And we'll be back. Perhaps we'll take the woman next time."

The other kidnapper laughed, nodded.

"Don't sleep, old man. Because when you do—"

Sonny begged for the Virgin's understanding as he shot them both.

Their bodies sank beneath the muddy water.

LAWYERS' TONGUES

BY THOMAS ADCOCK

Gentilly

I hope that the one of my relations who come across this gift find a very exlent use for it since the old bag I hereby confess to steal it from was a lowdown evil person who actually deserve what I imagine they going to do to me up to Angola after they catch up to me, which is stick me with the ugly needle and put me down like a cat . . .

Maybe there was ten thousand dollars' worth of "gift" slipping around in my hands, maybe twenty. A sheaf of beautiful green-gray bills fluttered to the floor, along with Frank's last letter to anybody. I stared at etchings of dead presidents on paper money. But all I could see, really, was the memory of my brother's face, how it so often wore the expression of a mutt dog expecting to be cuffed.

My brother wrote letters practically every day of his life, always on lined paper torn from the Big Chief notebooks he bought from Bynum's Pharmacy. Frank bought Big Chiefs like other people buy newspapers and chewing gum.

I picked up his letter from the floor.

Probly you going to come across this here loot, Wussy Wally. You being the onlyest one of our so-called family ever care to be buzzing around my bizness . . .

He always wrote in jet-black Sheaffer Skrip fountain pen ink. His handwriting was strangely elegant; surely that would seem most odd to those who didn't care to know anything about Frank besides the worst thing about his record in life.

He called me "Wussy Wally" only when it was just the two of us. I imagine Frank believed his little brother would be embarrassed otherwise. So I was properly Walter, or sometimes Walt, when anybody else was around.

I considered the private name a gesture of my brother's affection and gentleness. For indeed, I did care to know about the thoughtful dimensions of an angry man's life.

Frank was right. Nobody else cared anything about him beyond keeping him far away. All our uncles and aunts and cousins kept their doors shut to Frank—and, by extension, to me too. This was due to Frank's light fingers. As Aunt-tee Viola said for the whole bunch of our relations, "That boy Frank, he'd steal anything but a red-hot stove."

But he was more than a thief, of course. Just as surely as crooks in high places got where they are because of doing some good things for people now and then. A man's life is not so petty it can be measured up at the end as all good or all bad. Frank was plus and minus like anybody else, except for cheap schooling and black skin, which of course magnifies all minuses.

When I recollect his plus side, I would describe Frank as a philosopher. The things he said!

Such as things he'd whisper in the dark of night when we were boys in a shared room, me in one twin bed drifting off to sleep, Frank in his—only I can't recall ever seeing him sleep. Frank would be sitting up, sounding out important thoughts before scratching them into a Big Chief by the light of a radio dial.

One night it was, "It's a damn lie they say down to Asia Baptist Church about God create us all equal. But anyhow, every life is a big deal."

Another night, "Since I am only a poor man walking around to save on funeral expenses, maybe I ought to find a way of doing somebody a good deed when I leave. That sound like suicide. Well, suicide is just a trick played on a calendar."

And another night, "I am too sad to be dangerous. I am sad as a dead bird in a birdbath."

The night I especially remember from back in those years came the summer when Frank turned sixteen—on his birthday, actually. Mama said he was a man now according to the law, and that a man didn't need his mama's birthday fuss anymore. Just about everything was a fuss for Mama by then. She had the sugar, and it was taking her down fast and furious, even faster than diabetes killed Daddy six years before.

So Frank and I went out and had a birthday party, thanks to thirty-one dollars I'd squirreled away for the big occasion. Frank knew how to spend it, due to his knowledge of where a couple of teenage boys could purchase whiskey and the attentions of certain ladies who frequented the alley behind the Star Lounge on Senate Street.

I remember Frank grabbing hard on my arm when a police siren sounded faintly in the distance. The party was over for some reason; I didn't bother to ask why, as my brother was long in the habit of cringing and fleeing whenever a siren went off. I remember a party lady's voice calling out behind us—"Where y'all going, baby?"—as we sprinted together up the alley and around over to Harrison Avenue toward home.

It was the hottest night I have ever known, running

aside. So hot the chameleons that usually skittered across the screens outside our bedroom windows were hanging loose by their sticky little toes, and I swear they panted like hounds under a porch. I don't believe I slept any more that night than Frank did.

In one of the tiny hours, Frank whispered something that froze the sweat on my neck. He cursed the city is what he did.

The page where he wrote down that curse must have floated off with Katrina someplace, along with all the rest of Frank's life collection of Big Chiefs. But I don't need that long-lost page to remind me of what he said.

"New Orleans be a jazzy town," he said, "full of dead markers, a funeral urn of polished-up brass on top a flowery grave, and underneath the box going rotten."

So there I was in our old room in the old house—what was left of it—with all that money slipping and sliding through my shaking hands. I stepped over to a smashed-out window and took a sneaky look through a slit in the plywood cover to make sure no wrong numbers were out there in the street or the yard picking through trash or casing storm-bashed houses or otherwise prowling around.

Up and down DeSaix Boulevard and pretty much all over Gentilly, variously wrecked homes were still waiting on overpriced contractors to show up, a whole year after that bitch Katrina. Gangs of discriminating thieves and expert metal-strippers seemed to know exactly which houses were worth their while. My suspicions were the same as the neighbors' suspicions, what was left of the neighbors: Maybe the wrong numbers knew where to go because when they weren't contracting, they were thieving.

Nobody was prowling around outside.

I stepped back to where I was when I came across the money and Frank's letter—stooped in front of my grandfather Benjamin Masson's chifforobe, going through the drawers and shelves after anything worth keeping before the unhappy need of my cutting it down with a rented chainsaw.

That chifforobe and the matching cherry wood blanket chest and Mama's wide bureau, as we called it, along with the bed frame with the carved headboard and footboard, were Masson family heirlooms. They'd all been handed down to Daddy as Benjamin's wedding gift. The heirlooms crowded up my parents' first little bedroom in the St. Bernard projects, which is where I lived for the first ten years of my life until we left.

We didn't go far, at least not by the lights of Frank and me, resentful of being told we shouldn't be playing with the project kids we ran with since now we'd moved up in the world. But Daddy was proud to leave the apartment in St. Bernard and move off Gibson Street not so many blocks to DeSaix Boulevard. He had enough to buy a small house there, a wood one painted pink with two bedrooms and a Queen Palm in the front and two Chinaberry trees in back.

"Little no-account niggers," Daddy called the St. Bernard kids we weren't supposed to play with anymore. Never mind they came in approximately the same good-to-bad ratio as everybody else in New Orleans, little or big. Never mind that Daddy and Mama and all us Massons have been called that same hurting word at one time or another; never mind that everybody else on our new block, save for the Spagnuolo family, had to sit way up in the balcony at the Circle Cinema.

So anyway, what was I doing there with a chainsaw?

It was hard enough years ago to haul that chifforobe and

the rest of the bedroom suite out of Gibson Street and onto Daddy's pickup for the short drive to Gentilly. Daddy called it a bedroom *suit*. It was even harder to get the whole cherry wood shebang jiggled through the front door and the narrow foyer of the pink house. Daddy and two of his work crew buddies from the parks department grunted clear through a Sunday on that job.

Now, thanks to that hellbat Katrina, there was no way of removing the family heirlooms out from the pink house. The cherry wood was all waterlogged, too swollen up to get through the door frames. Everything had to be cut into pieces, and the pieces carted out to the curb to wait a minor eternity for the garbage haulers to come fetch the mess.

The cutting job fell to me for two reasons. First, I'm handy. Second, the house was automatically deeded over to me as next of kin by the state of Louisiana when its previous orphaned owner was convicted and sent up to Angola for what he did to a white woman by the name of Eugenia Malreaux, who lived uptown on St. Charles Avenue in a big old place with her prize tulip trees in the back garden.

What in the name of Heaven I was doing hanging on to the pink house and the heirlooms these past years I do not know. I didn't need a house. I have my own very nice little house uptown. And I didn't need a *suit* for my bedroom.

Before Katrina, my wife Toni was after me to rent out the pink house. But I always managed to stall by reminding her about Mama and Daddy both dying there in the cherry wood bed, both blind and crippled up from the sugar and helpless to keep from soiling themselves. And then how Frank took over the house after Mama died, and moved into our parents' own room at night to sleep in the big cherry wood death bed—leaving me to wonder what he might be cursing there in the dark . . .

. . . And how Frank took care of me in that house all the while I went through high school, then Xavier. And then on top of that, three years of law school at Loyola. No thanks to any of the cold relations who turned their backs on a pair of orphan boys. Just us two against the world, Frank and Walter.

I only worked part-time construction jobs in my school years, and I didn't manage to get half what I thought I might in scholarship money. But Frank always came up with the rest, always on the promise that I would not ask where the money came from.

It was hard for Frank to be as responsible as all that. But not as hard as the rest of his life. This was a capital-B bone of contention between us.

Frank claimed he was halfway a regular citizen for bringing me up, and so anything outside of his role of being a big brother was none of my business. It didn't sit well with me to be shut out like that. So to spite him, I did the meanest thing I could think of doing.

The day after commencement at Loyola, I marched down to the Orleans Parish District Attorney's Office with my law degree and got myself hired. I could just as easily have taken a job as a public defender. Frank never said anything about my spiteful choice, but I know I hurt him.

The white man who hired me at the D.A.'s office soon thereafter prosecuted my brother and sent him up to Angola, where they eventually put him down like a cat for stealing Miss Malreaux's money and afterwards splitting her head open with an axe.

Even though the crime scene investigators never found that axe and had to rely on the coroner's analysis at trial, the prosecution case against Frank was sufficiently solid. More solid, I admit, than a lot of cases I have prosecuted myself. People go to prison and get the needle for pitifully little evidence, really. All colors of people.

Frank had long been working handyman jobs at the big Malreaux house—earning money for my tuition at Loyola University School of Law, no less. So Frank had access to the place. The forensics squad came up with a smudged thumbprint they claimed was Frank's, right there on the dial of a private safe in the brick shed where Miss Eugenia was known to keep large amounts of cash. Add to that, investigators found a considerable number of Miss Eugenia's jewelry items inside a chifforobe drawer in the pink house.

They didn't find the looted cash, though. Frank, of course, denied stealing money or jewelry from Miss Eugenia, just like he denied stealing anything else in his life. He'd wear that bad-dog look on his face when confronted on matters of theft, which was as close as he'd come to admitting his light-fingered predilection—until his last letter, that is.

Certainly he denied murdering Miss Eugenia. Which flew in the face of jewelry found in the chifforobe. Which Frank's court-appointed lawyer might have said flew in the face of common logic, therefore constituting reasonable doubt in the mind of a juror. Because why would a murderer keep mementoes of his victim in the same place he kept his socks and boxer shorts?

At first, I thought it would be no problem to chainsaw the bedroom suit. Maybe in the past it was all worth some serious antique money. But the value was surely gone now—now that all that cherry wood was so nasty and swollen and probably full of termites, too. It was junk and nothing more. No problem.

But there I was in my dead brother's house, in the room where he used to sleep as a free man. Sentiment hammered me. The rented chainsaw seemed as disrespectful to Frank's house as Mother Nature had been.

Speaking of a hellish vandal woman, I took a long moment to gaze around the bedroom after a knock-down drag-out with Katrina.

Schaefer Skrip bottles by the dozen had flown around like stones in the hurricane, smashing into walls where splattered ink adhered to glass shards and blue and yellow labels. The floor was a carpet of Budweiser cans, crushed the way Frank crushed them with his big right hand, sodden Camel butts and moldy paperback books with underlined pages. Crime novels mostly. The door to the hallway was cracked in two and the plaster ceiling had gone pulpy like ricotta cheese.

Then I read the next parts of Frank's last letter.

Evil and lowdown ain't my view alone of Miss Eugenia Malreaux. It's what the old bag son Philip call her. He told me things about his mama make you toss a meal. Told me when he was just a boy she'd come wake him up in his bedroom some nights wearing nothing but a peek-a-boo and she poke where she ain't got bizness poking. Philip tell on her to his daddy one day. Then soon as daddy leave the house that lowdown Miss Eugenia take a strap to Philip and nearly skin him alive.

Oh yes, Philip he told me lots of things about the grand life up on St. Charles Avenue where it all look peace and quiet respectable. He said he like it better where we live in Gentilly on account of pain and awfulness can't be hid away so easy.

Also Philip said he like talking to me whenever I come

by to work for his mama in the garden since I understand the two of us is in the same boat—a couple of mens waiting around for the rest of their life to happen. Philip, he couldn't get enough of that sad sack talk and start coming by to drink with me at the Star Lounge, my little briar patch by good old St. Bernard.

I always feel sorry for Philip when he come slumming, a puffy little white guy in there with us Negroes. But I don't feel sorry enough to forget about asking him where do they hide the money up to his place on St. Charles. And he told me. Told me his mama keep a wall safe in the very last place I'd ever think to look, which is the garden shed behind the tools.

Also, he told me how he steal money from the evil lowdown old bag first as a boy, then as a grown man when he hide it down to the bank on Poydras Street where he keep a safety box in the vault on account of he trusts banks even if his mama don't . . .

Because Frank had secured them so carefully in a false compartment he'd constructed in the back of the chifforobe, the only thing in the room that wasn't ruined by greasy water were the Big Chief pages of his long letter. Oh—and the money, which made me nervous on many levels and which trembled my hands to the point where I couldn't help but spill the cash over the muck of cans and butts.

What especially unnerved me was my own larcenous first impulse on seeing all that green: how I'd spend it on my own selfish self, or at least pay off my bills. Which is not the way a sworn man of the law such as I am, after all, is supposed to think. The first thing I am obliged to do under the circumstances of tainted money is turn it in lickety-split, along with anything else incriminating, such as Frank's letter of a singular confession to theft in this particular instance.

But somehow I knew I wasn't going to feel so obliged. Maybe this was because of the crappy trial that Frank endured; not quietly, as they often tied him down on the defendant's chair and stuffed a bailiff's hanky in his mouth when he cursed the judge too much. Maybe it was because of my own rage that I had to keep bottled up since I myself am part of the crappy system, prosecution side. Maybe it was because of the parade of incompetent drunkards Frank kept hiring, since that's all he personally knew of the city's criminal defense bar and refused to consult me on the matter of his defense.

"Sorry, my Wussy Wally, but I ain't about to trust nobody who work for the Man going to get me needled for a lawyer reference—not even my own brother." Frank had told me this on the one occasion he agreed to see me in his cell.

Or maybe I was feeling rebellious against the whole crappy system, because once again Aunt-tee Viola spoke for the whole bunch of my cold relations when she came on the bus to the D.A.'s office on South White Street, right in the middle of my brother's highly publicized axe-murder trial, for an approving look-see. She told me, "Walter, we're so proud of you for rising above your brother's miserable failure of a life." I bottled up what I thought right then: In my brother's case, the words *South* and *white* were not harbingers of justice.

No doubt I was seriously conflicted because of my guilt for spiting Frank. It was a guilt settled in for life after I read through the transcript of his trial in the Superior Criminal Court of New Orleans, especially the part I can't help but remember by heart:

Mr. Masson: I want another attorney.

The Court: Well, I don't think I'm going to do that.

Mr. Masson: Y'all go ahead and have your trial if you want, but leave me out of it. You can sentence me, hang me, stick a needle to me, do what you want. If you don't give me no other lawyer, I ain't taking part in this stupidity. I already told you I didn't steal no money and I didn't bash the brains out of no white lady. Go on now, have court without me. I don't care.

The Court: It's your life that's involved. Don't you care about that?

Mr. Masson: I care about my life just as much as you care about it.

The Court: Don't you want to protect it?

Mr. Masson: Do you want to protect it?

Late as I was, I was finally doing the right thing by Frank, and set about business.

First, I confirmed with the senior barflies at the Star Lounge that a puffy-faced white guy used to pal around there with my brother.

"Oh, he still comes by here," according to somebody called Shug. "Real wormy kind of a man, just sit over to the end of the bar and complain. I ain't saying we don't got our share of complainers, but things that guy said—well, seems to me he was creeped by his own life."

Before I left, Shug told me, "Your brother was all right, you know? Sure, I know what they say he did. But that's lawyers making the charge. You know what your brother said about lawyers one time?"

From whispers of a long-ago night I had a fair idea.

"The Devil makes his Christmas pie with lawyers' tongues," said Shug. "That's Frank's own words. Oh, but he could talk some."

Next, I searched for a record of a safe deposit box rented to one Philip Malreaux, after which I pulled a few strings, thanks to my official capacity as a lawman, and quietly obtained a court order to open it up and inspect the contents. I had a fair idea what I'd find.

It was not difficult to crack Malreaux after a long talk at the Star Lounge, accompanied by a fifth of Johnnie Walker Red, which mostly he drank while softly weeping as I told him what I'd found—and what I made of it. As I was looking into Malreaux's white face, I saw my dead brother's own black dog face; it was as if the two of them, Philip and Frank, were some old married couple who came to resemble one another.

I asked Malreaux if he'd care to tell a detective to back up my theory of what really happened to the lowdown woman who shattered his life as bad as Katrina shattered the city. He took a long pull of Johnnie Walker before saying, "Yeah, that'd be all right."

As we rode in a taxi together down to police headquarters on South Broad Street, Malreaux said, "You being Frank's brother, I offer my word of honor—I'll protect you like Frank protected me."

That's when I realized we both knew the all-around score: He knew that I knew that he knew.

"Deal," I said to Malreaux. "Just say what I tell you to say."

Finally, I had a little talk with the boss—the man who had hired me and sent Frank to Angola.

"You found *what?*" he said, annoyed. I had interrupted the tuna sandwich he was eating at his desk.

"The axe."

"Don't matter about a murder weapon all this time after the fact."

"It matters if it's new evidence—grounds for a new trial for my brother."

"Who is a dead and gone man."

"True, but that doesn't mean the case is. Besides the axe, there was a whole lot of cash in Philip Malreaux's box."

"I don't see how that matters." The boss used the back of his hand to wipe a string of tuna off his lip. "That money could have come from anywhere, anytime."

"Including it could have come from Eugenia Malreaux's wall safe, a strong possibility I'm having the forensics squad consider."

In the worst way, I wanted Frank's name cleared. Frank might have said I wanted this in the *best* way.

And—hoo-whee!—what would my aunt-tee say if things turned out to clear Frank? What would any of my chilly relations say when it was written up in the newspapers the way I reasoned how things really went down in connection with the death of Eugenia Malreaux?

Frank helped himself somehow to Miss Eugenia's wall safe, that's for certain. But legally speaking, maybe there was a way of muddying up certainty. That thumbprint of Frank's? He must have brushed the dial of that safe a hundred times reaching for tools to tend the old lady's tulip trees. Frank's fingerprints that no doubt would be found all over the murder weapon? Well, of course Frank's prints are on that axe—probably a hundred times over the years of pruning trees.

But why would Frank murder Miss Eugenia anyhow? If it

was true what was said at his trial and he'd stolen jewelry from her before, then he hardly needed a goose that laid golden eggs to be dead. Philip Malreaux, on the other hand, had plenty of motive, which he'd been brooding over since his awful boyhood; since the first night his mama raped him.

Philip's fingerprints were never found on the wall safe in the brick shed. Why not? Maybe he was careful to wear gloves. But if Philip's fingerprints showed up on the axe, which was likely, it was for the simple reason that nobody but the owner of a safe deposit box account is allowed to put anything into it. So why would he do that?

Maybe Philip Malreaux came across that axe before the police did and ran down to the bank with it, thinking his buddy Frank Masson must have got liquored up and killed Miss Eugenia on account of hearing so many stories about the old bag that you could toss your lunch.

Having seen a bunch of loose ends in every single criminal matter that ever crossed my desk at the D.A.'s office, I was unsurprised by the case of my own brother and his wormy pal. For instance, how come Frank took the fall for murdering Miss Eugenia? Well, maybe it was his way of doing a good deed for somebody before playing a trick on the calendar.

And there's the little matter of what everybody overlooked right from the jump: What about old man Malreaux, by which I mean Philip's daddy? Mightn't the old man himself have gone crazed over all the years of carrying around the sickening knowledge of what went on in his house?

But mostly my theorizing was informed by what I alone knew about—namely, Frank's last letter and the money that came with it, and the contents of my long conversation at the Star Lounge with Malreaux. Three things I was not bringing up with the boss.

"My brother was no killer, he was just sad," I continued. "Sad as a dead bird in a birdbath."

"He was sure as hell a thief, I am sorry to inform you, Walter. And even if this Philip Malreaux was in on the crime like you are intimating, even if he was the one who did the whacking on his mama's skull—well, as party to felony theft when the axe fell, you know your brother was equally guilty of murder."

"But we don't know that the theft and the murder occurred at the same time," I said. "Or if Frank was even involved in the theft part."

"Then how come that jewelry ends up in his bedroom?"

"He could have come by it honestly," I lied. I thought about the Devil and his Christmas pie. "He could have bought it off Malreaux."

"Sure, and boar hogs might grow teats some day . . . Are you talking like reasonable-doubt talk, Walter?" he asked. "Because if you are, I don't like hearing that from a man supposed to be a prosecutor."

He glared at me while taking a last chew of sandwich, like it was me he wanted in his teeth.

"Especially when we're talking a heinous crime I prosecuted myself," said the boss, "and which I don't especially want to open up again. You get me?"

I said I sure did.

"Reasonable-doubt talk," added the boss, "that could imperil a man's career around here."

And so, under threat as I considered myself to be, I had the right to remain silent, except for resigning from the Orleans Parish District Attorney's Office.

The very next day, I found office space for no rent: The pink house in Gentilly. I am today waiting on contractors to come renovate the place as the offices of Walter Masson, Esq., criminal defense counsel.

I already have two clients: the late Frank Masson, whose case I am taking pro bono, and Philip Malreaux, who has the wherewithal to pay me handsomely.

That's part of the deal I struck with Malreaux.

As for all that money in the chifforobe, I am keeping it, in a kind of solidarity with my big brother.

AND HELL WALKED IN

BY JERI CAIN ROSSI

Bywater

The rain will never stop.

And her landlord would never fix the air conditioner, she thought, while she sat naked at the kitchen table fanning herself, sweating and stinking. As the bath water faucet dripped, she took two ice trays from the refrigerator and emptied them in. She stepped into the claw-foot tub filled with bath water and ice cocktail, lay back, and submerged, eyes open. Through the ripples, she looked up at her drowning reflection in the full-length mirror on the ceiling. Her long black tresses floated around her lily white flesh like the passion of Ophelia.

Her ex was bartending at the Sugar Park, a dive bar at Dauphine and France Streets in the Bywater, what was left of it. She went in to use the ATM and there he was, not looking so good—not that anybody was looking good since the storm of two-thousand-ought-five. Curious, she sat down for a nightcap. He walked over to her stool like it was the last few steps to the electric chair. He politely asked what she wanted and she politely told him red wine. Like he didn't know, the coward. That was their drink. She had an urge to lunge over the bar and rake his face for treating her like a stranger, like their time together didn't matter.

"Why, thank you so much," she said, sugary sweet when

he returned with the beverage. At least she could savor the pleasure of having him serve her.

His new girl, an emaciated brunette, walked out of the kitchen like a coiffed skeleton in a red halter dress. Her scapulae jutted and the vertebrae stretched like a mountain ridge down her back. *They must be doing coke*, she noted. The brunette had those deer-caught-in-the-headlights eyes. They were more bugged-out than usual. Yeah, coke or crystal meth, and lots of it. The brunette sat at the other end of the bar near the TV. She had no jealousy for this girl, this brunette girl, she told herself. She started to chew her fingernails, then caught herself.

Thinking back on it, there was nothing heroic about their affair, her and her ex. It was cowardice on both accounts. He was a charming heartbreaker trying to extricate himself from another fling that had run its course and she was the willing vehicle of his getaway. Just to be a bitch. The luxury of it. There's something alluring about being on the arm of a good-looking heartbreaker, like having something in your pocket everybody wants. And they indeed made quite an enviable ruckus, staggering around the Quarter arm-in-arm, howling merrily—beautiful, barefoot, and besotted. However, his attention began to waver toward the end of the summer. In fact, the night before the storm he made his move for the brunette.

That was months ago, and her insides were still charred like so many buildings in the neighborhood. There's nothing like knowing where you really stand when your man goes off with another girl during a cat-five hurricane, leaving you to die. She took a long gulp of Vendage and shuddered at its horribleness.

Maybe she read it somewhere in a book at the Isle of

Salvation Botanica, maybe she imagined it, but this is what she figured: She'd fuck a hundred men. Each man would be a pin stuck deep into her ex's cheating voodoo-doll heart. Each seduction would be a ritual to cleanse herself of his brutal rebuff. Then she wouldn't want him anymore. Furthermore, she imagined her indifference would revive his interest, because that's how it is with heartbreakers. He would be cursed to want her forevermore. And all evidence of the hurricane would go away as if it didn't happen. The shotgun houses would rebuild the way they were before. The people would come back. The music would play. Paradise would return.

One hundred men.

And she set off on her goal with abandon, especially in those first months. National Guardsmen, Louisiana SWAT, Texas Rangers, NOPD, animal rescue workers, paramedics, firemen. The second wave brought in demolition and salvage crews, construction workers, electricians, Latin migrant workers. Her bed was open to musicians, artists, poets, the drunken, the sad, the crazy. Men she would have never slept with before the hurricane. Men who would never have slept with her before the hurricane. By her calculation, she was at ninety-nine. She had been one man short for weeks now, peculiarly relishing the idea that with one more fuck her suffering would be over. So why did she hesitate? She stared deep into her wine glass.

"Gigolette!"

There was Jimmie Lee. The most beautiful boy in town. He waved at her drunkenly from the pool table, wearing a T-shirt with a frog drawing on it. To be anywhere near this creature was to be blessed by the gods. Pretty, pretty Jimmie Lee. Like many youth in New Orleans, he started carousing early.

He was everything innocent and pure yet wicked that was the Big Easy. A naughty manchild. Girls giggled and blushed when they passed him, peering back to see if he was looking at them. Men measured him with their eyes. Jimmie Lee flirted with everybody, but he wasn't a heartbreaker. More like a boyfriend to the world. He was the one good, true thing that seemed untouched by the storm. Everybody looked after Jimmie. He was like something holy.

She took her drink and sauntered over to him. Jimmie Lee leaned against the table aiming his shot with the pool stick, a cigarette butt with a long ash resting precipitously between his lips, ash stains on the green cloth. The balls clacked and, as drunk as he was, he still managed the solid into the hole.

"Who's winning?" she asked.

"Me!" he chirped.

"Who are you playing?" She glanced around.

"Myself!" The ash fell on the pool table.

Her cruel lover and his skinny brunette were necking at the bar, for her benefit no doubt. That's what wild animals do.

"Oh fuck it all to hell," she said under her breath.

Jimmie Lee looked at her, put down the stick, grabbed his beer, and took her by the hand. "I want to show you something."

He took her to the door and outside. Even at night, the weather was oppressively sauna-like. He took a swig of his beer.

"What, Jimmie Lee?"

He giggled like a little mischievous boy, then pulled her close and kissed her. It was like a third-grade kiss behind the magnolia tree in the school yard.

"Don't be silly, Jimmie Lee. You're too good for me."

She looked into his handsome brown eyes under the luminescent, almost full moon. He wiggled his eyebrows in his comical, precocious way. They both started laughing. The more they laughed the funnier and funnier it seemed. They laughed harder and harder there on the street at the corner of Dauphine and France in the Bywater, where before the storm, teenagers from the projects used to die with regularity from gangland drive-bys—neighbors would wake up and find a dead body on their lawn. Yet they laughed. A few blocks away across the Industrial Canal was the Lower Ninth, where the frail had floated in their attics, unable to breech their roofs during the storm. Laughed and laughed. They hugged long and hard.

"Let's go to a hotel and use their pool," he said.

"You got one in mind, Jimmie Lee? It's 3:00 in the morning."

"We could go swimming in the river."

"Are you out of your mind?" The undertow was notoriously fierce. The Mississippi was like a snake that swallowed its prey whole.

He pulled out a joint. "Well, how about we smoke this in my car?"

I walk along the street of sorrow
The boulevard of broken dreams
Where gigolo and gigolette
Can take a kiss without regret
*So they forget their broken dreams**

She could hear the phone all the way up the stairs. She was coming home from waiting tables at Elizabeth's Diner near the levee. The voice on the phone wouldn't stop crying. A tugboat captain, the voice sobbed, reported a body caught on a floating tree near Poland Avenue Wharf in the late morning.

Her instinct was to get drunk. She listened to her instinct. She parked her bike at the corner of Lesseps and Burgundy and entered BJ's, an old neighborhood dive bar, and proceeded to wallow. It was a skill she was good at. Several of the colorful older regulars had disappeared since the storm, but there was always another drunk to spring up and take the vacant barstool. She sat at a table away from the new faces.

A great many drinks later, the welcome feeling of indifference washed over her. Indifference over losing electricity every other day. Indifference over having to ride the bus for miles to find a decent grocery store. Indifference over nobody knowing what they were doing or how they were going to do it. She reckoned New Orleans as the best loverboy in the neighborhood who all the husbands cornered and mutilated while the wives wailed.

"Why are you crying?" He was dripping wet, his sparkly brown eyes mischievous. She jumped up and held him. Hard. He smelled of Old Man River.

"You've got a lot of explaining to do. Everybody thinks you've drowned."

The strains of a brass band reached a crescendo. The bar door opened and a second-line entered loudly, marching drums, trumpets, tuba, trombones, good-time people swaying with the good-time music, customers smiling, waving their drinks as they danced.

"See what you're missing?" she yelled to him over the cacophony.

* * *

She looked long and hard in the bathroom mirror and didn't like what she saw. *I wonder if I'll die tonight*, she thought, and sat on the toilet. *Now that's a sign you're wasted*, she mused, *when you actually sit on the toilet at the Abbey*.

Back in the bar, the jukebox was screaming a Tom Waits song about the end of the world. She spied Wyatt nursing a cocktail in the corner and sauntered over.

"That really sucks about Jimmie Lee," he said after hugging her.

"Don't tell anybody," she whispered in his ear, "but he's in hiding."

Wyatt looked at her, incredulous.

"He's too embarrassed."

"You mean it's a hoax?"

"Just like Tom-fucking-Sawyer."

Wyatt grinned ear to ear. "I'm going to kill him!"

They laughed and drank with renewed vigor. They drank all night long and made out at the bar. She'd already slept with Wyatt. He had been number forty-six or so.

By the time they decided to part company the next morning, it was already humid and scorching. The thought of her air conditioner still on the blink prompted her to order an ice-cold cocktail in a to-go cup. She remembered the pill someone had given her the night before and popped it in her mouth. As she walked down the street, she heard the low purr of a muscle car. It stopped next to her.

"Gigolette!"

She leaned into the open passenger window. "Aren't you dead? Did you fall off the dock or jump?" She grabbed his cigarette and took a drag.

"Funny girl. Thirsty?"

"Always."

She climbed in and they barreled down to the Saturn Bar on Saint Claude. They sat in a booth drinking whiskey, smoking Camels, and listening to George Jones on the old dime jukebox. The pill took effect, making the music sound like she was in a tunnel. She looked at her hand and it seemed a mile away.

"You're really gone, aren't you, Jimmie?"

"Yes, I'm surely dead."

"I must be crazy then."

"I like you because you're crazy, girl."

"I've been a terrible, terrible person. Horrible. I'm just a wreck, Jimmie. Sometimes I think I stick around just so another hurricane can finish the job." She wiped her brow. "Your funeral's tomorrow. You coming?"

He took a drag off his Camel. "I think it's going to storm again."

She sat down on a stone bench in front of the mortuary in Metairie. The service was proceeding inside but she couldn't bring herself to go in. Instead, she remained outside and smoked cigarettes. A pair of crows landed near her, cawing loudly. Thunder sonic-boomed in the distance.

"You going in or what?"

"You asshole, Jimmie! This prank has gone on long enough. You're coming with me now." She took him by the arm and pulled him to the front door. The crows shrieked as she opened the door and marched to the chapel.

"Look who I found!" she announced loudly to the room. Jimmie Lee's grandmother, mother, stepfather, sisters, aunts, uncles, other relatives, friends looked up. The priest paused. Jimmie Lee's cousin Ronnie slipped his arm out of hers and coughed. The priest held up the Eucharist and the service resumed. She watched Ronnie walk away to sit down with a girl who glared at her. She felt bewildered and faint, and ran outside to the parking lot as the rain came down.

She woke up suddenly from an afternoon nightmare about trapped, dying cats and dogs howling from the evacuated houses around her. Drenched in sweat, she arose and started the bath water.

She was depressed in the first place, so it was hard to differentiate the new despair from the old. Everything was a chore. Everything was broken. Someone opened the door to Paradise, and Hell walked in.

After the bath she donned a leopard-print wraparound dress with strappy high heels, barelegged. Too hot for stockings. Her long black hair reached to her lower back. The Latin migrant workers, brought in to secure blue tarps over roofless houses, wolf-whistled after her.

Drinking was a crutch, yes, but it got her through the day. Just for today, she would drink just for today, one day at a time. Maybe tomorrow would be better. Maybe she should sell everything and move west. West of Eden.

"Maybe you should slow it down, lady," said the new bartender. New bartenders were the worst. She hated the new faces that appeared daily in the city. New faces from the rest of America, dull uninspired faces. She surveyed the bar and noted the appalling number of strange men. They all seemed to be staring at her. New predatory faces contending for spoils. Modern carpetbaggers descending upon a modern Reconstruction.

Wyatt sat next to her.

"You okay?"

"I'm ghastly, thank you for asking."

"That was a bit of a fiasco at the funeral the other day. You've sure been acting loopy, come to think of it. Even more than usual."

"It's my fault he's dead."

Wyatt put his arm around her. "Come on, now, we all feel helpless about it."

"I was with him that night. Just before."

"Then what happened? What happened to you and Jimmie Lee down by the levee?"

Jimmie started the car, a rebuilt Mustang.

"Maybe we should ride around so we get some breeze," he said, and pealed out into the late night. They drove around the Bywater, sharing the joint, then headed over the Industrial Canal to the Dead Zone. It was black as black can be. No streetlights, nothing. Just the gleam of the waxing moon on the eerie razed stubble of a landscape that was once a neighborhood. Acres of toxic silt. Mountains of trash. Even the crows wouldn't land here.

Jimmie parked near the levee and turned the headlights off.

"If they build a casino on this land, I swear I'll torch it myself," he said, lighting a cigarette.

Tears welled in her eyes inexplicably. "I think I'm cracking up." Jimmie took her hand and caressed it. "You can lean on me, girl." He handed her his cigarette.

She took a drag, wiping her eyes. "You think the city is finished, Jimmie?"

"Hell no. If yellow fever, fire, and Betsy didn't wipe us out, Katrina won't either. But the government might." He gave her a toothy smile.

His handsome gaze lingered. Their breath quickened, and she leaned toward him. They kissed and embraced under the moonlight in the Mustang parked in the Dead Zone with an urgency like it was wartime. And it was.

Later, she opened the door from the backseat and looked for her panties. Jimmie sat there with his Wranglers unzipped, smoking a cigarette.

"You sure got a tiger in your tank," she said automatically. She said that to all the men. She found her panties in the front seat and put them on.

"You may want to keep those off. I'm not finished yet," he said tenderly, putting a hand on her back. She brushed it away.

"This was a mistake," she snapped.

"Why?" Jimmie asked in a puzzled voice.

"*Why why why*. Don't be so clingy." She couldn't believe what she was saying, but she couldn't stop herself.

They rode in silence to Montegut Street.

"Please stay," Jimmie said low, as he stopped near her gate. She wouldn't look at him.

"Go cool yourself off, Jimmie. I'll talk to you tomorrow."

She got out and walked to her door. The Mustang squealed away loudly.

Wyatt sighed long.

"Someone told me they found his clothes all neatly folded on the rocks down there at the Riverwalk. You know how crazy a kid he was; he probably tried to swim across the river to Algiers. Nobody ever makes it. The current lost him. Hell, the hurricane lost him."

She left Wyatt and wandered down by the Riverwalk, desolate at this hour. Clouds moved fast across the moon. *Is this where you did it, baby? Just like you to go skinny-dipping in the River Styx*, she thought. She walked down the steps to the water. She used to drink wine here with her ex. There was a figure sobbing.

"Jimmie Lee?"

She looked closer; it was the brunette her ex had been seeing.

"He set me up. The bastard!" she sobbed. "He called and asked me to meet him, and when I walked into the bar, there he was all cozy with some new fat rich cunt from New York who thinks she's going to save New Orleans. He wouldn't even look at me." The brunette shuddered as she cried.

"That's really tough, kid," she said, as she sat down on a step and lit a cigarette. Lightning flashed in the direction of the Gulf, followed by the low drones of thunder.

"You must really hate me," said the brunette when the sobs receded.

"No, I hate myself," she replied, and offered the brunette a cigarette.

"I'm sorry about your friend," the brunette said, taking the offered cigarette. "Does anyone know how he ended up in the river?"

She took a long drag and stared at the light dancing on the river currents. A breeze came off the water, small respite to the burning.

"He was number one hundred," she said finally.

The former rivals sat side by side smoking cigarettes. Watching the shadow of a barge in the dark moving quickly and silently up the river.

Here is where you'll always find me
Always walking up and down

But I left my soul behind me
*In that old cathedral town**

*From the song "Boulevard of Broken Dream." Words by Al Dubin, music by Harry Warren; © 1933 Warner Bros., Inc. All rights administered by WB Music Corp., lyrics reprinted by permission of Alfred Publishing Co., Inc. All rights reserved.

NIGHT TAXI

BY CHRISTINE WILTZ

Lakeview

Mike left his office at the shipping company at 5 o'clock sharp, his senses dull from another day of taking orders, checking invoices, and listening to the pursers gripe about prices going up. Didn't they know? It's what prices do. He always left work vaguely angry. All day counting the big money, all night counting the stingy tips. When he thought about driving the cab, trying to make ends meet, which they never did because the price of everything kept going up, he would get so worried he'd forget about being angry.

It had been worse since the hurricane. He was one of the lucky ones, his house was still standing; the floodwaters had leveled out with barely a centimeter to spare under his floorboards. The roof had nearly blown off. He and his wife prayed for no rain as they waited for their name to come up on any one of several roofers' lists, not likely until spring, while Mike often spent the midnight hours covering the mold with toxic goop to keep it from getting the upper hand.

Too many people hadn't come back yet, or they couldn't come back because they had no place to live. Mike did the work of two, sometimes three people at the shipping company, but his paycheck was still the same amount, as if nothing had happened. His initial gratitude had worn thin. Each night as he left his office to drive to the yard to claim his cab, to drive sometimes for two hours without a fare, to pick up irritable people who thought disaster warranted cheaper fares, he found it harder and harder to remind himself how lucky he was. Only the thought that he could have died, his family could have died, put him in the proper attitude of thankfulness. He had to be careful. The death thoughts could get hold of him in spite of his deeply rooted Catholic faith. They could take over his mind so that he wouldn't hear someone talking to him.

"Hey, Mikey," the man said, "remember me? Mikey . . . ? Hey. *Mikey.*" His breath fogged in the cool air as he leaned into the open passenger window.

"Yeah, sure. The casino. Kenner."

Last week. Thursday night. The guy had flagged him as he drove by, same time, about 8:00, near the same place he was parked now, in front of Igor's on St. Charles. He'd taken him out to the 'burbs because Harrah's had been closed since the storm. He'd waited a couple of hours for him, then dropped him off at a worn-out building on Felicity Street, right off Prytania, where he had a room. "Up there," the guy had said, and pointed to the second-floor balcony, rotting wood and rusted wrought iron that you'd think would have ripped clear away in the killer winds and landed on the avenue. The big wad of money he pulled out to pay Mike looked worth a week at the Pontchartrain Hotel. What did Mike care? It was the best money he'd taken in since the hurricane had wiped out the tourist trade.

Mike turned around now as the guy dropped his big rear end on the backseat and pulled his legs in after him, the way a woman gets into a car. "The casino?"

"Nah." The guy's short thick arm pulled the door closed and rocked the taxi. "We're on another mission tonight, Mikey."

Mike frowned as he turned away to start the car. What's with this *Mikey*? he wanted to ask the guy. No one called him that, not even when he was a kid. Then he was the French *Michel*, his mother straight off the boat from Pau, France. He'd taken his fair share of abuse for having a girl's name. So he'd changed it to Michael. His license on the dash of the cab read *Michael Willet*, clear as day. Now here comes this slick-haired, stubby guy with his big hard-looking tub, one of those guys who pushes his stomach way out front, uses it the way other people use authority, takes up space with it, likes taking up as much space as he can, likes his tub of lard because it gives him a kind of presence he could never have as a thin man. And thinks it's cute to call him *Mikey*. Puts him in his place.

Mike let it go. After all, this was the third night he'd parked outside Igor's hoping to run into the guy again. He started driving. "Where to?"

"Lakeview, Mikey. We're going to Lakeview. West End and Filmore."

Mike turned into the St. Charles neutral ground, stopped on the streetcar tracks they said would be out of commission for a year. He jerked around in his seat. "Lakeview? There's nothing out there." He could hear his voice echoing back at the guy, heard the whine in it. He hated going into the devastated areas where the water had gone up to the roofs, moved houses off their foundations, killed anything it touched except the damned mold spores. They were everywhere, waiting to go into your lungs, attach to your sinuses, take over your body. When he and his wife had made the obligatory tour of destruction soon after they returned to New Orleans, it reminded him of that horror movie he wished he'd never seen, *Invasion of the Body Snatchers*. He felt as if his body was being taken over, like one of the pod people, even when he wore a respirator.

"We need respirators," he told the guy.

That got him a laugh. "It ain't gonna kill you, Mikey. It's the land of opportunity out there. Some of us sees it, some of us don't. Don't worry, you can stay in the car. It ain't like I need a bodyguard." He snorted a big laugh over that one.

Mike turned his attention back to the street. Anger filled his chest, turned his olive skin a shade darker. He knew the guy was taking a shot at his thin frame, his body that looked weak, his slouchy posture, rounded shoulders, a body type that could catch attention coupled with the right attitude, like the young Brando or James Dean. Especially if the man was strong, and Mike was stronger than he looked. His thinness was sinewy, his muscles taut like rope, and his grip—try to get out of his grip. Like that amped-up gutter kid a couple of weeks ago who reached over the seat to take Mike's money pouch while he was making change. He grabbed the kid's thick wrist. The kid twisted and pulled, but all his amphetamine energy couldn't break Mike's hold. The way he ran off clutching his arm to his chest, Mike might have broken a bone.

At heart Mike was not a violent man. The thought of violence of any kind, even verbal, horrified him. His wife had insisted he carry a gun when he drove the cab. She'd gotten so worked up about it that he'd given in, but he kept the gun in the trunk, in the wheel well.

He made the U-turn heading toward the interstate. He spoke with his head slightly to the right so his coated, low-pitched voice would travel to the backseat: "Yeah, but if you did need a bodyguard, I could be your man. I'm even licensed to carry a gun."

The words sounded as empty to him as he knew they were, so he was surprised when the guy took him seriously. "That right? I guess you can't be too careful driving a cab these days." He shifted in his seat. In the rearview mirror Mike saw him lean forward. "You wear it on you?"

"No," Mike said low, without turning his head. The blower in the dashboard muffled him.

"What's that?"

"I said no, I don't talk about where I keep the gun."

The man leaned back. He laughed. "Yeah. You right, Mikey. Don't talk about the gun. Just show it when you need it, huh?" He chuckled a little more, his mouth closed, like it was his own private joke.

Mike felt his face heat up again. Fuck him. He turned the blower up another notch.

Mike headed toward the St. Charles ramp. Traffic was light, not many cars waiting underneath the overpass to get onto the ramp. The lights didn't work. One of them was on the ground. They were replaced by stop signs on short tripods. He stopped in the left lane behind a car that waited for a lone driver to cross the intersection in front of him. The car traveled slowly. In his peripheral vision, Mike saw a dark sedan pull behind the truck in the right lane. Mike knew the car without looking at it directly. It was his family car. His wife was at the wheel, no one in the passenger seat. He glanced; she glanced too, but turned away quicker than he did. He sensed the tension. Her mortification. He risked a look into the backseat. His daughter sat behind his wife, not looking his way, thank God. She had two friends with her, and she was reaching across one of them. He thought he could hear them laughing and talking through the glass, but he was only putting sounds to their animation. His head felt as though it was underwater. With effort he began to turn away, as though struggling against a current. His daughter, tight in her seat belt as she reached across to her friend, suddenly slammed herself hard against the seat back. He thought she would look at him then, but her head tipped backwards as she laughed. Her long gangly arms, arms like his, reached again, and the sedan moved up to where the truck had been. He could feel the sweat on his forehead. Twelve years old, the age of irreversible humiliation. His wife had told her never to tell anyone her father drove a cab.

"Hey, Mikey."

Sweet Jesus, there was someone in the car with him.

"We never gonna get there unless you stop dreaming your life away, Mikey."

"What?" He'd heard the guy perfectly. He touched the knob on the dash and turned the heat down as he eased off the brake. His wife was up the ramp before he reached the stop sign.

The moron in the back repeated his piece of sarcasm.

It had cut close to the bone. "I heard you the first time," Mike said with a certain amount of viciousness, but he mumbled.

The man leaned forward saying, "What?" When Dean or Brando mumbled, no one said, *What?*

Mike lifted his head to throw his voice behind him. "What kind of opportunities you got out in Lakeview at night?"

His wife must have taken the girls out to eat. It was funny how the people who'd come back didn't seem to like staying home. The few restaurants open were more crowded than ever, as though everyone wanted to see who had dared to return, bump shoulders with them. He wondered where his son was. Talk about attitude.

"Whew, Mikey," the guy was saying, "you really don't want to go to Lakeview, do you?"

"I don't care about going to Lakeview. I just asked you a question."

"Okay, okay . . ." He started to say something else, but Mike broke in.

"Look. My name isn't Mikey." He pointed at the license. "Michael, see? Or Mike."

"Okay, Michael it is." He deepened his voice. "A little touchy, huh, Mi*chael?*" The dramatic tone was followed by a high-pitched, strangled chuckle way back in his throat. The guy was his own best audience. "Did you know that woman in the car back there or something?"

Mike's eyes flicked to the rearview mirror and made contact, a split second when all his anger, his attitude slipped away, gone through the looking glass, and left him slumped in the front seat of his taxi.

"My wife." Out before he could stop it, as if he had no will left. He gave a short laugh.

"What's the matter? She not talking to you?"

"Not much." He nosed the taxi into the curve that took them toward Lakeview. "Not these days."

"You mean, since the storm?"

"Yeah, I guess."

"So the storm's *your* fault?" That high strangled laugh again.

"No. Come on—everyone's on edge since the storm."

"Yeah, sure."

"You don't get it, do you? You're not from here." Mike looked in the rearview to see if the guy was shaking his head or something, some indication he'd heard him, but he was gazing out the side window. "Are you?"

"No."

"Where're you from?"

"Jersey."

"Just down here to make a buck, huh?"

"Yeah."

Boy, it burned Mike up. *Some of us sees it, some of us don't.* That kind of arrogance, the guy was probably gouging the money out of people. Riding around in cabs, going to the casino—money to burn.

Mike exited the interstate and drove slowly along West End Boulevard. It looked as though most of the debris had been bulldozed out of the street since he'd last come through here, but if he went too fast he might drive into one of those crater-sized potholes the storm had left all over the city, as if it had blown out the asphalt with its explosive winds, the same way it bombed through houses and tore huge trees whole out of the ground. You could bust a tire if you missed one of those holes in the dark, do some serious damage to your car.

Mr. *Sees-it* was still looking through the window into a night so dark the skeletons of houses loomed like blackened ghosts. Mike jumped in his seat as a mountainous mass appeared ahead on his left in what had been the half-block-wide green space between West End and Pontchartrain boulevards. Once he was up on it, his headlights revealed a giant mound of debris. The green space, which Mike knew was now black even in the daylight from the toxic water, had become a dumping ground. He'd heard on the radio that the amount of debris already collected in the city was a year's worth of garbage in Manhattan. The landfills couldn't take any more.

Mike jumped again; his eyes had drifted from the road and caught the edge of a rift in the concrete. Sees-it said, "You sure you know where you're going? I can't see a fucking thing."

"Yeah, I know where I am. Filmore's just up there."

The man faced forward now, sitting up so he could clutch the back of the front seat. His nerves had got him. He was nuts to want to come out here at night. Mike had heard the looters came out after dark. Like cockroaches. They crawled through places most humans wouldn't go, searching out anything that might turn a dollar. They stripped the plumbing, the light fixtures, the copper flashing, chimney covers, eating a house down to the bare bones. Who knew what kind of *opportunity* this cockroach in the back of his cab could find at night. Mike should have said no. To hell with the extra buck. He rubbed his hand over his face. Christ—couldn't he think about anything other than money?

"Here's Filmore." He made a right turn and slowed the taxi to the speed of a gimpy pedestrian. "Where to?"

"Uh, General Diaz, General Haig, Argonne. One of those."

"If you'd told me that to begin with, I could have gone straight to Canal Boulevard."

"Yeah."

"It's your money."

Roach Man scooted to the edge of the seat, his antennae tuned. "They're in a service alley behind one of the houses they're gutting."

They crossed Canal Boulevard. Mike stopped at the General Diaz alley, but it was a dead end in the dark. The guy mumbled something that sounded like, "Motherfucking spics."

"What?"

"You think we'd see a lantern in all this pitch black."

Mike rolled past the intersection of Filmore and Marshal Foch. Just before Argonne, they saw a soft glimmer of light, presumably from a lantern, a quarter-block down the alley.

The guy opened the cab door. "I'll be fifteen, maybe twenty minutes. If it's gonna take any longer, I'll come let you know." Outside, he stood for a moment to zip up his cheap windbreaker. His new white sneakers shone in the dark. Even with the windows up, Mike could hear the crunch as he walked down the alley, the poisonous wasteland dried to a crisp in the drought since the hurricane.

Mike decided to turn the taxi around so he'd be pointed back toward the interstate. The quicker he could get out of here the better. His lights picked up the sheetrock dust surrounding several houses as he made a wide circle at the intersection. The dust coated Argonne; a lot of house gutting going on back here. He could smell the dust in the air. He didn't know if it meant people were trying to come back or trying to crowbar the money out of the insurance companies' tight fists. The latest word was they wouldn't pay off unless the house was gutted. What people were being put through, like puppets on a string.

Mike parked at the mouth of the alley but left the engine running for the heat. He could make out the top edge of the carport where the light came from; he could see that it leaned sharply, but he didn't notice anyone or any shadows, only a halo of light illuminating a small area of the alley.

Mike didn't like the finger of fear running up his spine. He had a bad feeling sitting out here in a dark ghost town with lots of good hiding places. He needed to be alert, to hear the slightest sound in the dark. He cut the engine, cracked his window open enough to hear a different quality of silence than that in the car, and pulled the collar of his jacket up around his neck. Somehow his passenger was up to no good, maybe the whole bunch of them, whoever it was that found cover in the shambles of other people's houses. Guilt rose in him like bile that he would have a payday, likely a good one, from this opportunist.

The guilt stole into his awareness. If it wasn't guilt about not making enough money, it was guilt about taking it from the wrong people, guilt about the way he made it. How did the straight-A Jesuit student, the kid with so much promise, end up driving a taxi at night? He rubbed his hand over his face, something he did so often now it was like a tic. The worst thing about driving the taxi, it gave him too much time to think. He wished he had a button on the side of his head he could turn to the *OFF* position.

Behind him came a sharp crack that sounded like a pistol shot. His body jumped with enough force that he hit his head on the ceiling of the cab. He whipped around. Another crack and the limb of a dying camphor tree fell to the ground inches away from his rear bumper. He slumped into his seat, limp, wasted. As if he could stop his racing heart, he pressed his hand against his chest. He glanced down the empty alley, checked his watch. It had been fifteen minutes. Where was this guy? His heart wouldn't slow down; his throat was tight. Christ, he thought he was going to die.

Mike was afraid of death. He thought about it a lot and wondered if other people did. No one ever talked about it much, but then neither did he. Stories he'd heard about people dying for a few minutes before being pulled back into life—the white light, the feeling of peace, of someone, God, beckoning from the light-filled tunnel—he wanted to buy it.

The nuns at Holy Cross, even the sometimes cynical Jesuits, had assured him there was an afterlife. But Mike feared death would be painful and messy and final. He would die and there would be nothing. When he was a boy, he would look into the sky, stare deeply into the heavens, his mind traveling into an infinity of nothing as long as he could stand it, before panic set in and he returned to earth. He could never keep going to find out if anything might be there to make him believe; his heart would begin to pound unnaturally and he would think he might die.

Had the nuns put this fear of death in him with their talk of eternal damnation? Wasn't he supposed to have developed a fear of God, not of nothingness? Had the Jesuits used subliminal messages in the religion classes? Had it been the Sunday trips to the cemetery, rain or shine, to visit the dead, his morose grandmother pulling him along by the hand, telling him to keep up? Or could it have been his father's stories about the war, about watching men die, about saving men whose bodies were already dead from paralyzing wounds? Mike would go to bed sometimes thinking about how he might die. His father's talk of heroism, the great terribleness of war, and the glory of it all would swarm in his head. "No guts, no glory," he liked to say, speaking about it the way Mike later heard men talk about their college football days, as though life beyond could never live up to such thrilling times. He tried to imagine a natural death, in his sleep, but all that did was make him try not to close his eyes.

Mike pulled up a short laugh. Here he sat, waiting for a man who might be dangerous, in an area people referred to as looking war-ravaged, surrounded by streets named after generals and world war heroes and scenes of battle. His father's description of the fighting in the Argonne Forest was the most vivid—the guts and the glory.

The tic, his hand down his face. The war Mike remembered most was the one he hadn't gone to and that his father had never seen. Vietnam. When he got drafted, his father, not a man big on physical affection, had hugged him and regarded him with the utmost seriousness and pride. His son was going off to experience what he had experienced, even if it was a different kind of war. There would still be valor and Mike would be one of the proud who fought for his country.

Two weeks before he was to leave for Fort Polk, Mike's right foot swelled to twice its size. Tests were run, the diagnosis was gout, not so common in such a young man, the doctor said. He hobbled to the recruiting office downtown in the Customs building where he expected a delay in his orders. Instead he walked out with a 4-F.

His relief was so overwhelming that he went straight to a nearby French Quarter bar, where at 9:30 in the morning he drank one beer fast and the second one slowly and counted his blessings with every sip. It had nothing to do with whether he thought the Vietnam War was right or wrong. He hadn't been a particularly idealistic young man. For six weeks, since the draft notice, he'd been nearly sick with fear that he was going to die.

He went home and told his father the news, keeping his face and tone emotionless. His father briefly laid his hand on Mike's shoulder, but said nothing.

Thirty-five years later, Mike sat in the taxi he drove six nights a week, rehashing the scene from his own private war. His father's hand seemed to have left a permanent mark of shame. He wanted to believe that the gesture had been one of sympathy and even some relief, but he believed that his father knew his son was a coward. He'd never since had an attack of gout.

Mike hoped his own son never had to face a draft or go to war. With the war in Iraq and the world so unstable, he worried about it a lot. His wife told him he dwelled on morbid thoughts. His priest told him that older parents were often more fearful for their children. He told Mike not to let fear control him. But he couldn't tell him how. The world was a hotbed of fear. It thrived everywhere, like the mold and the cockroaches.

A man's cry jerked Mike back into the night. He looked into the alley as the guy was shoved from under the carport. He tried to break his fall but his arm twisted under him and he cried out again as the side of his face and shoulder hit the hard rough surface left by the flood.

Four men rushed into the alley, all shouting in Spanish. One kicked the guy, whose ass was still up in the air, onto his back. He raised his arms weakly as if to ward off what he knew was coming. They were all over him—no more shouting, only the sounds of the punches against his body.

As soon as it started, Mike swung the cab door open. He rushed into the alley. "Hey," he called, "hey, stop that!"

At the sound of his own voice, he hesitated.

"Hey!" he yelled again, and began moving forward. "Hey!"

He had their attention. The flurry of blows stopped and the four of them turned toward him.

"Let him go!" He went another couple of steps.

The guy tried to raise himself on an elbow. One of the men shoved him down.

"Mikey." The guy sounded far away.

Mike took another step and stood his ground. "Let him

go. Now!" No one made a move. "*Comprende?*" Mike yelled at them.

One of the men stood and Mike saw that he held something close against his thigh. He thought it was a gun. He froze. The man lifted his hand, and enough light from the carport caught it that Mike saw the blade clearly. Holding the knife at waist level, the man came toward him. He spoke hard, rapid Spanish and gestured with his free hand. He was telling Mike to go, no doubt about it, and when he thrust the knife forward and picked up his speed, Mike turned and ran back to the cab. He vaguely heard the guy on the ground calling, "Mikey, Mikey," so far away now. Mike gunned the engine. The car slid a little on the dusty street and covered four blocks before a thought crossed his mind. He slammed on the brakes at Canal Boulevard.

His heart was pounding, his throat almost closed. He stared at the cab's radio, not a blip from it all night. It went in and out; his cell phone was useless. He was alone, completely alone, an entirely new way of being alone, and he made a choice.

He took a deep breath as he stepped out of the taxi. He went around to the trunk. Wrapped in old rags, the gun sat deep in the wheel well beside the spare. Mike unwrapped it, put the rags back in the wheel well, and replaced the cover. He got in the taxi and drove to the Argonne alley.

The four men in the alley all turned when Mike drove up. He didn't see his passenger. He killed the engine and pocketed the keys as he got out of the cab. He held the gun pointed at the men. As he walked toward them, he asked where the other man was. He got close enough to see that the men were standing around a pool of blood that had soaked into the crust covering the alley.

"What did you do to him?" he demanded.

They were mute, staring at him, maybe afraid of his gun, maybe not. He could see their hands, empty, no knife showing.

"Where's the man?" Mike repeated.

"*El hombre,*" one of them said.

"That's right, *el hombre. Dónde está el hombre?*"

They all shrugged. One of them said something in Spanish Mike didn't understand.

"Do you speak English? Doesn't anyone speak English? *Habla inglés?*"

They stood there.

"Come on," Mike said, "You have to know something. Did he walk away? Did you kill him?" He thought a moment. "*Muerto? Hombre muerto?*"

This got them very agitated. They spoke among themselves, too fast for Mike to understand anything other than a word here and there—*hombre, casa, pistola.*

"Hey!" Mike waved the gun and took a step toward them, but he didn't want to get so close that they could jump him. They stopped talking and looked at him. He looked back. Hard. He didn't know what to do. If he stared them down, maybe they'd think he was dangerous, not desperate.

What seemed like a long time went by. Mike finally said, "If you killed him, I'll kill you." He hadn't known what he was going to say, but in that moment he thought he had it in him to shoot every one of them.

The tallest one spread his hands. "No," he said, "we don't kill him."

"Then where is he?" The man dropped his hands. Anger began to rise in Mike. "You speak enough English to know the word 'kill.' How about this? You don't tell where he is, I'll kill you."

The Mexican spread his hands again, his gesture of supplication. "Not so much English."

"Bullshit! Where did he go, you creeps?" With his free hand he pointed down the alley. "That way?" None of them looked. "That way?" The opposite direction. "That way?" He pointed at the house. *"La casa?"*

"Sí." The tall man nodded vigorously, *"La casa."*

"Buncha dumb Mexicans," Mike muttered.

He started toward the house, moving sideways so he could see them. On his way, he picked up a Coleman lantern that sat on an ice chest and walked around a high wood fence that leaned on the carport.

The back door of the house had been removed. When Mike held up the lantern, he could see straight through the gutted downstairs and out the front door, which stood wide open. The house wasn't large, and a quick walk through the lower floor did not reveal a body or his passenger bleeding to death from a stab wound.

The stairway was by the far wall near the front door. As Mike looked at it, he knew he'd been duped, sent into the house on a fool's errand. He tore through the house as he felt for his car keys. He arrived in the alley in time to see the last Mexican pull his foot into the cab and close the door. The vehicle roared off and Mike ran down the alley to Filmore Street. It was already a block away, but he stood in the middle of the street and shot twice at it. It fishtailed and he thought he'd hit it, but if anything, it moved away faster.

He pulled his keys out of his pocket and pressed the red alarm button, knowing it wouldn't work. The remote needed a new battery.

Mike stuck the gun in the back of his pants and walked back to the house in a silence more oppressive than the blackness of the night. He retrieved the lantern, glad for the warmth of its light and the slight hissing sound it made.

The Mexicans had cleared out the carport. The ice chest was gone and not a tool or piece of clothing was left, only a few rags hanging on the Page fence that separated it from the carport next door. Mike stood there, the lantern at his side, as if gathering his energy for the long walk ahead.

His whole body jerked when he heard the rustling in the weeds across the alley.

"Mikey, hey, Mikey." His fare emerged from behind a dead shrub and limped across to the carport. Mike held up the lantern expecting to see him covered with blood. Instead, he saw sheetrock dust and dirt, maybe a smear of blood on his dark blue jacket, and the evidence of hiding in a weed patch. He held one arm tight against his rib cage. "I was over on Argonne when I heard the shooting. I knew you'd come back, Mikey, I knew you'd come back with the gun." He grinned.

How could he know it? Mike himself didn't know it. He wanted to knock the grin off him. He didn't even know why he felt so hostile. "Your face is a mess," he said.

"Yeah, well, it wasn't much to begin with." He was grinning again.

"I thought they'd stabbed you."

The guy frowned. "They had a knife?"

"I saw a knife."

"Glad I didn't see it."

"Looks like you lost a lot of blood." Mike walked over to the stain.

"My nose," the guy said. "Bled like a son of a bitch. I think it scared them." He shrugged with one shoulder. "They stopped kicking me." He glanced down the alley where the cab had been. "So what, you leave the keys in the car?"

"Hot-wired."

He laughed, a short one, and clutched his arm tighter against his side. "Fuckin' spics. They can do anything." He tilted his head and looked at Mike, amused. "What I don't get—you had a gun on 'em, right?"

"I went in the house looking for you, moron."

He did his high-pitched laugh, keeping it in his throat to avoid hurting his ribs, and the night air sent it out, a sound to make the worst scoundrel's skin crawl. He grimaced when he forgot his hurt leg, doing a little hop on his good one.

"You're a bucket of cheer for a guy who just got the crap beat out of him."

He rubbed at an eye, as though drying it, but touched the open cut on his cheekbone and winced. "Yeah, well, Mikey, what you gonna do? I tried to talk them into staying, but they weren't buying it this time."

"This happened before?"

"No, I mean they been stranded out here since my truck broke down."

"So they decide to beat you up tonight?"

"I was supposed to get the truck Friday. I went to the casino Thursday night, remember? Lost the repair money. They said they'd wait till today."

"I don't get it," Mike said.

The man's good humor seemed to be deteriorating. He said crossly, "I been at the casino all weekend and lost most of their pay, too. They're illegals. What they gonna do but beat me up?"

They started walking.

A block later, the guy's amusement recovered, he said, "Not only that, I been taking cabs all over the place. Fuckin' expensive."

"I guess you get off cheap tonight."

"Fuckin'-A. I gotta walk home." He tried to elbow Mike, but Mike moved away from him. "Don't be a sour puss. Come on, find us a bar. Buy me a drink. The spics get to party in a hot taxi."

The guy was strangled with laughter until they got to the intersection of Filmore and General Diaz.

After that they walked awhile in silence, until he added, "Look, Mikey, that was a real stand-up thing you did, come back to get me."

"Sure."

"No, I mean it. Four of them, one of you. Even if you had a gun. You didn't know what kinda weapons they had. You saw a knife. Hell, they had crowbars, sledgehammers, all kinda stuff."

"I never thought about it."

"That's what I mean. You come back for a guy you don't know, some fare you picked up. You coulda just gone home. That's real stand-up stuff." He brushed his knuckles across Mike's arm. "I appreciate it, man. I mean it." He limped along, grunting every few steps with the effort.

It was true, he'd gone back without a thought for his own safety. He couldn't just run away from a man getting kicked like that, who could have been killed. He would never have known whether the guy was dead or alive. His thoughts careened around his brain, and his emotions with them—afraid when he shouldn't be, not afraid when there was good reason. Maybe he didn't think right, not like other people. Maybe he'd gone back because the guy was a fare, no other reason than still hoping for a payday.

Christ, where was that button on the side of his head? He needed to turn it off.

"Yeah, I guess they could have killed you."

"Nah," the guy said, "I'm the meal ticket."

"What do you mean?"

"Not much of a businessman, are you, Mikey?" The arrogance—Judas Priest, Mike wanted to kill the asshole. "I get the work, collect the money, they gut the houses, I pay them."

"The way I read it, you're lucky they didn't kill you."

"Whatever you say, Mikey. You saved my life, okay? I'm telling you I appreciate it."

He said that, and all Mike felt was the weight of the gun against his back. "I didn't save your life. They let you go before I ever got back."

"That's what I mean. They could have killed *you.*"

"You're right, they could've. Instead, they took all their belongings, all those crowbars and sledgehammers, their ice chest, clothes, and they took the first ride out they could get."

The guy stopped dead. "So what's your conclusion here? You scared them off?"

"No, *hombre*, I'm suggesting that you need to reconsider just who the meal ticket is. The Mexicans have *vamoosed*. They aren't coming back."

"Okay, I get it. You don't need to tell me three ways to Sunday . . . Fuckin' asshole," he added under his breath. He started walking again.

Mike clutched the guy's shoulder and stopped him. "You calling *me* an asshole?" He held the lantern up so it lit the man's face.

"Get that thing outta my face." He pushed Mike's arm away and started moving again, limping down the street a little faster, trying to get away from Mike.

The lantern swinging at this side, Mike took a long step and caught up with him. "What's your hurry? We got a long way to go. You better pace yourself."

"Pace myself right outta this goddamn place," he mumbled.

"What—back to Jersey?"

The guy walked, his head down. He grunted with each step.

"You mean you're leaving the land of opportunity? One small setback and that's it? What about that house back there? The one the Mexicans didn't finish gutting." Mike had read all the warnings about rip-off contractors.

The big businessman tried to go faster, but Mike lengthened his stride and walked comfortably next to him. "All you have to do is go down to Lee Circle and hire another crew at the gas station." The illegals gathered there every morning, holding up signs for work.

The man wouldn't talk to him. He was going to leave the city, leave people who had paid him in good faith.

"You have any other houses lined up?" He waited a second then went on. "How 'bout it, buddy. You gonna return the money?" He held the lantern up again, leaning so he was in the man's face.

He didn't see it coming. The guy from Jersey back-fisted him. Mike felt a tooth go. Blood filled his mouth.

The man grabbed the lantern from Mike's hand. "Who's gonna make me, huh? You?" He swung the lantern and threw it. It shattered against the side of the house they stood next to. Mike smelled gas. All the dry debris beside the house burst into flame. It pushed Mike back several steps, into the street.

The man was on him, hands all over him, feeling for the gun. As hard as he could, Mike kicked him in the shin of the bad leg. The guy landed full weight on his ass, yelling and wrapping both arms around his broken ribs.

Mike rushed forward as if he could stop the fire. But the heat stopped him first. The house had already caught; it would burn to the ground faster than he could get help.

Mesmerized by the fire, Mike felt the hand at his back too late. Jersey had the gun. Mike turned and caught his forearm, twisting the weapon away from them both. It fired off to the side. Mike kept twisting, the man's thick forearm held against him. They stayed like that, both of their bodies tense, unmoving, until the tree next to them caught fire. Without much strength behind it, Jersey kneed Mike in the groin. Mike lost his balance but didn't release his hold. He pulled Jersey with him as he fell against the tree. Both their jacket sleeves caught fire, but Jersey's cheaper one went up faster and hotter. He started screaming. Mike released him, moved away from the tree, and started tearing off his own jacket. The man seemed almost frozen. He pointed the gun at Mike, still screaming. Mike threw his jacket to the ground. He watched his passenger shake the gun at him and waited for the bullet. But then he realized something else was going on. The man finally shook the gun free. The flesh of his hand went with it. Then the flames from the tree jumped to the man's back, and in a moment the screaming stopped.

Mike watched until most of the body had melted away, until the stench of burning flesh was no longer overpowering. He kicked the gun out into the street. It was still hot. After it cooled, he picked it up, wiped the grip off on his trousers, and put it back in his waistband. He started walking toward West End, death all over him. His mind, for once, was still.

ANNUNCIATION SHOTGUN

BY GREG HERREN

Lower Garden District

"I swear I didn't mean to kill him."

If ever a person was meant to come with a warning label, it was my tenant, Phillip. He'd been renting the other side of my double shotgun in the Lower Garden District for two years now, and while he was a good tenant—always paid his rent on time, never made a lot of noise in the wee hours of the morning, and even ran errands for me sometimes—chaos always seemed to follow in his wake. He didn't do it intentionally. He was actually a very sweet guy with a big heart, a great sense of humor, and he was a lot of fun to have around.

Every morning before he went to work, he'd come over for coffee and fill me in on the latest goings-on in his life. I usually just rolled my eyes and shook my head—there wasn't much else to do, really. For all his good heart and good intent, somehow things always seemed to happen whenever he was around. Bad things. He attracted them like a magnet attracts nails.

I looked from the body on the kitchen floor over to where he was standing by the stove and back again. I knew I should have evicted him after the hurricane, when I had the chance. *I don't need this,* I thought. My evening was planned to the second. My new book, the latest (and hopefully biggest-selling) suspense thriller from Anthony Andrews was due to my editor in three days. I was finishing up the revisions, and when I was too bleary-eyed to stare at the computer screen any longer, I was going to open a bottle of red wine, smoke some pot, and throw the third season of *The Sopranos* in the DVD player. A very nice, pleasant quiet evening at home; the kind that made me happy and enabled me to focus on my work. When Phillip called, panic in his voice, demanding that I come over immediately, I'd thought it was a plugged toilet or something else minor but highly annoying. I'd put my computer to sleep and headed over, figuring I could take care of whatever it was and be back at the computer in five minutes, cursing him with every step for interrupting my evening.

A dead body was the last thing I was expecting.

"Um, we need to call the cops." I shook my head, forcing myself to look away from the body and back over at Phillip. I felt kind of numb, like I was observing everything from a distance that I wasn't a part of. Shock, probably. Phillip's eyes were still kind of wild, wide open and streaked with red, his curly hair disheveled, his face white and glistening with a glassy sheen of sweat. "We need to call the cops like right now." I raised my voice. "Are you listening to me?"

He didn't move or answer me. He just kept standing there looking down at the floor, occasionally shifting his weight from one leg to the other. There was a bruise forming on his right cheek, and his lips looked puffy and swollen. I peered back at the body. I hadn't, in my initial shock and horror, recognized the man sprawled on the floor with a pool of blood underneath his head. "You killed Chad," I heard myself saying, thinking, *This can't be happening, oh Jesus, Mary, and Joseph, this isn't happening.*

Chad was his scumbag boyfriend.

"We can't call the cops. I mean, we just can't," Phillip replied, his voice bordering on hysteria. "Please, Tony, we can't." His voice took on that pleading tone I'd heard so many times before, when he wanted me to do something I didn't want to. He was always wheedling, dragging me out to bars against my will, urging me on until I finally gave in. He could always, it seemed, wear me down and make me go against my better judgment. But this was different.

A *lot* different.

This wasn't the same thing as a 4 in the morning phone call to pick him up at the Bourbon Orleans Hotel because he'd somehow lost his pants. Or to come bail him out of Central Lockup because he'd pissed in public in a drunken stupor. Or to help him buy his car out of the impound lot where it had been towed. Or any number of the minor crises that seemed to constantly swirl around him, like planets orbiting the sun.

Chaos.

"What happened?" I asked. I was starting to come back into myself. I've always managed to remain calm and cool in a crisis. Panicking never makes any situation better. A crisis calls for a cool head, careful thought, the weighing and discarding of options. I started looking around for the phone, cursing myself for not bringing my cell with me. We had to call the cops, and soon. The longer we waited, the worse it would be for him.

"You didn't hear us?" Phillip stared at me. "I don't see how—you had to have heard us, Tone. I mean, he was yelling so loud . . ." He shuddered. "Are you sure you didn't hear anything? He came over in one of his moods, you know how he gets—*got*—and you know, just started in on me. I was making him dinner . . ." his voice trailed off and he made a limp gesture with his hand toward the top of the stove.

I noticed a pot of congealing spaghetti floating in starchy water and another one with skin starting to form on what looked like red sauce. "We've got to call the cops, Phillip. We don't have a choice here."

"He started hitting me." He went on as if I hadn't said a word, beginning to shake as he remembered. "Yelling and screaming. You didn't hear? You had to have heard, Tony, you had to have heard."

"I was working. I had the headphones on." I always put on headphones when I am writing so I can shut off all external distractions and focus. The littlest thing can take me away from my work, so I try to avoid all outside stimulus at all costs. The iPod had been a huge help in that regard.

"And I just pushed him away and he slipped and hit his head on the table." Phillip started to cry. "Oh, Tony, what are we going to do?"

"We have to call the cops. Where's your phone?"

"We can't call the cops!" His voice started rising in hysteria. He buried his face in his hands. "I can't go to jail again. I just can't. I'd rather die than do that."

I looked at him, starting to get exasperated. Even now, in a panic and terrified, he was handsome, with his mop of curly brown hair and finely chiseled face with deep dimples and round brown eyes straight out of a Renaissance painting of a saint. He was wearing a tight sleeveless T-shirt that said, *NOPD—Not our problem, dude*. Phillip always wore T-shirts a size too small, to show off his defined arms, strong shoulders, and thickly muscled chest. I'd been attracted to him when he first moved in, and even considered trying to get him into my bed for a few days. Seeing him shirtless and sweating in the hot August sun as he moved in certainly was a delectable sight; almost like the opening sequence of one of your better gay porn movies. Yet it didn't take long for me to realize that as sexy and lovable as he was, I just couldn't deal with the chaos that followed him around like a dark cloud. No, I'd spent most of my adult life getting chaos *out* of my life, and wasn't about to let it in again just so I could fuck the hot guy who lived next door. I didn't mind listening to his tales of woe every morning—but that was as involved as I got. Just listening to him some mornings was tiring enough.

"So, what do you suggest? We dump the body in the river?"

Phillip let out a big sigh and smiled. "Oh, I knew you would understand! You're the best! I knew I could count on you!"

I stared at him. He could *not* be serious. "That was sarcasm, Phillip." I looked down at Chad again, and my stomach lurched. I'd never liked Chad, couldn't understand what Phillip saw in him, and every day for the month or so they'd been dating I told Phillip to dump him at least once. He was a jerk, an arrogant ass who thought because he was handsome and had a nice body he was better than other people, as though spending hours in the gym every week somehow gave him the right to treat people like something he'd stepped in. He'd been awful to Phillip almost from the very start of their relationship. He seemed to take great pleasure in tearing Phillip down in front of people, and I could only imagine what he was like in private. After a while, I gave up trying to get Phillip to wake up and see Chad for the loser he was. I just wanted to scream at Phillip, *Get some goddamned self-esteem!* After Chad hit Phillip the first time, I was ready to kill the son of a bitch myself—but ultimately decided he wasn't worth it.

And now, as I looked down at the pool of blood under his

head, I realized I wasn't sorry he was dead. The world was a better place without the arrogant son of a bitch.

"I wasn't serious."

"Come on, Tony, we can't call the police." Phillip shakily lit a Parliament. "You know what that's like. Even if they believe me, that it was self-defense and an accident, it's still going to be a big mess." He shuddered again. "That night I spent in Central Lockup—Tony, if I go back there, if I have to spend one night there again, I'll kill myself. I will. And you know how the cops are. You *know.*"

He had a point. I didn't blame Phillip one bit for not having any confidence in the New Orleans Police Department. No one really did after the hurricane and all the allegations of police looting and car thefts and so forth, whether they were true or not. Their reputation hadn't exactly been great before the storm either. Phillip might be right—getting the police involved would probably only make matters worse. He needed to protect himself. They'd been pretty awful when he'd been arrested that one time. And, as it later turned out, he'd spent the night in jail for something that was merely a ticketing offense. He'd been a hysterical mess when I bailed him out. I'll never forget the look on his face when they finally let him go, and the stories he told me about that night in jail made my blood run cold.

"We'll call the police and then call a lawyer." It sounded reasonable to me. "I won't let you go to jail," I said, as though I had any control over what the police would do. The more I thought about it, the less I liked it.

"I can't afford a lawyer." Phillip worked at the Transco Airlines ticket counter out at the airport. He made a decent living—always paid his rent on time—but there wasn't a lot of money left over for extras. I was always loaning him a twenty when he fell short. "And what if they don't believe me? What if they arrest me? I don't have bail money. I'll lose my job. My life will be ruined."

"We can't just dump the body somewhere," I replied, it finally beginning to dawn on me that he was completely serious. *He wants me to help him dump the body.* "They'd find out, and that would just make things worse." I shook my head. "Phillip, this isn't something we can just cover up. They always find out . . . and then they definitely wouldn't believe you."

"You've said a million times that anyone can get away with murder if they're careful." He crossed his arms. "I mean, you write about stuff like that all the time, right?"

I looked at him. "Murder? I thought you said it was self-defense?" I chewed on my lower lip.

"We could dump him in the Bywater. We could make it look like it was a mugging, couldn't we? How hard could it be?"

"Phillip . . ." I sighed. I could think of at least a hundred reasons off the top of my head, minimum, why that wouldn't work, but there wasn't time to go through them all. Besides, I knew Phillip. He wasn't going to listen to any of them. "We can't dump him in the river. We need to call the police." I looked back down at Chad's staring eyes, and noticed the congealing blood again. "Oh my fucking God, Phillip! *How long has he been dead?*"

He bit his lips. "Um, I didn't know what to do. I freaked!"

"How long has he been dead?" I gritted my teeth.

"Maybe about an hour." He shrugged. "Or two."

My legs buckled and I had to grab the edge of the table to keep from falling to the floor next to Chad. We couldn't call the cops. It had been too long. I could hear the homicide detective now, see the look on his face: *And why did you wait so long to call us? Why didn't you call 911?* It looked bad. What if Chad hadn't died instantly? What if they could have saved him? *What if he'd bled to death?*

And once the history of physical abuse came to light—and there were any number of Phillip's friends who'd only be too glad to tell the cops all about it, not realizing that they'd be sealing Phillip's indictment, thinking they were helping by making Chad look bad, like he deserved killing.

Phillip was going to jail.

Jesus FUCKING Christ.

I was going to have to help him.

"What are we going to do?" he asked, his voice hinting at rising hysteria once again. "I'm telling you, Tony, we can't call the police! I can't go to jail, I can't." He suddenly burst into tears, covering his face with his hands, his shoulders shaking.

"Well, the first thing is, you need to calm the fuck down," I snapped. My head was starting to ache. I definitely didn't need this shit. I was on deadline—I couldn't exactly call my editor and say, *Sorry, I need a few more days, I had to help my tenant dispose of a dead body and come up with a story for the cops.* I raced through possibilities in my mind; places to dispose of the body where it might not be found for a while. Almost every single one of them was flawed. Seriously flawed—though an idea was starting to form in my head. "Is Chad's car here?"

Phillip wiped at his nose. "Uh-huh."

"Well, we're going to have to get rid of that, too." I refrained from adding *dumbass*, like I really wanted to. But there was no sense in getting him all worked up again, since he seemed to finally be calming down. And if we were going to do this—and, more importantly, get away with it—I needed him calm. "Give me a cigarette." I'd managed to finally quit a few months earlier, but I needed one now. *Get ahold of yourself, look at this as an intellectual puzzle, shut off your emotions.* I lit the Parliament and sucked in the bitter smoke. I took a few deep breaths and decided to try one last time. "Phillip, we really should call the cops. I mean, if this was self-defense—"

"What do you mean, *if* it was?" Phillip's brown eyes narrowed. He pointed to his cheek, which was purple. "He slugged me again, Tony. He threw me against the wall—I can't believe you didn't hear him screaming at me."

I hadn't, though—no shouting, no crashing, no struggle. Sure, I had the headphones on, but—no, it was probably self-defense, there was no reason to doubt Phillip. Chad was an egotistical bully with no problem using his fists whenever he decided Phillip had looked at him cross-eyed. I looked down at the pale face, the sticky pool of blood under his curly brown hair. His eyes were open, staring glassily at the ceiling. He was wearing his standard uniform of Abercrombie & Fitch sleeveless T-shirt and low-rise jeans, no socks, and boat shoes.

"What exactly happened here, anyway?" None of this made any sense. But then, death rarely does.

"I don't know, it all happened so fast." Phillip's voice shook. "Chad called and wanted to come over. I said okay, even though I was kind of tired. So I started making spaghetti. He came in the back way—" he gestured to the door I'd come through, "and he just started in on me. The same old bullshit, me cheating on him, me not being good enough for him, all of that horrible crap." He hugged himself and shivered. "Then he got up and shoved me into the wall and punched me—" he touched his cheek again, "and was about to punch me again when I shoved him really hard, and he fell back and hit his head on the edge of the counter . . . Then he just kind of gurgled and dropped to the floor." He gagged, took some breaths, and got control of himself again. "Then I called you."

Two hours later—what did you do for two hours? "Well, good enough for him," I finally said, stubbing the cigarette out in an overflowing ashtray on the counter.

"Are you going to help me?"

"Give me another cigarette and let me think, okay?"

The plan was simplicity itself. Once I'd smoked two or three cigarettes, I'd worked it all out in my head. I looked at it from every angle. Sure, we'd need some luck, but every plan relies on luck to a certain degree. The Lower Ninth Ward above Claiborne Avenue was a dead zone. Hurricane Katrina had left her mark there, with houses shifted off foundations, cars planted nose-down in the ground . . . and bulldozing had recently begun. I'd clipped an article out of the *Times-Picayune* that very morning on the subject, thinking it might be useful with my next book. Out in the shed behind the house, I still had the remnants of the blue tarp that had been our roof after the one-eyed bitch had wrecked it on her way through. I had Phillip help me get it, and we rolled Chad up in it. We carried the body out into the backyard, and then we cleaned the entire kitchen—every single inch of it—with bleach. I knew from a seemingly endless interview with a forensic investigator with the NOPD for my second book that bleach would destroy any trace of DNA left behind. I made Phillip wash the pots and pans and run them through the dishwasher with bleach. When the kitchen was spotless and reeked of Clorox, I checked to make sure the coast was clear.

The Lower Garden District, before Katrina, had been a busy little neighborhood. We weren't as fabulous as the Garden District, of course; when Anne Rice still lived here, I liked to tell people I lived on a street called Annunciation, about "six blocks and six million dollars" away from her. We didn't have the manicured lawns and huge houses you would see above Jackson Avenue; we were the poorer section between I-90 and Jackson. Around Coliseum Square there were some gigantic historic homes, but most of the houses in our neighborhood were of the double shotgun variety, like mine. Our section of St. Charles Avenue—about four blocks away from my house—was where you'd find the horror of chain stores and fast food that you wouldn't find further up the street.

But I liked my neighborhood. There'd always been someone around—kids playing basketball in the park down the street, people out walking dogs, and so forth; the normal day-to-day outside ramblings of any city neighborhood. The floodwaters from the shattered levees hadn't made it to our part of town—we were part of the so-called sliver by the river. When I'd come back in October, the neighborhood had been a ghost town. And even though more and more people were coming back almost every day, it was still silent and lifeless after dark for the most part.

Tonight was no different. Other than the occasional light in a window up and down the street, it was as still as a cemetery. We carried Chad out to his car and started putting him in the trunk. The way things were going, it would be just our luck to have a patrol car come along as we were forcing the body in the blue tarp burial shroud into the vehicle, and I didn't stop holding my breath until the trunk latch caught.

No one came along. The street remained silent.

Then Phillip got behind the wheel of Chad's Toyota to follow me through the city. "Make sure you use your turn signals and don't speed," I cautioned him before getting into my own car. "Don't give any cop a reason to pull you over, okay?"

He nodded.

I watched him in my rearview mirror as we drove through the quiet city. There were a few cars out, and every once in a while I spotted an NOPD car. The twenty-minute drive seemed to take forever, but we finally made it past the bridge over the Industrial Canal. I turned left onto Caffin Avenue and headed into the dead zone past the deserted, boarded-up remnants of a Walgreen's and a KFC. It was spooky, like the set of some apocalyptic movie. We cruised around in the blighted area, my palms sweating, until I found the perfect house. There was no front door, and there were the telltale spray-paint markings on the front, fresh. It had been checked again for bodies, and the three houses to its right had already been bulldozed; piles of smashed wood and debris were scattered throughout the dead yards. Several dozers were also parked in the emptied yards, ready for more demolition.

I pulled over in front of the house and turned off my lights. I got out of the car and lit another cigarette. We wrestled the body out, and lugged it into the dark house, which stank of decay and mold, rotting furniture scattered about as we made our way through it. We found the curving stairway to the second story, and carried him up. The first bedroom at the top of the stairs had a closet full of moldy clothing.

"Okay, let's just put him here in the closet," I said, panting and trying to catch my breath. Chad weighed a fucking ton. "But put him down for a minute."

Phillip let go and the body fell to the floor with a thud. I had the body by the shoulders, and I staggered with the sudden weight. The tarp pulled down, exposing Chad's head, and then I couldn't hold him anymore, and he fell, dragging me down on top of him.

"FUCK!" I screamed, looking right into Chad's open eyes. His mouth had come open as well, and in the moonlight I noticed something I hadn't seen before.

There are bruises on his neck. Bruises that look like they came from fingers around his neck, choking the life out of him. A chill went down my spine. *What the fuck—*

I looked back up at Phillip. I could almost hear him saying again, *You've said a million times that anyone can get away with murder . . .*

No wonder he hadn't wanted to call the cops.

It hadn't been an accident. It hadn't been self-defense.

It *was* murder.

And I'd helped him cover it up. I was an accessory after the fact.

And even if I cooperated, testified against him, I might have to serve time myself. At the very least, author Anthony Andrews would get some very nasty publicity.

Does he know? I thought, my heart racing. *Can he tell that I've seen? It was awful dark, and I only saw because my face was right there by Chad's.*

"Are you okay? Jesus, I'm sorry!"

He doesn't know I know. Thank you, God.

Phillip grabbed me under the arms and lifted me up to my feet without effort. He started dusting me off. "Are you okay?"

"Didn't know you were so strong," I said. I forced a smile on my face. "I'm okay."

"Don't you want to put him in the closet?" he asked. "Or can we just leave him here?"

"No, he needs to go in the closet, just in case. Let's do this and get out of here," I said, managing to keep my voice steady. *I can't let him do this, I can't let him get away with this, but I've got to get out of here. Think, Tony, think, there must be something I can do . . .*

We shoved him in, standing up, and wedged the door shut.

"All right, now we have to get rid of his car, right?" He gave me a smile. "This means so much to me, Tony, you have no idea." He gave me a hug, almost squeezing the breath out of me.

How come I never noticed how strong he is before now? Aloud, I said, "Well, maybe we could just leave it here after all." I shrugged. "I mean, they probably wouldn't think anything about it, really."

Phillip raised an eyebrow. "But you said—"

"No, no, I know, we can't leave it here." I gave him a ghost of a smile and tried to keep my voice steady, even as I thought, *I am alone in an abandoned house in an empty neighborhood with a killer.* "I'm just a little—you know . . ." I tried to make a joke. "This isn't exactly my normal Tuesday night routine." I gave a hollow laugh. "No, we can't leave the car parked out in front."

"Okay."

"We'll leave the car in the Bywater," I went on, my mind racing, trying to think of something, some clue, to leave behind. If they didn't find the body, he'd get away with it, but how to tip them off and leave myself out of it . . . ? "With any luck, the tires and everything will be stripped in a few days. If and when the cops finally find it, the body will be gone, and Chad will have just disappeared from the face of the earth."

"Won't they check the house for bodies before they bulldoze?"

"They already checked this house—they marked it as clear." I'd picked the house for that very reason. I felt sick to my stomach. Oh, yes, the plan was clever. I'd outsmarted myself, that's for damned sure. Tomorrow morning the bulldozers would level the place into a pile of rubble, and when the backhoe cleared it into a dumpster, if no telltale body parts fell out, that would be the end of it. Nope, Chad would be off to the dump, hopefully to be incinerated, and all Phillip would have to do was pretend he'd never seen or spoken to Chad again. Sure, they'd check his phone records and see that Chad had called, but all Phillip had to do was say they'd argued and Chad said he was going out in the Quarter. Besides, it would probably be days before anyone even noticed Chad was missing—and it wasn't like the post-Katrina police force wasn't already spread thin. Even before the storm, they weren't exactly a ball of fire.

And Phillip was obviously a lot smarter than I'd given him credit for.

We left the car on Spain Street on a dark block on the lake side of St. Claude. I'd told Phillip to leave the windows down and the keys in the ignition. Someone would surely take that invitation to a free car. The police wouldn't be looking for the vehicle for days, maybe even weeks—if ever. Maybe I could report the car stolen?

But that wouldn't lead them back to Phillip.

Phillip got into my car and we pulled away from the curb. "Some adventure, huh?" he said, rolling down his window and lighting another cigarette. "Thanks, man." He put his free hand on my inner thigh and stroked it, giving me the smile I'd seen him use a million times in bars. I knew exactly what that smile meant, and my blood ran cold. "Do you really think we'll get away with it?"

"As long as you stick to your story and don't freak when the police come by to interview you—if they ever do," I replied, knowing that he wouldn't freak. Oh no, he was much too clever for that. How could I have missed that before? If the body disposal went as planned, it could be days, even weeks, before anyone even notified the police. Chad worked as a waiter in a Quarter restaurant, and from all appearances, never seemed to have any friends. Who would miss him? He wouldn't show up for work, they'd write him off—people tend to come and go quickly in New Orleans, especially now—and that would be the end of it. Unless a family member missed him, filed a missing-persons report, and really pressed the cops—which wouldn't do much good, unless his family was wealthy and powerful.

You have to hate New Orleans sometimes.

As we drove down Claiborne, the one thing I couldn't stop thinking about was those bruises on Chad's throat, and the two hours Phillip had waited before he called me. His story was a lie. No one freaks out and stays alone with a dead body for two hours. And I hadn't heard anything. Sure, I'd had the iPod on pretty loud, but I'd heard their fights before. As for the bruise on his cheek, the cut lips—maybe he'd done that to himself somehow, as he tried to figure out a way to get me to help him. There was no way I would ever know what had finally pushed Phillip over the edge, why he'd decided that Chad had to die rather than just breaking things off with him. Or maybe the story he'd told me was partially true—maybe Chad had hit him, he'd fought back, knocked him down, and Chad had hit his head on the table on the way down. But Phillip had definitely finished him off by choking him.

I fell for his story like an idiot, worried as always about poor dumb Phillip in a jam, and now I am an accessory after the fact.

Just get home, get away from him, and make an anonymous call to the police, tip them off. As long as they find the body before it's too late . . .

I glanced at Phillip. That was a good idea. Just get away from him and make the call.

Thank God I'd never followed up on the attraction I'd felt for him when he first moved in.

I pulled up in front of the house and turned the car off. I gave him a brittle smile. "Here we are."

Phillip gave me that look again. "Thanks, Tony. You really are a good friend." He leaned over and kissed me on the cheek. "Whew. Some night, huh?"

"Um, yeah."

He got out of the car and stretched, his muscles flexing and rippling in the light from the streetlamp. Before, I would have admired their thickness and beauty. Now, all I could see was their strength, and it terrified me. "Man, I'm beat." He gave me that smile again, and this time it curdled my blood. "Mind if I come in for a while? You have any pot? I could use some."

Fuck!

"Phillip, I'm really wiped and just want to go to bed." I faked a smile. "Wait here and I'll roll you a joint." I climbed the steps to my side of the house as quickly as I could. I unlocked the door and walked into my living room. The lights were still on; I hadn't turned them off when I'd rushed over there. My computer screen glowed, my bag of weed still sitting there on my writing table where I'd left it. My hands shook as I reached into a drawer and pulled out my rolling papers. *Just roll the damned thing and give it to him and then call the cops.*

I jumped as the front door opened.

"Thanks, man," Phillip said, as he shut the door behind him. "I know you're tired, buddy, but I just need some company for a little while."

I barked out a little laugh as I fumbled with the paper. "Yeah, it's been kind of a weird night, huh?" *Hurry, hurry, roll it and get him out of here.*

"I'm really sorry, Tony," Phillip said as I finished rolling the joint, licked it, and handed it over to him. "You're such a good friend. I don't know what I ever did to deserve you."

That makes two of us, I thought. *Just take your joint and get the fuck out of my house.*

He sat down on the couch and stretched out, giving me that smile yet again. He patted the couch. "Why don't you sit next to me, Tony?" He twirled the joint in his fingers. "Got a light?"

The easier to choke me? I swallowed and handed him the lighter. My heart was racing and I sat down, trying to keep my legs from touching his.

He took a long hit, held it in for a while, then blew it out in a plume. He offered me the joint, which I declined. He took another hit, pinched it out with his fingers, and put it on the coffee table. "You know what?"

"What?"

"I've always wondered about something but I never felt right asking." He smiled at me.

Stay calm, keep cool, don't alarm him in any way. "What's that?"

"How come we've never hooked up?" I felt his arm slide around my shoulders, and out of the corner of my eye I saw his big hand on my shoulder.

I swallowed. "I—I don't know."

"I mean, I've seen how you look at me sometimes." He leaned into me, his face close to mine. "Don't you think I'm hot, Tony? Don't you want to fuck me?"

Oh God, no, this isn't happening. Get him out of here!

He kissed me on the cheek, his left hand moving to my chest.

"Phillip, no." I tried to pull away from him, but he had a firm grip on my shoulder.

"You know you want it," he whispered.

"No." I pushed his hands off me and stood up. "I think you should leave." I was shaking, my stomach churning.

He stood up as well, his face unreadable. "Come on, Tony." He reached for me and put his arms around me, pulling me close.

"Let me go!" I tried pushing him away, but he just laughed and gripped me tighter, and as he pulled me in I knew he was stronger than me, and I wondered if this was the last thing Chad had seen before the hands went around his throat and started choking the life out of him, Phillip's face moving in closer and closer as everything went dark and he slid to the floor . . . and my heart started pounding, this was it, I was going to die, he was going to kill me, too . . .

"Phillip, *don't!*" Adrenaline coursed through my body as I planted my hands on his chest and shoved with every ounce of strength in my body.

He stumbled backwards, opened his mouth, his face shocked, and gasped, "Hey!" just as the back of his legs hit the coffee table.

I watched. It seemed as though time had slowed down, as though the entire world had somehow moved into slow motion.

He fell, his arms pinwheeling as he tried to catch himself.

The back of his head hit the edge of the mantelpiece with a sickening crunch.

And then he was sprawled on my floor, his head leaking.

He let out a sigh and his entire body went limp, his eyes staring at the ceiling.

"Oh. My. God," I breathed, as I stepped forward and knelt down, placing my fingers on his carotid artery.

No heartbeat.

He was dead.

"I swear I didn't mean to kill him!"

I sank down onto the floor in a stupor and started laughing hysterically.

Who was I going to call?

LOOT

BY JULIE SMITH

Garden District

Mathilde's in North Carolina with her husband when she hears about the hurricane—the one that's finally going to fulfill the prophecy about filling the bowl New Orleans is built in. Uh-huh, sure. She's been there a thousand times. She all but yawns.

Aren't they all? goes through her mind.

"A storm like no one's ever seen," the weather guy says, "a storm that will leave the city devastated . . . a storm that . . ."

Blah blah and blah.

But finally, after ten more minutes of media hysteria, she catches on that this time it might be for real. Her first thought is for her home in the Garden District, the one that's been in Tony's family for three generations. Yet she knows there's nothing she can do about that—if the storm takes it, so be it.

Her second thought is for her maid, Cherice Wardell, and Cherice's husband, Charles.

Mathilde and Cherice have been together for twenty-two years. They're like an old married couple. They've spent more time with each other than they have with their husbands. They've taken care of each other when one of them was ill. They've cooked for each other (though Cherice has cooked a good deal more for Mathilde). They've shopped together, they've argued, they've shared more secrets than either of them would be comfortable with if they thought about it. They simply chat, the way women do, and things come out, some things that probably shouldn't. Cherice knows intimate facts about Mathilde's sex life, for instance, things she likes to do with Tony, that Mathilde would never tell her white friends.

So Mathilde knows the Wardells plenty well enough to know they aren't about to obey the evacuation order. They never leave when a storm's on the way. They have two big dogs and nowhere to take them. Except for their two children, one of whom is in school in Alabama, and the other in California, the rest of their family lives in New Orleans. So there are no nearby relatives to shelter them. They either can't afford hotels or think they can't (though twice in the past Mathilde has offered to pay for their lodging if they'd only *go*). Only twice because only twice have Mathilde and Tony heeded the warnings themselves. In past years, before everyone worried so much about the disappearing wetlands and the weakened infrastructure, it was a point of honor for people in New Orleans to ride out hurricanes.

But Mathilde is well aware that this is not the case with the Wardells. This is no challenge to them. They simply don't see the point of leaving. They prefer to play what Mathilde thinks of as Louisiana roulette. Having played it a few times herself, she knows all about it. The Wardells think the traffic will be terrible, that they'll be in the car for seventeen, eighteen hours and still not find a hotel because everything from here to kingdom come's going to be taken even if they could afford it.

"That storm's not gon' come," Cherice always says. "You know it never does. Why I'm gon' pack up these dogs and Charles and go God knows where? You know Mississippi gives me a headache. And I ain't even gon' *mention* Texas."

To which Mathilde replied gravely one time, "This is your life you're gambling with, Cherice."

And Cherice said, "I think I'm just gon' pray."

But Mathilde will have to try harder this time, especially since she's not there.

Cherice is not surprised to see Mathilde's North Carolina number on her caller ID. "Hey, Mathilde," she says. "How's the weather in Highlands?"

"Cherice, listen. This is the Big One. This time, I mean it, I swear to God, you could be—"

"Uh-huh. Gamblin' with my life and Charles's. Listen, if it's the Big One, I want to be here to see it. I wouldn't miss it for the world."

"Cherice, listen to me. I know I'm not going to convince you—you're the pig-headedest woman I've ever seen. Just promise me something. Go to my house. Take the dogs. Ride it out at my house."

"Take the dogs?" Cherice can't believe what she's hearing. Mathilde never lets her bring the dogs over, won't let them inside her house. Hates dogs, has allergies, thinks they'll pee on her furniture. She loves Mathilde, but Mathilde is a pain in the butt, and Cherice mentions this every chance she gets to anyone who'll listen. Mathilde is picky and spoiled and needy. She's good-hearted, sure, but she hates her precious routine disturbed.

Yet this same Mathilde Berteau has just told her to *promise* to take the dogs to her immaculate house. This is so sobering Cherice can hardly think what to say. "Well, I *know* you're worried now."

"Cherice. Promise me."

Cherice hears panic in Mathilde's voice. *What can it hurt?* she thinks. The bed in Mathilde's guest room is a lot more comfortable than hers. Also, if the power goes out—and Cherice has no doubt that it will—she'll have to go to Mathilde's the day after the storm anyhow, to clean out the refrigerator.

Mathilde is ahead of her. "Listen, Cherice, I *need* you to go. I need you to clean out the refrigerator when the power goes. Also, we have a gas stove and you don't. You can cook at my house. We still have those fish Tony caught a couple of weeks ago—they're going to go to waste if you're not there."

Cherice is humbled. Not about the fish offer—that's just like Mathilde, to offer something little when she wants something bigger. That's small potatoes. What gets to her is the refrigerator thing—if Mathilde tells her she needs her for something, she's bringing out the big guns. Mathilde's a master manipulator, and Cherice has seen her pull this one a million times—but not usually on *her*. Mathilde does it when all else fails, and her instincts are damn good—it's a lot easier to turn down a favor than to refuse to grant one. Cherice knows her employer like she knows Charles—better, maybe—but she still feels the pull of Mathilde's flimsy ruse.

"I'll clean your refrigerator, baby," Cherice says carefully. "Don't you worry about a thing."

"Cherice, goddamnit, I'm worried about *you!*"

And Cherice gives in. "I know you are, baby. And Charles and I appreciate it, we really do. Tell you what—we gon' do it. We gon' go over there. I promise." But she doesn't know if she can actually talk Charles into it.

He surprises her by agreeing readily as soon as she mentions the part about the dogs. "Why not?" he says. "We can sleep in Mathilde and Tony's big ol' bed and watch television till the power goes out. Drink a beer and have the dogs with us. Ain't like we have to drive to Mississippi or somethin'. And if the roof blows off, maybe we can save some of their stuff. That refrigerator ain't all she's got to worry about."

"We're *not* sleepin' in their bed, Charles. The damn guest room's like a palace, anyway—who you think you is?"

He laughs at her. "I know it, baby. Jus' tryin' to see how far I can push ya."

So that Sunday they pack two changes of clothes, plenty for two days, and put the mutts in their crates. The only other things they take are dog food and beer. They don't grab food for themselves because there's plenty over at Mathilde's, which they have to eat or it'll go bad.

The first bands of the storm come late that night, and Charles does what he said he was going to—goes to bed with a beer and his dogs. But after he's asleep, Cherice watches the storm from the window of the second-floor living room. The power doesn't go off until early morning, and when the rain swirls, the lights glint on it. The wind howls like a hound. Big as it is, the house shakes. Looking out, Cherice sees a building collapse, a little coffee shop across the street, and realizes how well built the Berteaus' house is. Her own is not. She prays that it will make it. But she knows she will be all right, and so will Charles and the dogs. She is not afraid because she is a Christian woman and she trusts that she will not be harmed.

But she does see the power of God in this. For the first time, she understands why people talk about being God-fearing instead of God-loving, something that's always puzzled her. You *better* have God on your side, she thinks. You just better.

She watches the transformers blow one by one, up and

down the street, and goes to bed when the power goes out, finding her way by flashlight, wondering what she's going to wake up to.

The storm is still raging when she stirs, awakened by the smell of bacon. Charles has cooked breakfast, but he's nowhere to be found. She prowls the house looking for him, and the dogs bark to tell her: *third floor*.

"Cherice," he calls down. "Bring pots."

She knows what's happened: leaks. The Berteaus must have lost some shingles.

So she and Charles work for the next few hours, putting pots out, pushing furniture from the path of inrushing water, gathering up wet linens, trying to salvage and dry out papers and books, emptying the pots, replacing them. All morning the wind is dying, though. The thing is blowing through.

By 2 o'clock it's a beautiful day. "Still a lot of work to do," Charles says, sighing. "But I better go home first, see how our house is. I'll come back and help you. We should sleep here again tonight."

Cherice knows that their house has probably lost its roof, that they might have much worse damage than the Berteaus, maybe even flooding. He's trying to spare her by offering to go alone.

"Let's make some phone calls first," she says.

They try to reach neighbors who rode out the storm at home, but no one answers, probably having not remembered, like Cherice and Charles, to buy car chargers. Indeed, they have only a little power left on their own cell phone, which Cherice uses to call Mathilde. The two women have the dodged-the-bullet talk that everyone in the dry neighborhoods has that day, the day before they find out the levees have breached.

Though they don't yet know about the levees, Cherice nonetheless feels a terrible foreboding about her house, acutely needs to see how badly it's damaged. She doesn't have much hope that the streets will be clear enough to drive, but she and Charles go out in the yard anyhow to remove broken limbs from the driveway.

"Let's listen to the car radio, see if we can get a report," Cherice says, realizing they've been so preoccupied with saving the Berteaus' possessions, they've forgotten to do this.

She opens the car door, is about to enter, when she feels Charles tense beside her. "Cherice," he says.

She turns and sees what he sees: a gang of young men in hooded sweatshirts walking down the street, hands in their pockets. Looking for trouble.

Charles says, "You go on back in the house."

Cherice doesn't need to be told twice. She knows where Tony keeps his gun. She means to get it, but she's so worried about Charles she turns back to look, and sees that he's just standing by the car, hands in pockets, looking menacing. The young men pass by, but she goes for the gun anyway.

By the time she gets back, Charles is back inside, locking the door. "Damn looters," he says. "Goddamn looters." And his face is so sad Cherice wants to hug him, but it's also so angry she knows better. "Why they gotta go and be this way?" he says.

They listen to the Berteaus' little battery-powered radio and learn that there's looting all over the city, crime is out of control. "Ain't safe to go out," Charles says grimly. "Can't even get home to see about our property."

She knows he's sorry they came, that they didn't stay home where they belonged. "I'm gon' fix some lunch."

So they eat and then go out in the backyard, and clean it up the best they can, even try to get some of the debris out of the swimming pool, but this is a losing battle. After a while they abandon the project, realizing that it's a beautiful day and they have their dogs and they're together. Even if their house is destroyed.

So they live in the moment. They try to forget the looting, though the sound of sirens is commonplace now. Instead of Tony's fish, they barbecue some steaks that are quickly defrosting, and Cherice fixes some potato salad while the mayonnaise is still good. Because they got so little sleep the night before, and because there's no electricity, they go to bed early.

Sometime in the night they awaken to a relentless thudding—no, a pounding on the Berteaus' door. "I'm goin'," Charles says grimly, and Cherice notices he tucks Tony's gun into the jeans he pulls on.

She can't just stay here and wait to see what happens. She creeps down the stairs behind him.

"Yeah?" Charles says through the door.

"I'm the next door neighbor," a man says. "I've got Tony on the phone."

Charles opens the door and takes the man's cell phone. He listens for a while, every now and then saying, "Oh shit." Or, "Oh God. No." Cherice pulls on his elbow, mouthing *What?* to him, terrified. But he turns away, ignoring her, still listening, taking in whatever it is. Finally, he says, "Okay. We'll leave first thing."

Still ignoring Cherice, he gives the phone back to the neighbor. "You know about all this?" he says. The man only nods, and Cherice sees that he's crying. Grown man, looks like an Uptown banker, white hair and everything, with tears running down his cheeks, biting his lip like a little kid.

She's frantic. She's grabbing at Charles, all but pinching

him, desperately trying to get him to just finish up and tell her what's going on. Finally, he turns around, and she's never seen him look like this, like maybe one of their kids has died or something.

He says only, "Oh, baby," and puts his arms around her. She feels his body buck, and realizes that he's crying too, that he can't hold it in anymore, whatever it is. Has one of their kids died?

Finally, he pulls himself together enough to tell her what's happened—that the city is flooded, their neighborhood is destroyed, some of their neighbors are probably dead. Their own children thought *they* were dead until they finally got Tony and Mathilde.

Cherice cannot take this in. She tries, but she just can't. "Eighty percent of the city is underwater?" she repeats over and over. "How can that be?"

They live in a little brick house in New Orleans East, a house they worked hard to buy, that's a stretch to maintain, but it's worth it. They have a home, a little piece of something to call their own.

But now we don't, Cherice thinks. *It's probably gone. We don't have nothin'.*

In the end, she can't go that way. She reasons that an entire neighborhood can't be destroyed, *something's* got to be left, and maybe her house is. She wants to go see for herself.

"Cherice, you gotta pay attention," Charles says. "Only way to go see it's to swim. Or get a boat maybe. There's people all over town on rooftops right now, waitin' to be rescued. There's still crazy lootin' out there. The mayor wants everybody out of town."

"That's what he said *before* the storm."

"He's sayin' it again. We goin' to Highlands tomorrow."

"*Highlands?*"

"Well, where else we gon' go? Mathilde and Tony got room for us, they say come, get our bearings, then we'll see. Besides, Mathilde wants us to bring her some things."

There it is again—Mathilde asking a favor to get them to leave. So that's how serious it is. Well, Cherice knew that, sort of. But it keeps surprising her, every time she thinks about it.

"How we gon' get out with all that lootin' goin' on?" she says. "Might even be snipers."

"Tony says the best way's the bridge. We can just go on over to the West Bank—we leavin' first thing in the morning. And I mean *first* thing—before anybody's up and lootin'. Let's try to get a few more hours sleep."

Cherice knows this is impossible, but she agrees because she wants to be close to Charles, to hold him, even if neither of them sleeps.

De La Russe is in the parking lot at the Tchoupitoulas Wal-Mart, thinking this whole thing is a clusterfuck of undreamt-of proportions, really wanting to break some heads (and not all of them belonging to looters), when Jack Stevens arrives in a district car. Sergeant Stevens is a big ol' redhead, always spewing the smart remarks, never taking a damn thing seriously, and today is no different.

"Hey, Del—think it's the end of the world or what?"

De La Russe is not in the mood for this kind of crap. "There's no goddamn chain of command here, Jack. Couple of officers came in, said they got orders to just let the looters have at it, but who am I s'posed to believe? Can't get nobody on the radio, the phones, the goddamn cell phones—" He pauses, throws his own cell across the concrete parking lot. It lands with something more like a mousy skitter than a good solid thud.

He has quite a bit more to say on the subject, but Stevens interrupts. "What the hell you do that for?"

"Why I need the goddamn thing? Nobody's gonna answer, nobody fuckin' cares where I am, nobody's where they're supposed to be, and I can't get nothin' but a fuckin' busy anyhow. Nothing around here . . . fuckin' . . . *works!* Don't you . . . fuckin' . . . get it?"

"Del, my man, you seem a little stressed."

De La Russe actually raises his nightstick.

"Hey. Take it easy; put that down, okay. Ya friend Jack's here. We gon' get through this thing together. All right, man?"

For a moment, De La Russe feels better, as if he isn't alone in a world gone savage—looters busting into all the stores, proclaiming them "open for business"; whole families going in and coming out loaded down with televisions and blasters and power tools (as if there's gonna be power anytime soon), right in front of half the police in the parish. Sure, De La Russe could follow procedure, order them out of there, holler, *Freeze, asshole*! like a normal day, but which one of 'em's gonna listen? In the end, what's he gonna do, shoot the place up? It's not like he's getting any backup from his brother officers and, as he's just told Stevens, it's not like he can get anybody on the goddamn phone anyway. Or the radio. Or anyhow at all.

"Now, first thing we're gon' do is go in there and get you another phone," Stevens says.

De La Russe knows what he means, and he's not even shocked. What's going on here is nothing short of the breakdown of society, and he thinks he's going to have to roll with it. Something about having Stevens with him is kind of reassuring; he *is* a sergeant—not Del's sergeant, but still, if he heard right, a sergeant in the New Orleans Police Department has just told him to go into Wal-Mart and loot himself a phone.

Just to be sure, he tries something out: "Loot one, you mean."

"Hell no! We're gonna *commandeer* you one." And Stevens about kills himself laughing.

They hitch their trousers and push past several boiling little seas of people, seemingly working in groups, helping themselves to everything from baby food to fishing poles. Nobody even glances at their uniforms.

"Why are we bothering with the goddamn phone?" De La Russe asks. "Damn things don't work anyhow."

"Yeah, you right," Stevens says. "But just in case." He turns to the busy knot of looters on the small appliances aisle and grabs himself one at random—a woman. Just shoves an arm around her, gets up under her chin, and pulls her against his body. De La Russe sees her pupils dilate, her eyeballs about pop out of her head with fear. Stevens whispers something in her ear and she nods.

When he lets her go, she reaches in the pocket of her jeans and comes out with a cell phone, which she hands over, meek as you please. Stevens passes it to De La Russe. "Now ya back in business." He swings his arms wide. "Anything else ya need?"

De La Russe feels sweat break out on his forehead. His scalp starts to prickle, and so do his toes. His heart speeds up a little. Weirdest part of all, he's actually having a sexual reaction; he's getting hard. Not all the way hard, just a little excited, like when he sees a woman he likes, maybe lights a cigarette for her, brushes her thigh, but that's all, no kiss or anything. A woman who isn't his wife but someone who's not supposed to get him excited. This is how he feels now, except with sweat and prickles. Because he's pretty sure this is not an idle question Stevens is asking. Thing about Stevens, there's rumors about him. About how he makes stuff disappear from the property room, shakes suspects down for drugs, little stuff that tells you a lot.

Thing about De La Russe, he's not above the same kind of thing. And he doesn't need rumors, he's been disciplined and everybody knows it. Yeah, he's been clean since then, but he's starting to feel this is something else again, this thing he's looking at. This thing that's nothing less than the breakdown of the social contract. It's just occurring to him that people are going to profit from this, and they're not just gonna be the Pampers-and-toothpaste thieves. He decides to get right down to it.

"What are you saying, sergeant?"

"Hell, Del, it's the end of the world and you're callin' me sergeant—what's up with that shit?" But he knows perfectly well.

De La Russe smiles. "I was just wondering if I heard you right." He waits for an answer, not allowing the smile to fade. Keeping his teeth bared.

"Remember that little eBay bi'ness you told me you and ya wife was runnin'? How she goes to garage sales and finds things she can sell to collectors? And then you photograph 'em and get 'em on up online? Y'all still doin' that?"

"Yeah. We still doin' that. Why?"

Stevens looks at him like he's nuts. "Why? Think about it, Del. You can sell just about anything on eBay." He pauses, does the wide-open this-could-all-be-yours thing again. "And we got access to just about anything."

De La Russe is getting his drift. His mind's racing, going instantly to the problems and working on solutions. He shrugs. "Yeah? Where would we store it?"

"Glad you axed, bro. Just happens I already hooked up with a lieutenant who's got a room at the Hyatt." The Hyatt has become the department's temporary headquarters. "He's got access to a couple other rooms we could use. And I don't mean hotel rooms. Storage rooms. Pretty big ones. We keep it there for now and when things get back to normal, somebody's garage, maybe."

De La Russe narrows his eyes. "What lieutenant?"

"Joe Dougald."

The patrolman almost does a double take. "Joe Dougald? You're dreaming. Guy's a boy scout."

Stevens hoots. "Yeah? Ya think so? I been doin' deals with Joe for fifteen years. Trust me. We can trust him."

De La Russe isn't sure if he even trusts Stevens, much less Dougald, but what the hell, the regular rules just don't seem to apply now that the apocalypse, or whatever this is, has come crashing in on them. And he's got two kids in Catholic school, with college looming. *That's* not going away.

He assesses the place. "Let's start with little stuff that's easy to carry. IPods, video games, stuff like that. Electronics, small appliances. Hey, do they have jewelry here?" He gives a little snort. Wal-Mart jewelry isn't going to make them rich, even if it exists. "Watches, maybe?"

Stevens smiles as if he likes the way De La Russe is getting into this. "This ain't the only store in town, ya know. And stores ain't the only sources we got. You're from the Second District, right? People there got real nice taste."

De La Russe decides he's just fallen into a real deal. Here they are, right this minute, he and Stevens, policing Wal-

Mart and helping themselves while they're at it. He sees how he can patrol his own district, get credit for coming to work, arrest a few of the real looters—the street guys—and help himself to whatever he wants while everybody's still out of town. How come he hadn't thought of it first?

It's early the next day when De La Russe sees the black couple—oh, excuse *him*, the two African-Americans—packing up their car in front of the biggest-ass goddamn house in the Garden District, or so near it doesn't matter. What the hell are they thinking? There aren't any cops around here? He decides he's really going to enjoy this.

He parks his car and strolls up all casual, like he's just gonna talk to 'em. "How y'all?" Dicking with them.

They go rigid though. They know from the get-go he's trouble, and it has to be because of their guilty little consciences. "What y'all doing?"

"Leavin'," the man says. "Gettin' out of town quick as we can. You want to see some ID? My wife works here and the owners are in North Carolina. So we rode out the storm here." He starts to put his hand in his pocket, maybe to get the ID, and that gives De La Russe an excuse to slam him up against the car, like he thinks the guy's going to go for a weapon.

He pats the man down, and sure enough, there is one. Doesn't *that* just sweeten this whole deal. Worth a lot to a couple guys he knows. "You got a permit for this?"

The guy doesn't answer, but his wife pipes up: "It's not ours. It belongs to Tony. My employer. When the looters came . . ."

De La Russe smiles. ". . . ya thought it might be okay to steal ya boss's gun, huh? You know how pathetic that story sounds? Know who I think the looters are? Yeah. Yeah, I guess ya do. Let's see what else ya got here."

The woman says, "My boss, Mathilde . . . she asked me to bring—"

"Mrs. Berteau," the man says. "My wife works for Mathilde Berteau."

"Right," says De La Russe. "Y'all get in the backseat for a while."

"What about . . . ?" The woman's already crying, knowing exactly what's in store for her. He grabs her by the elbow and rassles her into the car, shoving her good, just for the fun of it.

"What about what?"

"Nothin', I just . . ."

The husband is yelling now. "Listen, call the Berteaus. All you have to do is call 'em, goddammit! Just call 'em and let 'em tell you."

"Like there was the least chance of that," Cherice says ten months later. The encounter had led to the misery and indignity of incarceration for three days and two nights, plus the humiliation of being accused of looting—almost the hardest part to bear. But she has survived, she and Charles, to tell the story at a Fourth of July barbecue.

"Know why I was wastin' my breath?" Charles chimes in. "'Cause that peckerwood was enjoyin' himself. Wasn't about to ruin his own good time."

She and Charles are living in Harvey now, in a rental, not a FEMA trailer, thank God, until they decide what to do about their gutted house. Their families have all heard the story many times over, but they've made new friends here on the West Bank, people they haven't yet swapped Katrina yarns with. Right now they have the rapt attention of Wyvette Johnson and her boyfriend Brandin. Cherice didn't catch his last name.

Wyvette gets tears in her eyes. "Mmmm. Mmmm. What about those poor dogs?"

This annoys Cherice, because it's getting ahead of the way she usually tells it. But she says, "I nearly blurted out that they were there at the last minute . . . before he took us away. But I thought they'd have a better chance if he didn't know about 'em. *Last* thing I wanted was to get my dogs stole by some redneck cop." Here she lets a sly smile play across her face. "Anyhow, I knew once Mathilde knew they was still in the house, that was gon' give her a extra reason to come get us out."

"Not that she needed it," Charles adds. "She was happy as a pig in shit to hear we'd been dragged off to jail. I mean, not jail, more like a chain-link cage, and then the actual Big House. I ended up at Angola, you believe that? The jail flooded, remember that? And then they turned the train station into a jail. Oh man, that was some Third World shit! Couldn't get a phone call for nothin', and like I say, they put you in a cage. But one thing—it was the only damn thing in the city that whole week that worked halfway right. Kept you there a couple days, shipped you right out to Angola. But they got the women out of there just about right away. So Cherice was up at St. Gabriel—you know, where the women's prison is—in just about twenty-four hours flat. And after that, it wasn't no problem. 'Cause they actually had working phones there."

Wyvette is shaking her silky dreads. "I think I'm missin' somethin' here—did you say Mathilde was *happy* y'all were in jail?"

"Well, not exactly," Cherice says. "She was *outraged*—'specially since I'd been there for two days when they finally let me make the call. It's just that outrage is her favorite state of mind. See, who Mathilde is—I gotta give you her number; every black person in Louisiana oughta have it on speed dial—who Mathilde is, she's the toughest civil rights lawyer in the state. That's why Charles made sure to say her name. But that white boy just said, 'Right,' like he didn't believe us. Course, we knew for sure she was gon' hunt him down and fry his ass. Or die tryin'. But that didn't make it no better at the time. In the end, Mathilde made us famous though. Knew she would."

"Yeah, but we wouldn't've got on CNN if it hadn't been for you," Charles says, smiling at her. "Or in the *New York Times* neither."

Wyvette and Brandin are about bug-eyed.

"See what happened," Charles continues, "Cherice went on eBay and found Mathilde's mama's engagement ring, the main thing she wanted us to bring to Highlands. Those cops were so arrogant they just put it right up there. In front of God and everybody."

"But how did you know to do that?" Wyvette asks, and Cherice thinks it's a good question.

"I didn't," she says. "I just felt so bad for Mathilde I was tryin' anything and everywhere. Anyhow, once we found the jewelry, the cops set up a sting, busted the whole crime ring—there was three of 'em. Found a whole garage full of stuff they hadn't sold yet."

Brandin shakes his head and waves his beer. "Lawless times. Lawless times we live in."

And Cherice laughs. "Well, guess what? We got to do a little lootin' of our own. You ever hear of Priscilla Smith-

Fredericks? She's some big Hollywood producer. Came out and asked if she could buy our story for fifteen thousand dollars, you believe that? Gonna do a TV movie about what happened to us. I should feel bad about it, but those people got *way* more money than sense."

Right after the holiday, Marty Carrera of Mojo Mart Productions finds himself in a meeting with a young producer who has what sounds to him like a good idea. Priscilla Smith-Fredericks lays a hand on his wrist, which he doesn't much care for, but he tries not to cringe.

"Marty," she says. "I *believe* in this story. This is an important story to tell—a story about corruption, about courage, about one woman's struggle for justice in an unjust world. But most of all, it's the story of two women, two women who've been together for twenty-two years—one the maid, the other the boss—about the love they have for each other, the way their lives are inextricably meshed. In a good way.

"I want to do this picture for *them* and . . . well . . . for the whole state of Louisiana. You know what? That poor state's been screwed enough different ways it could write a sequel to the *Kama Sutra*. It's been screwed by FEMA, it's been screwed by the Corps of Engineers, it's been screwed by the administration, it's been screwed by its own crooked officials . . . *Everybody's* picking carrion off its bones. And those poor Wardells! I want to do this for the Wardells. Those people have a house to rebuild. They need the money and they need the . . . well, the lift. The *vindication*."

Marty Carrera looks at the paperwork she's given him. She proposes to pay the Wardells a $15,000 flat fee, which seems low to him. Standard would be about $75,000, plus a percentage of the gross and maybe a $10,000 "technical consultant" fee. He shuffles pages, wondering if she's done what he suspects.

And yes, of course she has. She's inflated her own fee at the expense of the Wardells. She thinks she should get $100,000 as an associate producer, about twice what the job is worth. And not only that, she wants to award the technical consultant's fee to herself.

Marty is genuinely angry about this. She's roused his sympathy for the wrongfully accused couple, and even for the beleaguered state, and he too believes the Wardells' story—or more properly, Mathilde and Cherice's story—would make a great movie for television.

However, he thinks Ms. Smith-Fredericks is a species of vermin. "After looking at the figures," he says, "I think I can honestly say that you seem uniquely qualified to do a piece on looting."

But she doesn't catch his meaning. She's so full of herself all she hears is what she wants to hear. She sticks out her hand to shake

Well, so be it, Marty thinks. *I tried to warn her.*

His production company doesn't need her. So what if she found the story and brought it to him? He's not obligated to . . . Well, he is, but . . .

"Marty," she says, "we're going to be great together."

He shakes her hand absentmindedly, already thinking of ways to cut her out of the deal.

ANGOLA SOUTH

BY ACE ATKINS

Loyola Avenue

The child was small and black, shirtless, wearing only a filthy pair of Spider-Man pajama bottoms and carrying a skinned-up football. His fingers still felt numb from holding his mother's hand all night and he now found himself standing on top of the interstate overpass looking down at a maze of swamped streets.

For a long time now, since the morning heat started shining hard off the top of the downtown buildings, he'd been watching the man with the gun.

The man was white and wearing green, a big plug of tobacco in his left cheek. To the child, it seemed his eyes were superhuman, taking in everything in their thick mirrored lenses and occasionally shouting to a group of shackled men who sat and slept.

He kept the gun tight in both hands and would walk from the beginning of the chain of men—bearded and smelling of rotten eggs and garbage—to the end, his boots making hollow sounds on the overpass. His steps seemed like a drum over the murmur of men and families who'd found refuge on the high ground.

By early afternoon, the child stood close to the railing, trying to catch the breeze that would sometimes come across his face, his eyes lazily opening and closing, watching the waves break and shift on top of the roadway and on the parched roofs of partially sunk buildings and shotgun houses.

He felt his fingers slip from the sweaty hand of his mother and he wandered, walking and swaying, toward the man with the gun.

The boy tugged at the rough material on his leg and the man stared down at him, his silver glass eyes shining an image of a grinning child back at him.

He looked at the twin images of himself and said: "Mister, when you gonna fix our city?"

Jack Estay woke at 5 a.m. to the sound of the big yellow locomotive's engines chugging away and keeping the entire station juiced with power. He took the twelve-gauge from his lap, stood from where he'd fallen asleep in a chair the night before, and washed himself in the lavatory.

At 5:15 he walked five men caught looting a Vietnamese restaurant (they'd been found eating dried shrimp and guzzling bottles of 33 beer) down the endless train platform and into the holding cells fashioned with chain link, metal bars, and concertina wire. In each of the sixteen cells there was one portable toilet.

Orleans Parish Prison sat filled with water, so it was the best they could do.

As Jack locked up and walked the line back to the old Amtrak station, men and women hollered and yelled. A homeless man on the way tried to piss on him, but his short quick stream stopped shy of Jack's leg.

Jack looked at the man and spat some brown juice at the base of the cell.

Another guard called out to him about the next row of cells. "That one has AIDS," the thick-bodied woman said. "Be careful."

Most of the prisoners were looters, some stole cars, some broke into mansions, and about ten had tried to kill folks. Mainly taking shots at cops who were trying to rescue people from their swamped neighborhoods.

"Hey, Audie Murphy!" yelled a man with a long gray beard stained yellow. "Go suck a turd."

Jack walked into the wide expanse of the train station, the newspaper racks selling a copy of *USA Today* from August 26, a picture of Martha Stewart on the cover with a big shit-eating grin on her face.

Welcome to Angola South read a cardboard sign by the door.

Jack got a break just before sundown.

He used his cell phone to call his father back on Grand Isle, a man who'd been left alone to pick through the wreckage of a shrimp company he'd owned since '64, surviving even Hurricane Betsy. His dad told him that every boat they owned, the refrigerated warehouse, and their stilt house had all washed out into the Gulf.

"Say hello to Mama for me," Jack said before ending the call and heading out in his truck along the river.

Jack rode through the city and drank a cold Budweiser, a cooler in the back of his Chevy loaded down with ice brought in by the Indiana National Guard. The radio carried nothing but news, so he shut it off and just drove slow out Canal Street past the carnival of TV trucks and reporters camped out on the neutral ground. At one point, he slowed, noticing a leg sticking out from under a tarp.

But raising his sunglasses, he saw it was only a mannequin. He glimpsed a couple of cameramen in the shadows laughing and pointing.

He drove on.

Rampart at Canal was the foot of the swamp, water all the way to Lake Pontchartrain. He turned around and crossed back through the Quarter, found higher ground and crossed Rampart further downriver, ending up at the corner of St. Louis and Tremé, right by the old housing projects, St. Louis Cemetery, and the looted-out Winn-Dixie. All along Tremé, tree branches and drowned cars filled the road. Birds and loose trash skittered in the warm breeze.

Jack polished off the Bud and pulled a plug of tobacco from his pouch. Sitting on his hood, he brushed off the brown pieces of Redman from his mustache and spit into the swampy water covering his truck tires.

The warm air was calm. The city completely still, with huge clouds above the Central Business District. A skinny, mangy dog wandered past him.

An old black man on a bicycle peddled through the foot-deep water and waved.

The only sound came from helicopters loaded down with machine guns passing over the Mississippi and the Lower Ninth Ward looking for bodies and looters. An old-fashioned Army Jeep passed, driving in reverse with a young kid in the passenger seat wearing an NOPD shirt and Chinese hat. He eyed down his rifle, scoped a bird on the cracked cemetery wall, and then, satisfied he had the shot, dropped the gun at his side.

Jack spit and smiled.

He wasn't even back at the train station for his next shift when he saw the smoke curling and twisting like a mythical snake. Jack followed the smoke and called in on his handheld radio, arriving before the firetrucks at a block of row houses at Oretha Castle Haley Boulevard and Jackson Avenue. Two of them burned, crackling and popping as only ancient wood can. Hard and buckling, turning to coal-black smoke.

Six firetrucks. And then seven.

The sun set through leafless oaks, the light orange and slatted and broken through black smoke. A helicopter passed overhead and dropped a huge bucket of water on the dying buildings. The falling water stirred up dead leaves and stale wind and fell with a whoosh.

Dried pieces of debris and smoke blocked out the sun.

"So you were scared?" Jack asked the pretty girl from Indiana.

"Hell yes, I was scared," she said.

It was the next day at sunset and they talked at an old convent in the Bywater near a statue of the Virgin Mary.

"They dropped us off in the middle of the night," she said, smoking. Her hand shook a bit. "The water was up past the transport's tires and you couldn't see two feet in front of your face. No moon. Nothing."

The girl was pretty. Blond and muscular with brown eyes. She wore camouflage but sat like a girl, on her butt with her knees pulled up to her chin. Jack met her when she'd delivered the ice.

He turned away when she exhaled.

"You want one?"

"I don't smoke."

She nodded. "So they dropped us off on the high ground," she said. "When was that, a few weeks ago?"

"Last week."

"Last week," she repeated, thinking. "And they dropped us off, like I said. On the high ground. Well, we didn't have orders or anything. We just sat there."

"All night."

"All night," she said. "We could hear gunshots and people yelling. Families passing us on boats and little pool floats . . . So anyway, I finally fall asleep and I hear something at the edge of sleep. You know how that can go? Kind of a dream but you're awake. And it's a trudging sound through the water and this heavy breathing. I couldn't see anything. It was so dark I wasn't sure if it was just in my head."

"What was it?"

"You'll laugh at what I thought it was."

"What did you think it was?"

"Demons."

"What was it?"

"Horses."

"You religious?" Jack asked.

The pretty Indiana girl stubbed out her cigarette on one of the statue's base stones and tucked back on her uniform hat. "Not at all."

At midnight there was a riot. A man who'd shot at the police from the top of the hot sauce factory in Mid-City had decided to lock himself in the portable toilet.

A few minutes before, he'd stuck his penis through one of the holes and told a female guard to "suck it" as he masturbated with his eyes rolling up in his head. Instead, she'd whacked it hard with a billy club and then two of the other inmates in an adjoining cell had started climbing the chain link and screaming at the guards.

The guards were able to mace the two on the walls but the man who'd started it all had run and shut himself in the toilet.

Jack said: "Give me the hose."

Guards pulled the hose from the edge of the train platform and ran the nozzle to Jack.

"Turn it up." And he unlocked the gate and walked inside and thumbed open the toilet's door.

The flush of water blew the man against the back wall of the toilet and washed him outside in a long brown stream until he rolled and crawled to the far corner of the cell.

"Goddamn!" the man yelled, curling into a ball. Both hands on his privates, his brown pants at his knees.

"Turn it down," Jack said.

You wrote a report, fingerprinted them, and then tagged them. Pink for federal cases, green for misdemeanors, and red, yellow, and blue for different kinds of felonies. They were locked up, given something to eat, and then shipped on buses by gun bulls out of the Louisiana State Penitentiary in Angola the next morning.

"Move 'em in, herd 'em out," Jack always said.

A few days before, a two-time loser had driven a stolen car to the drop-off zone at the old Amtrak station, walked up to the front desk, and asked the warden for a one-way train ticket.

The warden, ten years on the job running Angola, asked for his driver's license and registration, and it wasn't but a second later that he nodded to Jack and another guard. "*Yes sir. Yes sir.* One-way ticket to Angola coming up."

They took him to the platform and locked him in with a French Quarter street musician who'd been caught stuffing his pockets with cold medicine and NoDoz at what was left of the Walgreens on Canal.

The next day, transport carriers and Humvees passed by the Convention Center carrying soldiers with farm-boy grins and buzz cuts. They waved and smiled in a slow, steady parade, most of them carrying cameras and camcorders aimed at all the wreckage.

Jack watched another Humvee roll by the La Louisiane Ballroom—two skinny, goofy kids giving a thumbs-up—where the Guard held two prisoners. The officers came from Arkansas and rolled their own cigarettes and wore sunglasses like Jack.

"Y'all got to clean this up?" Jack asked.

"Good God Almighty, I hope to hell not."

Jack eyed the mess and walked under the shaded outdoor roof. There were: folding chairs and MRE packs, spoiling milk and open Heineken bottles, inflatable mattresses, CDs, overnight cases, water jugs and suitcases, rotting food and bottles of urine and piles upon piles of garbage, a faded World War II veteran's hat, baby blankets and some kid's New York Giants helmet, jumper cables, unopened bottles of Corona, and hotel beach chairs.

A chopper's propellers beat overhead and along the Mississippi.

Jack picked up the vet's hat, studied the gold pins, and placed it back, softly, on the chair.

In an old pile of dog food sat an empty bottle of champagne. Veuve Clicquot Ponsardin. Forty-five-dollar label.

There were millions of flies and the foul smell of rotting food and human waste. Jack reached into his pocket for a bandana and covered his mouth. He felt lunch back up in his throat.

From the other side of the building, one of the Army men yelled: "It's a grand ol' ballroom, ain't it?"

There was better cell phone coverage up on the overpass, and even though I-10 didn't go anywhere, Jack would drive his truck up there, heading north toward the airport until the water started coming up at the Metairie Cemetery. And he'd sit there and call his dad and talk about busted boats and files lost at sea and insurance folks who wouldn't respond to messages. Mostly he'd eat MREs with the sun going down, occasionally giving directions to rescue workers from other states who didn't know the damn interstate was closed.

It was a week or so after the storm when he felt that bullet zip by his ear and heard the sharp report of a pistol.

He rolled off the hood and found his footing.

Reaching into the passenger seat, he pulled out a rifle and duck-walked back behind the concrete barrier. He didn't have field glasses or a scope but could pick out the rough-shadowed shape in the sun setting through the endless marble mausoleums.

Another shot pinged off the concrete.

With breath held, he took aim and shot.

He heard a scream.

Jack jumped over the barricade and moved across the interstate and into the waist-deep water, rifle in the crook of his arm, his eyes following the shadowed shape through the rows of crypts and canals of golden water under oaks.

The water grew up to his chest and he waded into the city, breathing hard, and stopped to listen, slowing down his heart and lungs, hearing that splashing frantic sound in the distance, and then he turned and took in another row of mausoleums, another grand monument to wealth, another angel, another sphinx, another proud man in marble staring down with sad dead eyes.

He lost the sound.

He heard birds and a siren, and standing there he knew he was lost. He could not see the road or even find it. He only saw the sun, the giant glowing orb of light painting everything orange and gold and making all the dead things shine so soft.

Jack spat some tobacco juice into the stale water and walked, wiping his mustache with the back of his hand, following the rows. Past a giant monument to the lost Confederate dead and then past a small statue of a fat man holding a quill pen.

The light was dull orange now. The bearded trees giving long shadows.

The sound of birds.

And then a sucking sound of rotten, slow breath.

He turned blind down a waist-deep path. In the shadows, only the thinnest sliver of gold light ran down the middle of the still brown water, almost an arrow.

At the top step of a marble crypt sat a young boy, maybe ten, holding his swollen belly, covered in blood. He breathed thick and hard and wet and he watched Jack come down the waterway and soon emerge on a bottom step, and then another, until the man grew tall and towered above him.

Jack placed his rifle on the last step. His clothes dripping.

The boy pushed himself against the locked glass doors to the long-dead family, each of their names and dates of life written in gold on marble.

Jack took off his shirt and pressed it to the boy's stomach. He reached for his radio but it had been shorted out. "I'll fix it," he said to the boy, even as the long shadows covered the lost cove. "I'll fix it."

Jack stayed there until the boy's head grew cool in the dark, a soft green-marbled moon shining on the cemetery water like silver.

MARIGNY TRIANGLE

BY ERIC OVERMYER

Faubourg Marigny

Pretty and sad, like New Orleans
—The Iguanas

Ask me, things started to go to shit *way* before the hurricane. The Pizza Kitchen killings, for instance. Well, what would *you* have done? One of your coworkers, that sullen kid from the Iberville projects, that dishwasher you hired, him, he was a friend of a friend and needed a break, knocks on the door as you're getting ready to open for lunch, him and a couple of his equally sullen, hunched-up, shifty friends, course you let 'em in. And then he pulls a nine and ties you and everybody else in the place up, and executes all y'all with a shot to the backa the head using a raw peeled potato as a silencer, for eighty-eight dollars and change. And somebody else, who got lucky and missed her bus and was a little late to work that day, finds five bodies a few minutes later, still warm and oozing.

And this on a beautiful Thanksgiving weekend morning, clear blue Creole sky in the French Quarter, for God's sake, well, felt like the beginning of the end to me. Maybe more so 'cause it was a rare day off for me, and I'm taking the kids on a little stroll through the Quarter, pointing out this and that historic feature, and the difference between a slave quarters and a *garçonnière*, and I get the call to get on over there, sorry 'bout your day off, Reynolds, and I say, nah, I don't need no address, I'm *lookin'* at it, mac—and I am, standing across the street, taking in the crowd and the cop cars and emergency vehicles, and when I can't bear it no more, looking up again at the soft blue Louisiana sky, trying to put the two together.

Or maybe it was when those kids popped that priest, Father Peterson, off his bike further down in the Marigny, almost to Bywater. Out for a sunset ride, beloved in the neighborhood, and these punks just whacked the padre for kicks, far as we know, wasn't like nobody was ever arrested. And this sorta shit's why the town was deserted after dark in most neighborhoods long *before* the hurricane tore it up—and talking about *that*, parts of this town were always so raggedy-assed, you'd be hard-pressed to know what piece of decrepitude was there before or after Katrina: St. Claude, Tremé, St. Roch, St. Bernard, Central City, Desire. I mean, I *defy* you to tell me—

Or maybe it was Officer Antoinette Frank that broke my particular camel's back, where she and her cousin lit up her partner *and* the Vietnamese family they both moonlit for as part-time after-dark security. A *police* officer, sworn to serve and protect. She was that family's guardian angel, and she did them like that—and again, all for a few bucks, supposedly. The cousin said she thought they kept gold bullion in the back room, them being Vietnamese and all. Maybe. But who'd be that stupid? And what the real reason was, how'll we ever know? She's still on death row, Officer Frank, and the hurricane probably gave her another five years of undeserved life at least, delaying as it did every judicial proceeding large or small in the great state of Louisiana. And her, we *know* she done her daddy, too, filed a missing person's on him and moved right into his house, and they found his bones under it and didn't even bother to charge her with that.

You smell that? I don't mean that slop in the footlocker—a smell I could never possibly describe to a civilian, except to say you gotta burn your clothes after a crime scene like this. Never wear nothing you wanna hold onto to a crime scene, I tell the rooks. Nah. I mean *that*—the night air. Sweet. Jasmine. *Confederate* jasmine.

Now, I'm a Seventh Ward, all the way. That's the Creole ward, y'all, the Mighty Seventh. And I always lived in the Seventh Ward—always. Where I live since the hurricane, my mama's house. I mean, same house I come up in on Dauphine Street in the Marigny, the Triangle, between Touro and Pauger—a double camelback with a screened-in side gallery, that we all piled into since our place in Gentilly had thirteen inches of water in it . . . on the *second* floor. I lie in bed, windows thrown open in the nice weather, I can smell the jasmine, the coffee roasting down along the river, hear the carriages rattling home at night after a day in the tourist trade, the *clack clack* of the mules' hooves. I just lie there, I can hear the train whistle way down in the Bywater. Can hear the ferry boat horns out on the river. The out-of-tune calliope on the *Creole Queen*. All kinds of birds. The rain rattling in the gutters. The wind whipping the palm fronds. I don't know. Place makes my heart ache. Way it smells, way it sounds. Way it looks. No place as pretty and sad as New Orleans. Depending on if the sun's shining or not. You ever notice that? Sun's out, ain't no prettier place on earth. No place more . . . *resplendent*. But gray and gloomy, cloudy, rainy, this town is so shabby, dreary, and downright depressing, makes you wanna take morphine and die. As the old song goes.

If I believed in karma I'd be worried I'd come back as one of those mules. Those carriage mules. I would just hate like hell to come back as a mule.

It *is* a beautiful night. Despite this shit here. Sweet and soft, balmy. *Dark*. I know that sounds odd to say. The night is dark. But it is. Here in New Orleans, it is really dark. One or two things I know about New Orleans. The nights are *darker* here. I don't mean that metaphorically. I'm not talking about human darkness. About evil, or shit. I'm talking about the quality of the night. The *feel*. I been everywhere, all over this country. The Gulf of Mexico. Jamaica. I'm telling you. I seen a lot of darkness, stayed up a lot of nights. It's just a fact. The nights are darker here. *Palpably* darker. And thicker. You can reach out and stroke the darkness. Touch it. Run your hand over it, like somebody's skin, or a piece of soft cloth. Got a soft feel to it, New Orleans nights. The nights are always soft here. No matter what else has happened. No matter what kind of horror show. The nights are always soft. I can't tell you how many times, how many blood-stained crime scenes I been privy to, how many murders. I just stepped away, stepped outside, into the night, and been struck by how thick and soft and sweet and downright dark the nights are here. Struck dumb. It's a mystery.

This, this here, ain't no mystery. Run of the mill lover's quarrel. Guy's wife and her girlfriend—by which I mean, her *girl*friend, her lesbian lover—decided they were tired of him. The three of them get to drinking and fooling around—fuckin' and fightin', really, what it amounts to—and one of them whacks him over the head with a hammer two times and then the pair of them stuff him in this here footlocker, pour cement in the damn thing, and push it out on the back porch. A few days go by, and a neighbor gets to smelling something ripe, drops a dime on them. And here I am. Do I know why, exactly? No. But I know what.

It ain't like TV. Most of the time, you do know who. You

don't know why, maybe, and you don't care. Means and opportunity is all that matters. That thing about motive? Fuck motive. People kill each other for no damn reason at all.

One or two other things I know about New Orleans. Termites and hurricanes. The intro and the outro, how it starts and how it ends. The micro and the macro. That's what gonna do New Orleans in. Not crime. Not fucked-up terminal stupidity like we got ourselves here. Termites and hurricanes. If you could beam me forward a hundred years from now, set me down right here in this spot a hundred years in the future, it wouldn't be here. No sir. Not just this house here, this rundown half of a double, lower Marigny, Spain Street shotgun. I mean New Orleans. Not here. Nothing. Just cypress swamp again. Malaria mosquitoes and alligators. Gulf water maybe, far as the eye can see, the Mississippi finally jumping its banks like it's been wanting to ever since it can remember, over to the Atchafalaya. Just nutria and gators and skeeters. But New Orleans? Not a chance. Gone like the lost city of Pompeii. Drowned like Atlantis. The termites and the hurricanes gonna take care of all *this* shit. The lost city of New Orleans.

Fifty years from now, I live that long, I'll be fishing off my roof.

Not that I don't love New Orleans. I do. But I'm a pessimist, I guess, especially about the capacity of human beings to solve their problems. Comes with the territory, I believe. Being a homicide detective. Makes you a little bit cynical about the human capacity. Makes you think maybe people ain't real bright. Otherwise why would they do the things they do? To themselves and others. Why would they live the way they do? Now there's a mystery for you. Not this sorry situation. All that's left to figure about this is which one hit him, and get the other to cop a plea and turn against her girlfriend to get a little something off the top of her sentence.

What else I know about New Orleans? One or two things. They got some scruffy white people here. Scary looking. Take these three. Just beat to shit, generally. I mean, the dead guy, the vic, literally. One of the women, the girlfriend, five-nine, two-fifty, told the parish deputies she was a man, and they *believed* her. And the other one, the wife. Kinda scrawny and twitchy. And why on earth didn't they get rid of the body? Oh, they were fixin' to, but just "hadn't got around to it." Even bought some fishing poles. They were gonna take the footlocker out in the Gulf and dump it overboard. Plus, they got to drinkin', to fuckin' and fightin' again, one thing and another, and just plum lost track of the time.

One or two other things I know about New Orleans is the pull of the past. Never been anywhere the past had such a pull on a person as here. If I had me a time machine, I'd wear it out, me, and I wouldn't be hitting no future button, no, no, no. Even if there was one. No, I'd dial me up *old* New Orleans. The French Opera House. Storyville. Lulu White's Mahogany Hall. The New Basin Canal. Not even that far back. I'd be just as happy to hitch a ride back to the '50s. South Rampart Street honky tonks and gin joints and every mobbed-up club in town before that self-righteous prick Jim Garrison shut them all down. Not that I could go in those places back then, not through the front door anyway. But still. All the glorious past.

So much gone now, so much vanished. The Dew Drop Inn. Old Chinatown where City Hall is now. The amusement parks at Pontchartrain Beach and Milneburg and Old Spanish Fort and Lincoln Beach. North Claiborne before they tore up the old oak trees with bulldozers and rammed the interstate down our throats. Funny they didn't run it through Uptown, ain't it? I suppose I could use that time machine to go forward to when somebody apologizes for that, huh? I could set it for, let's see, turn the dial to When Hell Freezes Over. I'll be there.

We used to all picnic on Mardi Gras day on North Claiborne, wait for the Indians to congregate. Still do, but instead of under the live oak trees, now it's in the shade of the freeway. Pathetic, huh? We're stubborn, or stupid. Set in our ways.

So much gone. I'd give anything to see the glorious past of New Orleans. The octoroon balls. The slave market. Congo Square. I'd wanna see all that. One of the perks of this job, it teaches you not to flinch. The glorious and horrible past of New Orleans. Almost makes you believe in karma, doesn't it? This beautiful place, paradise on earth, the City That Care Forgot, built on blood and tears and human misery.

I sometimes wonder if maybe that's why this job keeps me so busy. In the words of that great Southern writer, the past ain't never past, is it? But you knew that, didn't you? Don't need me to tell you. We all know that. No excuse, anyway. You can't be blaming karma when you kill somebody. You can't go crying about history when you blow some old lady away. Shoot some tourist in a cemetery, just some ordinary nobody checking out our great and glorious past. But still, I get to thinking sometimes, wondering when the past is gonna run its course here in the Crescent City. Wondering when we ever gonna get *past* the past.

Oh, I'd give that time machine a workout. Doesn't have to be so far back. I'd settle for thirty years ago, when the parades still snaked through the Quarter on Mardi Gras day. Hell, I'd settle for last Saturday night, about 10 o'clock, when all *this* bullshit went down.

I mean, it's not a mystery, exactly, but I'd still like to know. What was said. Did they plan to do him, the two of them? Did he know that she was more than just his wife's friend? Did he come home and catch them going at it? Or maybe he was into it and they weren't? Or they weren't anymore? How long, in the words of that old song, had this been going on, anyway? Kind of case that keeps them speculating at work, you know?

Homicide. *Our day starts when your day ends.* Some of us have that on a T-shirt. Baseball cap. People say it ain't respectful. But you gotta have a sense of humor in this job. I know that too.

ABOUT THE CONTRIBUTORS

Kim Sykes

THOMAS ADCOCK is an Edgar Award–winning author of six novels, including *Thrown-Away Child*, set in New Orleans. He is a reporter for the *New York Law Journal*. Twenty-five years ago, thanks to marrying the New Orleans–born actress Kim Sykes, the Crescent City became his second home.

Jay E. Nolan

ACE ATKINS covered the immediate aftermath of Hurricane Katrina in New Orleans and the Gulf Coast for *Outside Magazine*. The Pulitzer Prize–nominated journalist is also the author of four crime novels based in and around the city. He lives and writes in Oxford, Mississippi.

James Ezell

PATTY FRIEDMANN has lived in New Orleans all her life, except for slight interruptions for education and natural disasters. Her darkly comic novels include *Eleanor Rushing, Secondhand Smoke,* and *A Little Bit Ruined*. Her works have been selections of the Barnes & Noble Discover Great New Writers Program and Borders Original Voices, and Book Sense 76 picks.

Michael Riley

DAVID FULMER'S *Chasing the Devil's Tail,* a mystery set in turn-of-the-century Storyville, New Orleans, won a Shamus Award and was a finalist for a *Los Angeles Times* Book Prize, a Barry Award, and a Falcon Award. His Storyville novels *Jass* and *Rampart Street* have drawn high praise. He lives in Atlanta with his daughter Italia.

Mark Fair

BARBARA HAMBLY was born in San Diego, California, and originally trained as an academic historian. She lived part-time in New Orleans for three years while married to science fiction writer George Alec Effinger; she now lives in Los Angeles.

SylvesterQ.com

GREG HERREN is the author of six mystery novels set in New Orleans, including *Mardi Gras Mambo* and *Murder in the Rue Chartres* (forthcoming). He lives in the Lower Garden District of New Orleans and refuses to relocate. Ever.

Jim Burger

LAURA LIPPMAN, a Baltimore-based writer best known for her award-winning Tess Monaghan novels, believes New Orleans is the only other city where she could be happy for more than a few days, preferably December through March.

Renette Zimmerly

TIM MCLOUGHLIN is the editor of the multiple award–winning anthology *Brooklyn Noir.* His novel, *Heart of the Old Country*, was a selection of the Barnes and Noble Discover Great New Writers Program and won Italy's Premio Penne award. He was married in St. Mary's Chapel on Jackson Avenue in the Garden District.

Marcel.lí Sàenz

JAMES NOLAN, a fifth-generation New Orleans native, is a widely published poet, fiction writer, essayist, and translator. His collections of poetry are *Why I Live in the Forest* and *What Moves Is Not the Wind*, both from Wesleyan University Press. He is a regular contributor to *Boulevard*, and recent stories have come out in *Shenandoah*, the *Southern Review*, and the *Chattahoochee Review*. He lives in the French Quarter, and currently directs the Loyola Writing Institute at Loyola University.

© 2006 David G. Spielman

TED O'BRIEN moved, somewhat arbitrarily, from South Florida to New Orleans in 2000. He signed on as a bookseller and continues, post-Katrina, to live and work in the Garden District.

Eric Overmyer

ERIC OVERMYER'S plays include *On the Verge, Native Speech, In a Pig's Valise, In Perpetuity Throughout the Universe, The Heliotrope Bouquet by Scott Joplin & Louis Chauvin,* and *Dark Rapture.* At one point he had a home in the Faubourg Marigny on Kerlerec Street, and he has been a "near" Orleanian for twenty years.

Megan Jankowski

JERI CAIN ROSSI is the author of *Angel with a Criminal Kiss* (Creation Books) and *Red Wine Moan* (Manic D Press). Since Katrina, she has resided in San Francisco, but she left her heart on the wild streets of New Orleans. She dedicates her story in this collection to the loving memories of Jason and Tommy, two beauties who will always be young, sipping cocktails on Decatur Street.

Lynda Koolish

KALAMU YA SALAAM is a New Orleans–based editor, writer, filmmaker, and teacher. He is director of Listen to the People, a New Orleans oral history project; moderator of e-Drum, a listserv for black writers; and comoderator, with his son Mtume, of Breath of Life, a black music website. Salaam is also the digital video instructor and the codirector of Students at the Center, a writing-based program in the New Orleans public school system.

Lee Pryor

JULIE SMITH is the Edgar Award–winning author of two detective series set in New Orleans. A former reporter for the *New Orleans Times-Picayune* and the *San Francisco Chronicle,* she lives in the Faubourg Marigny section of New Orleans, which is much funkier than it sounds.

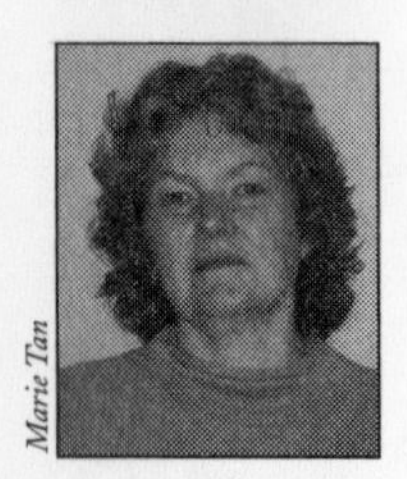

Marie Tan

MAUREEN TAN is the author of the critically acclaimed Jane Nichols suspense novels. Her focus on strong, independent female protagonists and Southern locales continues in *A Perfect Cover*—set in the Vietnamese community in New Orleans—and in her most recent book, *Too Close to Home.*

Qevin Oji

JERVEY TERVALON was born in New Orleans and raised in Los Angeles. He has written two novels set in New Orleans, *Dead Above Ground* and *Lita*. He's almost obsessed with Creole Cream Cheese, stuffed Mirliton (militon), and good grits.

Thomas Williams

OLYMPIA VERNON is the author of three critically acclaimed novels published by Grove Atlantic. Her first, *Eden*, was written in Uptown New Orleans and was nominated for a Pulitzer Prize. In 2006, *A Killing in This Town* was published to rave reviews. Vernon is a Louisiana native and is now the Hallie Brown Ford Chair at Willamette University.

Randy Moses

CHRISTINE WILTZ has written five books: a detective trilogy—*The Killing Circle, A Diamond Before You Die,* and *The Emerald Lizard*; a novel, *Glass House;* and a biography, *The Last Madam: A Life in the New Orleans Underworld.* All of her books are set in New Orleans, where she was born and still lives.

Also available from the Akashic Books Noir Series

D.C. NOIR
edited by George Pelecanos
304 pages, a trade paperback original, $14.95

Brand new stories by: George Pelecanos, Laura Lippman, James Grady, Kenji Jasper, Jim Beane, Ruben Castaneda, Robert Wisdom, James Patton, Norman Kelley, Jennifer Howard, Jim Fusilli, Richard Currey, Lester Irby, Quintin Peterson, Robert Andrews, and David Slater.

GEORGE PELECANOS is a screenwriter, independent-film producer, award-winning journalist, and the author of the bestselling series of Derek Strange novels set in and around Washington, D.C., where he lives with his wife and children.

BROOKLYN NOIR
edited by Tim McLoughlin
350 pages, a trade paperback original, $15.95
***Winner of SHAMUS AWARD, ANTHONY AWARD, ROBERT L. FISH MEMORIAL AWARD; Finalist for EDGAR AWARD, PUSHCART PRIZE**

Twenty brand new crime stories from New York's punchiest borough. Contributors include: Pete Hamill, Arthur Nersesian, Maggie Estep, Nelson George, Neal Pollack, Sidney Offit, Ken Bruen, and others.

"*Brooklyn Noir* is such a stunningly perfect combination that you can't believe you haven't read an anthology like this before. But trust me—you haven't. Story after story is a revelation, filled with the requisite sense of place, but also the perfect twists that crime stories demand. The writing is flat-out superb, filled with lines that will sing in your head for a long time to come."
—Laura Lippman, winner of the Edgar, Agatha, and Shamus awards

MIAMI NOIR edited by Les Standiford
356 pages, trade paperback, $15.95

Brand new stories by: James W. Hall, Barbara Parker, John Dufresne, Paul Levine, Carolina Garcia-Aguilera, Tom Corcoran, Christine Kling, George Tucker, Kevin Allen, Anthony Dale Gagliano, David Beaty, Vicki Hendricks, John Bond, Preston Allen, Lynne Barrett, and Jeffrey Wehr.

"Variety, familiarity, mood and tone, and the occasional gem of a story make *Miami Noir* a collection to savor." —*Miami Herald*

MANHATTAN NOIR
edited by Lawrence Block
257 pages, a trade paperback original, $14.95

Brand new stories by: Jeffery Deaver, Lawrence Block, Charles Ardai, Carol Lea Benjamin, Thomas H. Cook, Jim Fusilli, Robert Knightly, John Lutz, Liz Martínez, Maan Meyers, Martin Meyers, S.J. Rozan, Justin Scott, C.J. Sullivan, and Xu Xi.

LAWRENCE BLOCK has won most of the major mystery awards, and has been called the quintessential New York writer, although he insists the city's far too big to have a quintessential writer. His series characters—Matthew Scudder, Bernie Rhodenbarr, Evan Tanner, Chip Harrison, and Keller—all live in Manhattan; like their creator, they wouldn't really be happy anywhere else.

SAN FRANCISCO NOIR
edited by Peter Maravelis
292 pages, a trade paperback original, $14.95

Brand new stories by: Domenic Stansberry, Barry Gifford, Eddie Muller, Robert Mailer Anderson, Michelle Tea, Peter Plate, Kate Braverman, David Corbett, Alejandro Murguía, Sin Soracco, Alvin Lu, Jon Longhi, Will Christopher Baer, Jim Nesbit, and David Henry Sterry.

BALTIMORE NOIR
edited by Laura Lippman
298 pages, a trade paperback original, $14.95

Brand new stories by: David Simon, Laura Lippman, Tim Cockey, Rob Hiaasen, Robert Ward, Sujata Massey, Jack Bludis, Rafael Alvarez, Marcia Talley, Joseph Wallace, Lisa Respers France, Charlie Stella, Sarah Weinman, Dan Fesperman, Jim Fusilli, and Ben Neihart.

These books are available at local bookstores.
They can also be purchased online through www.akashicbooks.com.
To order by mail send a check or money order to:

AKASHIC BOOKS
PO Box 1456, New York, NY 10009
www.akashicbooks.com, Akashic7@aol.com

(Prices include shipping. Outside the U.S., add $8 to each book ordered.)